FORBIDDEN MONTANA LOVE

THE BURKES OF BURNSIDE CREEK, BOOK ONE

FIONA CULLEN

GRIZZLY DAMSEL PUBLISHING

Cover design by Cover Couture

Photographer: Wander Aguiar

Jefe
Thank you for all your
guidance, support and love.
I still hear your voice guiding me as I write.
I miss you every day.

WANT TO KNOW HOW IT ALL BEGAN??

Hi!
 If you're like me, you always want to know more about characters and how it all began! With that in mind, I wrote a special short story prequel that's only available for my newsletter subscribers called *Unexpected Montana Love*.

Unexpected is about Evelina, the Burke family matriarch and how she came to be in Montana.

I hope you are as curious as I was about her super romantic story with Lorenzo and join in the fun! Here's a link to the short story— Enjoy! Hugs,

Fiona

CHAPTER 1

THEODORA

T *hirty minutes of shame and then I'll be free...*

I tried to blend into the background as my captivating cousins sparkled and garnered all the attention. I knew my plan was working as I'd chosen Willow's most boring dress, a brown sack-like thing that hung off me and did nothing to highlight my curves. She was more slender and it made her look intriguing. I saw men's eyes skim over me as they focused on Willow, my blonde, beautiful-as-a-model cousin, and her sister Briar, equally as stunning with her black hair and red dress.

For this evening of humiliation—the last one I hoped I'd ever suffer with them—they had somehow wrangled invitations to the most exclusive resort in the valley, The Hill. I'd always considered it a pretentious name, but everyone who was anyone flocked here. I wish they'd chosen the Staggering Bull again. I'd garnered little interest there last year as I'd completed my requisite thirty minutes of torment.

Here at The Hill, there were too many strangers. Too many who weren't from the valley— who didn't know me and understand that they should leave me alone as I suffered in silence for thirty minutes. They'd approach and taunt and, God forbid, feel emboldened to touch me. I shivered in horror at the thought.

I should have known better when the teasing and taunting began a month ago about what I would need to do for the last time I attempted to make amends. As I looked at the floor, rather than at any of the leering men in the room, I buried a deep resentment that having to live with my cousins hadn't been enough of a punishment.

A headache bloomed from the laughter, the loud chatter, and the throbbing music that made me feel as though it was taking over my pulse, and I'd only just entered the bar. I cast a furtive glance to the outside patio area, but I knew that was foolish. It was far too cold to wander outside alone in Montana in January with no coat. Besides, I'd never escape my cousins when they were intent on a goal.

With a sigh, I walked with them to the bar, praying for a way to speed up the clock so I could return to my room and try to forget this evening had ever occurred.

~

NOLAN

I saw the small group of women sidle into the bar, my attention immediately caught by the blonde bombshell throwing out "fuck me" vibes. She swayed to the beat of the music, her hips gyrating enough to let a man know she'd fulfill the promise her body suggested. The black-haired woman beside her was attractive in a skanky way while the brown-haired woman was nondescript enough as to be a mouse and was just as easily forgotten. I'd been to The Hill enough times to know almost everyone here who was a local, but the mouse was

4

unknown to me, although the other two looked familiar. Probably women I wanted to forget from my high school days.

Sipping my scotch, I watched as they pushed through the press of people. Were they friends? If they were, why did the mouse seem so upset? I sighed, forced myself to stop staring at them, and looked into my glass, attempting to banish the anguish today always evoked. When would I overcome this agony?

I took a swallow of my drink and glanced down at the person standing beside me at the bar. Choking on my drink, I barely stopped myself from spitting it all over her. "Fuck me," I breathed as I stared down at the most perfect pair of tits I'd ever seen.

For a few seconds, my mind went blank as I gaped at the skin as white as marble with a few veins visible. I wanted to trace those veins with my tongue. A soft blush on her chest spread, giving her skin a gorgeous glow while her coral-tipped nipples puckered. I fought my most base instinct to duck my head and suck on her nipples then and there.

Instead, I forced myself to lift my gaze and meet her eyes. I jerked in shock. Rather than the blonde bombshell, the mouse stood with the neckline of her dress down. Why?

"Are you well?" I whispered as I heard her breathy gasps that sounded like cries of distress rather than any siren's call of passion.

"No," she breathed.

That one word cut me to my soul, and I shucked my jacket, slipping it over her shoulders and pulling it over her chest. I glanced around, surprised no one else had noticed her blatant display. She stood, trembling and frozen beside me.

"Come," I murmured. "Come with me." I faced her, momentarily struck dumb by her sage-green eyes that seemed to see into my soul. I cleared my throat and dropped my gaze to my hands holding my suit coat closed. "Come," I rasped, grabbing one of her hands.

"No," she said in a soft, throaty voice, her hand tugging on mine.

I stilled, frowning to see the panic in her eyes. Tilting my head down toward her as she was inches shorter than me, I stared at her in confusion. "Why? You want to stay here, exposed for all to see? The next man who approaches won't keep his hands off you."

She flushed and nodded, leaning closer to me. "If I take a step away, my dress will fall to the floor and then I'll be..."

My eyes flared with understanding. I took in her brown, sackcloth-like dress, shocked that anyone would have paid designer prices for such an ugly piece of clothing. Stepping closer, caging her in and making it appear we were having a romantic encounter, I held the sides of the jacket fanned out so she was completely concealed, but the jacket wasn't impeding any movement. I whispered in her ear, "Can you fix your dress now?" relishing the small shiver she was unable to suppress at the feel of my breath on her neck.

At her subtle nod, I remained in place, breathing in her intoxicating scent—a mixture of soap and sweet flowers. I inhaled again, the fragrance reminding me of summer days of long ago. Stifling a groan as her hands rose and brushed against my chest, I clenched my jaw to prevent leaning forward to kiss her. To throw her over my shoulder as I wanted to, and to carry her away. How had the mouse transformed into such a vixen?

Taking a stuttering breath, I looked over her shoulder and met the pouting glance of the sulking blonde who stood beside her. Rather than show any concern for the woman in my arms, the blonde appeared dismayed at her friend's rescue. When I heard a sigh of relief, I focused again on the woman in front of me. "Ready, *bella*?"

Her head jerked at my quiet endearment before she gave a quick nod. "Yes. Please get me out of here."

I settled the suit coat in front of her and buttoned it before reaching for her hand, holding it tight lest someone attempted to separate us as we snaked through the crowd. I ignored calls from friends and acquaintances, sighing with relief when we emerged onto the rear patio. Here, the loud, thrumming music was dulled and the sweet smell of a pine forest replaced the overheated, cloying stink of too many people in one space.

I released her hand for a moment, immediately grabbing it again when she tottered on her high heels. "Why do women always wear those stupid Louis-whatevers?" I asked as her heel caught in a patio paver.

She shrugged and shivered. "We do what's expected of us," she whispered, looking over her shoulder in trepidation. "Besides, these are knockoffs."

I shook my head at that information, as high heels were high heels in my life. They made a woman's legs sexy as sin, but I was thankful I didn't have to wear them.

"Do you want your friends to follow you?"

"Cousins. And no."

When she shivered again, I held out my hand. "Trust me. I won't hurt you." I stared deeply into her mesmerizing eyes, half hopeful she would call bullshit and scamper away. Instead, she let out a deep breath and nodded. "Damn," I murmured, clasping her hand again.

We walked slowly to the edge of the patio, only pausing when she realized there was a walkway leading to private residences. "I swear, bella, you're safe with me."

THEODORA

I stood, panting and feeling like I was going to hyperventilate as the most gorgeous man I had ever seen stared at me like I had five heads. How had my cousins maneuvered me to stand beside him? Why had he taken pity on me? I shivered again, not from cold, but from the latent heat I saw in his beautiful blue eyes.

He stood tall, so much taller than my five feet eight. He towered over me, sheltering me with his large shoulders and his fierce protectiveness. I hadn't felt like this since…I pushed that thought away. Those thoughts never helped.

He'd asked me to trust him. He swore I was safe with him. What kind of simple-minded fool believed a complete stranger? I knew what could happen. At best I could be raped. At worst, murdered. I stared up into his gaze, looking deeply into his eyes, and it seemed as though he understood the uncertainty and trepidation I felt. Glancing over my shoulder, I saw the large room with the frolicking party, and an all-consuming fear filled me at having to return there. At having to see my cousins again.

"Please," I whispered, my voice breaking and emerging even more scratchy than usual. "Take me away from here."

He nodded, the tension easing from his shoulders as his fingers clasped mine again. A tall man, he matched his strides to mine, aware of my inability to walk quickly in high heels. *Would a murderer be so considerate?* my racing mind asked.

We walked a fair distance, the path cleared of snow and ice and lit well enough that it appeared romantic rather than eerie. Still, I held onto his hand. When he turned onto a smaller path leading to one of the prestigious private cabins, I balked. "Who are you?" I whispered.

He chuckled, giving my hand a tug and urging me to continue to follow him. After extracting a key, he led me inside, turning on a few lamps. "Sit," he murmured, motioning to a large, overstuffed chair with ottoman. I sank into the comfortable chair, sighing with relief as I kicked off my shoes. When I saw him watching me with frank amusement, I blushed and moved my feet around, trying to find my shoes again.

"Leave them off. You should relax." After draping a throw blanket over me, he moved to the fireplace and set a match to the wood waiting to be lit. Unbuttoning the top buttons of his shirt, he turned to face me. "You are an enigma."

I blushed and shrugged as I huddled under the blanket. Although I was no longer cold, I relished the sense of security it offered. Perhaps it was fleeting, but I would cling to it. "I'm as much of a mystery as a box of chocolates."

He laughed, the full-throated, deep sound sparking tingles throughout parts of me I wished would remain dormant forever. My gaze roved over him, suddenly realizing my assessment of him as gorgeous didn't begin to do him justice. His thick, black hair was longer than the preppy haircuts I saw some men wear in town, but not so long as to tie back. A shadow of a beard—hinting that he needed to shave twice a day—enhanced his dark, good looks. Through his thin dress shirt, I saw muscles tighten in his chest as he swiped his hands together, and I suddenly wished one of those hands was still touching me.

"Now I wish I knew what that flush was for," he murmured.

"Why did you help me tonight?" I asked, tucking my legs up tight against my bottom. If I had any sense, I'd run out of this private cottage and find a way back to my room at the resort or to my uncle's house in town. Right now, my common sense was on vacation. In Fiji.

He sobered and stood. After studying me for a long moment, he moved to a nearby chair and sat down. Rather than curling into it and making himself comfortable, as I had, he sat on the edge of it, leaning toward me. "You were in distress. Someone wanted to shame you."

My breath caught. "How...?" I shook my head, unwilling to say more as I fought a tidal wave of embarrassment.

"How did I know?" He clasped his hands together and looked at the scuffed wood floor. "I know because no woman ever goes to a bar with the desire of acting like Lady Godiva. Not unless she's drunk or high. And the woman I saw entering the bar tonight,"—he nodded at me—"was neither."

"I'm surprised you noticed me," I said in a tart voice.

He shrugged. "I can imagine you are. You take great pains to remain invisible, don't you?"

I goggled at him. "I'm not the beauty of my family. In case you didn't notice, my cousins were with me tonight." I felt like I was on fire as he scrutinized me with unveiled interest.

"Oh, I saw your cousins tonight. It was hard not to be aware of them. But you—you are different."

I fought to suppress a shiver at his soft tone in his deep baritone. I ignored his comment about being different. I'd always been different, and I always would be. "Who are you?" I was a master at deflecting attention from myself, and I strived to continue that pattern.

Smiling, he said, "I'm Nolan Burke. I own the LBarM Ranch." He made a motion to indicate the area's most successful cattle ranch.

"You're a Burke?" I breathed. "But you're sixty and have ten children."

He laughed and eased back into his chair. "I hate to disappoint, but no, I don't. My dad's sixty and has seven children." He shrugged, a frown marring his beautiful face. "But I don't know where all my siblings are." He shook his head, cutting off my next question. "And no, he's not Nolan. He's Jameson." His gaze fixed on me again. "Care to explain what happened tonight?"

I curled farther into myself and shook my head. "No. I don't." When he stared at me with an expression indicating he'd be content to sit there the entire evening waiting for me to speak, I sighed. "It's nothing really. A little diversion they like to do every once in a while."

His black eyebrows shot up and his eyes glowed with shock. "Once in a while? You mean this has happened to you before?" At my mortified nod, he swore. "What happened the last time?"

"I've always lived through my half hour of humiliation and been allowed to retreat to my room. Few have taken liberties." I grimaced at my word choice. "It's only once a year."

"Once a year?" he asked. "Today? January fifteenth?" At my nod, he demanded. "Who are you?"

"Theodora Miller."

I'd never seen a person turn to stone until I saw him freeze in place. His eyes lost all luster and he paled to the point I thought he'd faint.

"Damn," he breathed. "You're his daughter and I just saved you."

I stared at him in confusion, my soul filling with horror at his next words.

"Your father killed my mother. I'll hate you forever."

CHAPTER 2

THEODORA

I sat in stunned silence as I listened to myself gasp and then attempted to catch my breath as I stared at the man in confusion. What did he mean? *I'd* killed my father. That's what my family had told me for ten years. It's why I had to pay a debt of honor every year to atone for what I did.

My palms started to sweat as I felt a panic attack threaten. *Dammit*, I swore to myself, *not now!* What could I do to get out of here? I didn't even know where *here* was. If I tried to find my way back to the main part of the resort, I knew my cousins would insist I finish my thirty minutes of mortification. It was the highlight of their year.

I closed my eyes in defeat. Not for the first time, I wished I'd moved away. That I'd changed my name and tried to start fresh. I should never have allowed my desire to regain my birthright to tether me to this backwater in nowhere Montana.

My breath caught and I bent forward, gasping.

"Nothing to say, bella?" he taunted. "No excuses?"

"I...I..." I closed my eyes and focused on my breathing as I'd learned to do. I cringed at the thought of this man seeing me at my worst twice in the matter of an hour, but there was nothing I could do. I imagined a beach with swaying palm trees. A river in a high mountain valley. Anything but the harsh reality of where I was. I focused on everything the counselor had taught me on overcoming a panic attack, although I was a bit rusty. I hadn't had one since I was eighteen.

"Bella?" he murmured as he crouched by me, flicking my hair up and turning his head upside down to stare at me. "Shit, what's the matter?"

"Panic...attack," I gasped out. I shrieked when he picked me up as though I weighed no more than a gallon of milk and turned me so that I was cradled on his lap as he sat in my chair. "No, this isn't proper."

He chuckled and wrapped the blanket around me. "Nothing about tonight's been proper." He ran a hand over my back and gently pressed so I'd rest my head against his strong chest. "Relax, bella. Relax," he soothed.

Taking a few shaky breaths, I breathed in deeply of his spicy, intoxicating cologne mingled with the healthy aromas of a man who worked. Sweat and straw and horses. I focused on him, rather than what had upset me, and ran my nose over his neck, inhaling his varying scents.

"What are you doing?" he rasped as his arms tightened around my back.

"Finding a way to relax," I murmured. "You smell good." I flushed beet red after blurting out that statement and wished a sinkhole would open up and swallow me whole. "I didn't mean to say that!"

"So I don't smell good?" he asked with humor lacing his tone.

I relaxed against him in defeat. "You smell like ambrosia."

"Hmm, not a word you hear every day," he teased. He

continued to run his hands over my back, and I felt myself slipping toward sleep. "Why'd you become hysterical?"

I froze, any lassitude evaporating with his question, and pushed against his chest to sit up. My hair felt like a frizzy mess, and I knew I always looked like a frightened hedgehog after a panic attack. I ducked my head, suddenly wishing the room was pitch black or that he was sitting far from me.

He grabbed my jaw, preventing me from turning away from him. "No, Theodora," he murmured, saying my name so it sounded exotic. "Stop hiding."

"Who are you to tell me what to do?" I snapped, anger erupting. Little did he know I hid behind anger as readily as I did shapeless, ugly clothes.

"The son of the woman your father killed."

Paling, I nodded and bit my lip. I shifted, whispering, "Let me up." I hated how quickly he released me, although I knew I should be thankful he was a gentleman. I stumbled upright and moved to the chair he had vacated, closer to the fire. Dragging the blanket behind me, I used it as a shield as I wrapped myself up tight. "My father died in a horrible car accident."

He nodded. "Yes. And killed my mother. He was speeding and out of control. He should never have been driving." Running his long fingers through his thick hair, he sat with his elbows on his knees. "I've always thought he was drunk, but a friendly sheriff wouldn't accuse him of it after he'd died."

"Drunk?" I gasped, shaking my head. "No, not drunk. He didn't drink. He was driving like a maniac because of me," I whispered. "I guess you really should hate me forever."

For long moments, the only sound in the room was that of the fire crackling and snapping. He stared at me in confusion and disbelief as I nodded.

"I killed him. I'm so sorry I never knew I caused your mother's death too."

∼

NOLAN

F*uck.* This woman was trying to upend everything I knew to be true. To strip me of my anger and hatred of her father. I firmed my jaw and stared at her as I shook my head. "No," I breathed, "you shouldn't have to bear his shame. That isn't right."

We both jumped as the door to the cabin slammed shut. I heard footsteps pound into the kitchen, and then the refrigerator door open and then crash shut with the sound of bottles clanging together. "Do you know who had the nerve to show their faces tonight at The Hill?" I heard Caleb call out. My best friend, who was also my cousin, was part owner of The Hill and this was his cabin. "Those two-faced bitches, the Miller sisters. They must have used fake names, because they sure as shit would never have been granted admittance otherwise." He groaned and stomped into the living area, taking a swig of beer from his bottle.

"Oh, sorry, didn't realize you had company," Caleb said. He stood looking like he'd just stepped out of a fashion magazine shoot, with a white button-down shirt, the top two buttons unbuttoned, and a form-fitting navy blue suit that made his shoulders appear even broader. He looked debonair. For a lawyer, I supposed it was appropriate. I knew he'd rather be in jeans and a flannel shirt, but he knew that would never fly as he sweet-talked guests at The Hill. His blond hair was disheveled, and I knew it was because he'd run his hands through it out of agitation, rather than from a romantic interlude. He always said he'd never date anyone he met here, as he refused to mix business with pleasure.

Caleb stared from me to Theodora and back again, his blue

eyes lighting with amusement. "Clearly you've not gotten to the kissy-kissy, pant-pant part of the evening."

"Quit being an ass, Caleb," I muttered and rolled my eyes, although I relaxed when I heard her giggle. "This is my cousin, Caleb Doyle." I addressed Theodora before speaking to him again. "Theodora Miller's visiting tonight."

Caleb had just taken a swig of beer, and he turned away to spit out his drink, choking and coughing. "What did you say?" he sputtered as he swiped at his mouth and chin, staring at the woman huddled on the chair near the fire. "Theo?"

"How do you know her well enough to call her Theo?" I demanded.

"Hey, calm down, big boy," Caleb said with a roll of his eyes. "She knows my dad. She's come into *D, D & Sons* a few times to see him." Caleb's dad, my uncle, was a lawyer, too, and one of the nicest men I'd ever met.

"I thought it was *and Son*," she said in a soft voice.

He raised his beer in a salute to her astuteness. "Yes, that it is. Ever since Brody decided to throw off the mantle of the law and sail around the world, it's been *and Son*." He pointed to himself. "God help the old man and my uncle." He stared from her to me, and I shook my head at him.

"I imagine you're wondering what I'm doing here," she said in a prim tone, a tone I was learning to loathe.

Caleb nodded. "That's the polite way of asking," he said with a wry quirk of his lips. "I never thought Nolan would go near you." He shrugged. "Well, not for a while yet."

I frowned at his cryptic comment and then focused on her. Caleb excelled at cryptic comments and loved seeing if he'd get a rise out of me. He said it was more fun than fishing could ever be.

"Ah, those unfortunate women you ran into tonight were my cousins. Mr. Burke was kind enough to save me from them."

Caleb raised his eyebrows and then blew into the top of his

now-empty beer bottle, making an annoying hooting noise he knew I detested.

"Caleb!" I barked.

He chuckled as though he'd completed his mission and set his bottle aside. Pulling out an ottoman, he sat on it, kicking off his shoes and staring at the pair of us. "It's the fifteenth." He said it as though he were talking about a sunny day in June. At my nod, he sighed. "You both decided to commemorate today at The Hill?" He looked from me to her and back again. "It's one hell of a coincidence."

I frowned as I stared at him. "What do you know, Caleb?"

He shrugged and said, "What I do know I can't reveal. Client confidentiality and all that." He waved his hand around. Never before had I found his blasé reference to his responsibilities as a lawyer so irritating.

"She's your client?" I asked in horror. "Not me?"

Caleb nodded. "Yep. Her dad set it all up before he died. Wanted to make sure she was taken care of." He looked from me to her and shrugged. "She was my dad's client until he semi-retired last fall. Now, she's my client, although we've never officially met."

"I'm your client," I hissed.

Caleb shrugged. "Everyone in this damn valley is my client. If there's ever a conflict of interest, you know I'll tell you about it and find another lawyer for one of the parties. You know you can trust me."

He stared at me for a long moment, and I nodded. I knew I could believe in Caleb. I'd always trusted Caleb, and I didn't know what I'd do if I didn't have him in my life.

I rose, pacing away. After approaching the fireplace, I stared down at her, momentarily mesmerized again by her eyes and the way she seemed to see into me. Taking a deep breath, I asked in a low voice, "Can I tell him about what happened?"

At her gentle nod, I turned to face my cousin, but remained

near her. "Theodora's cousins were shaming her tonight." I glared at him until the smug expression on his face disappeared at the way I said her name.

I looked at her. "Would you care to explain? I don't understand why they do it or why you put up with it." I grimaced as I saw her flinch at my blunt statement.

I saw her glance from me to my cousin, biting her lip in a way I found far too sexy. With a resolute sigh, I focused on Caleb as she began to speak.

~

THEODORA

I glanced from Nolan to his cousin Caleb, suddenly wishing I was back in Nolan's arms. I'd felt secure there, even if I knew deep inside he had every right to hate me. With a deep breath, I pushed my hair behind my ear and then fidgeted with a ring on my middle finger.

"My father died ten years ago. In the car crash." I paused, and my breath caught as memories of that night flooded back. The teenage angst I'd felt. The certainty that nothing could be worse than a fight with my best friend, Becky Thompson, after I caught her kissing my boyfriend, Sam Daniels. I thought I was devastated when I called my dad in hysterics. In my teenage naiveté, I thought my world had come to an end when I saw them kissing and I'd heard Sam say he could never like me like he liked Becky. Instead, I'd learned what true devastation was.

When I'd heard about my father's death, it felt as though I'd been turned to ice. I was so cold and emotionless. I soon realized I'd been turned to chipped glass instead that night. Fragile and never quite whole.

Taking a deep breath, I forced myself to continue speaking. "My father was racing to me." I shook my head. "And crashed.

Hit a patch of black ice or something. That's what I was told." I looked to Caleb, relaxing ever so slightly to see his subtle nod of agreement.

I gripped my hands together, my fingernails digging into my palms as I attempted to remain focused on that pain rather than the memory that had tormented me for a decade. "I lost everything that night. Including our family ranch."

Caleb squinted at me and appeared confused but remained quiet.

"My family told me that if I was good, and did what was required in the will, I had a chance of regaining the ranch when I turned twenty-four."

Nodding, Caleb said. "Yes. Next month."

"Yes," she whispered. "Next month, everything changes."

~

NOLAN

I waited for the conversation to continue, wondering why Caleb stared at me as though I should have understood a deeper meaning to Theo's last comment. Scratching at my head, I murmured, "Next month everything changes?"

At her nod, I frowned. "What does parading your tits around a bar full of randy men have to do with the will?" I saw Caleb's eyes bulge as he canted forward. I knew he was intrigued and interested even though he believed himself a jaded lawyer who couldn't be surprised by humanity's depraved actions toward each other.

She flushed and held the blanket to her chin even though I knew her dress was securely in place. "According to the codicil to my father's will, I have to agree to a ritual shaming every year on the anniversary of his death to fulfill the terms of the will and have a chance at regaining my birthright. It's a sort of homage to him. A penance."

"What?" Caleb breathed.

"You actually believed them when they told you that bullshit?" I roared. I took a deep breath when I saw her pale and hide even farther under the blanket.

"Nol," Caleb chided, casting me an annoyed glance before he focused again on Theodora. "What codicil?" he asked, staring at her intently.

"You're my lawyer. You should know all about it." She spoke with a defiant note to her voice as she glared at Caleb. "I only saw it once." She snapped as she met my doubt-filled gaze, "I read it. It was in my father's handwriting. It's what he wanted." She speared me with a scorn-filled glare that made my belly tighten in shame as she called me out for having doubted her reason for acting as she had tonight.

Caleb sighed and rubbed at his face. "I'm too tired to know heads from tails, but you have shocked me." He looked at me and then to her. "You seem to trust my cousin, even though he's an overbearing oaf who reeks of horse dung." He winked at her when that comment earned a reluctant smile and chuckle from her. "Come to my office tomorrow at eleven. Bring him if you want." He paused before adding, "I'd recommend you not bring your family."

I stared at Caleb a long moment, but he wore his inscrutable lawyer face. I sighed with frustration, but I knew I'd get no information out of him now. Although I was loath to admit it, Caleb was the most honorable man I knew, and it was one of the reasons he was my best friend.

"There's an extra bedroom here if you want to avoid the witches tonight." Caleb winked at Theodora and left on silent feet.

"Why does he detest my cousins?" she asked.

I sighed and plopped down on the floor, thankful for the small area rug. "They were known as the wicked witch of the east and west in high school." I nodded as she stared at me in shock. "You're young enough not to have been in school with them." I yawned, stretching with a groan. "God, they were awful. Made my sisters' lives a living hell too." I smiled as I crossed my feet at my ankles. "No one hates them like Cora, Caleb's sister."

"Why do you look so gleeful?" she asked as she curled into her chair.

"Because no one is better at revenge than Cora," I murmured. "God help the man she eventually marries." Yawning again, I glanced at her. "Do you want to stay here, or do you want me to take you back?"

Her eyes bore into me as though able to detect any deception. "There truly is a separate bedroom?" When I nodded, she smiled. "I'd prefer to stay here. I can always tell my cousins I had a wild night with the two of you." At my gasp, she flushed. "No need to look so horrified."

I rose, facing away from her as I battled images of holding her in my arms. Of having the right to touch her and kiss her and…. I took a deep breath, banishing any further thoughts. She was the cause of all of my family's troubles. I could never have anything to do with her.

"Come," I said in a low voice, wincing as it sounded more like a bark than a friendly invitation. "I'll show you to your room." I hoped she had the sense to follow and not attempt to speak to me any more tonight. For I feared if she did, I would break every vow and fuck her until I got her out of my system.

CHAPTER 3

THEODORA

The following morning, I woke feeling rested. I sat up with a start, the events of the previous night flooding back and shocking me. Had I really been in Nolan Burke's presence? I rubbed at my head, grimacing at my ratty hair. With a groan, I collapsed onto the most comfortable bed I'd ever slept on and tugged the heavy down comforter up to my chin.

Bright sunlight streamed in through the gauzy curtains, and it looked as though it was a gorgeous winter day in Montana. A cloudless, bright blue sky contrasted the white snow on the ground, and the brilliant sunlight made the day seem even brighter. The nearby trees were covered in fresh snow, and I had a sudden yearning to be young again and play in the snow. Anything to postpone my meeting with Caleb later today.

Rolling onto my side, I stared at the beautifully decorated room, complete with wingback chairs in light blue damask by the banked fireplace. As I looked around the room, I realized that although it was perfectly decorated, it was impersonal. There were no family knickknacks. No photographs or anything that gave it a sense of being a home. I hadn't felt that downstairs, but then I'd been distracted by Nolan.

At the knock on the door, I tugged the comforter even higher, with only my eyes visible. "Yes?" I called out.

"May I come in?" I heard Nolan's deep voice and fought a shiver.

"Yes."

I watched as the door silently swung open and he entered, carrying my suitcase. I sat up, no longer caring about the comforter. "How'd you get that?"

He grinned, and my breath caught at the teasing in his gaze as he looked me over. "Good night?"

I turned pink and patted at my hair before draping an arm over my chest while I plucked at the T-shirt I was wearing. I hadn't realized my nipples would harden with the cold. *It's the cold, dammit,* I told myself. *It has nothing to do with him.*

He chuckled and focused on my eyes. "It's ten. You might want to get ready for our appointment with Caleb at eleven."

"Ten!" I gasped, about to jump out of bed, realizing just in time I was only wearing a T-shirt. Just a T-shirt. "Do you mind?"

"No," he said, although his voice sounded tinged with regret. "And you can thank Caleb when you see him. He had the resort pack up your room and bring your things over. He has the ability to do that sort of thing."

No longer so concerned about my shower, I stared at Nolan in confusion. "Why? He's a lawyer."

"A lawyer and part owner of The Hill." He nodded as my mouth dropped open. "You should shoot for him, bella."

I watched him leave, the door not even making a click as it shut behind him. Caleb was part owner of The Hill? How rich was he? I thought of the handsome man I'd met the night before, of his humorous antics as he annoyed Nolan. He would be a perfect best friend. Whereas Nolan…

I sighed as I dropped my head in my hand. "Nolan's pure

trouble," I muttered to myself before I forced myself up to rush through a shower.

~

NOLAN

I knew Theo was nervous about her meeting with Caleb as I saw her clench and unclench her hands over and over again. I wanted to wrap her small hands in my huge paws, but I didn't have that right. I shouldn't even be here. I shouldn't speak to her. However, something about her compelled me to continue to spend time with her and learn all I could. For some reason, I couldn't stay away.

Today, she wore a pair of form-fitting jeans that hugged her ass in all the right places and a light blue T-shirt with a flannel over it. I hated that flannel. It concealed her luscious curves. Her cowboy boots were well-worn, and she seemed much more at home today than she had last night in her ugly designer dress and frou-frou shoes.

I tried to force myself to think about the price of feed or the concern for a fierce blizzard right at calving season, but all I could focus on was her. Her scent filled the cab of my truck, that elusive smell from my youth that always reminded me of summer days when Mama was alive. Damn, I needed to go to this meeting and get the hell away from her. She was nothing but trouble.

I drove slowly through Burnside Creek, our small town, careful not to speed as the sheriff loved to give out tickets. It was his favorite pastime in the summer as he padded the police budget on unsuspecting tourists' leaded feet. Snow piled up on the sidewalks, although all of the downtown businesses had a path cleared in front of their stores for pedestrians.

Founded at a crossroads in the late 1800s, Burnside Creek

had prospered as it catered to both cattlemen, homesteaders, and a nearby mine. The mines had long since petered out, but the ranching and farming communities had thrived, and the town with them. A few of the original clapboard buildings remained, including the first church established in town near the town square, although most were ruined in a fire around 1900.

Residents were proud of our small town, and the brick buildings shone in the mid-morning January light, a contrast to the pristine white snow and the robin's-egg-blue sky. I could see the café was doing a good business, as was the competing coffee shop. The hardware store was busy selling shovels, sleds, and ice melt, while the bookstore had an inviting display for kids and adults alike. We passed by the town square—where the farmers' market and summer concerts were held in warmer weather—en route to Caleb's office on the edge of downtown near the grocery store. Farther down the road, my friend Chase's dad once had a garage, but that had closed years ago after Mr. Harrington's untimely death and Chase's departure from town.

When we arrived at Caleb's, I hopped out, walking over to open Theo's door. After helping her down, I winged out my arm as Mama had taught me, and I walked with her to the lawyers' office. Being a Saturday, Caleb was waiting for us in the lobby. After we entered, he locked up and then motioned for us to follow him to his office.

"You look like hell," I said as I stared at him. "How much sleep did you get last night?"

He shrugged. "I can sleep later. I wanted to review this file." He held it up as he sat behind his desk, nodding with approval as I closed the door to his office. I'd learned you could never be too cautious.

"Should I be concerned?" Theodora asked, her purse propped on her lap.

Caleb sighed and leaned back in his chair, one ankle

balanced over his other knee. "Tell me what you know about your father's will."

I saw Theo frown as she focused on his question. I hated the doubt and uncertainty in her expression as she sat with stooped shoulders. She was a beautiful, bright woman who should never feel so diminished by life. My breath caught as I realized that no matter what I heard today, I wouldn't be able to hate her. Everything had changed.

I edged forward in my chair as I waited for her to speak.

"My father died. Due to his death, the ranch was lost but in a sort of forbearance or guardianship way until I turn twenty-four." She paused. "My father wanted me to have time to finish school and live a little before the responsibilities of the ranch were mine. That was one stipulation that couldn't be broken. I was to go to college."

"Yes," Caleb said, "your father wanted you to go to college and see if you wanted ranch life. Many who are born to it don't love it. You also had to live with family because you were so young when he died." He paused, waiting for a long moment before he said, "And the codicil. What did that say?"

She closed her eyes, and a tear leaked onto her cheek. "That if he suffered an unfortunate demise, I needed to pay him homage every year on the day of his death. To slight him by ignoring this request would result in my loss of right to inherit the ranch. That those who were my guardians had the right to determine what was appropriate for my homage." She opened her eyes, and I saw they were filled with unshed tears. "There's little I wouldn't do to save the ranch. That was our home."

Caleb grimaced and leaned forward, his elbows on the desk. "There is no codicil to the will, Theodora. Someone fabricated it. Your uncle, perhaps?" He shrugged as he looked at me. "Brothers often have the ability to forge their siblings' writing." He focused again on Theo. "Who is the executor of the will until you inherit?"

"My uncle," she whispered. "I think he would be mortified if he knew what my cousins had me do." She ducked her head. "I'm mortified. Uncle thought they took me out to dinner to celebrate the memory of my dad every year."

"I wonder," he muttered. Caleb shifted again and cleared his throat. "As you're most likely aware, your uncle wasn't willing to run the ranch these past ten years, nor pay anyone to run it for him. The cattle were sold when your dad died. The only thing he's managed to do is keep the fields in decent shape. He sells hay on years he'll make a profit."

"Yes, I know all this," Theodora whispered. "He shows me the deposits from the hay sales so I can see the additions to the ranch account."

Caleb squirmed a little. "I'm afraid your ranch account isn't worth much now."

"What?" she gasped. "But it's good land. My father ran a prosperous ranch. Dad told me he'd invested wisely and there was plenty for me in case...in case.... We rivaled the LBarM." She glared at me as though I were to blame.

I saw my cousin search for words, and I snapped, "Just spit it out, Cay. We don't need a thousand-dollar explanation."

"No one thought to look into your uncle as he was your family. Besides, it's illegal for the executor to take money out for his own personal uses. It appears he bled the ranch dry. The account that had millions in it when your dad died is nearly empty." He stared at her with a deep sorrow. "I'm sorry, Theodora."

She sat in stunned, devastated silence. "They stole my inheritance?" she whispered. "They belittled and humiliated me, knowing I'd have nothing at the end of it?" She shook her head. "But Uncle's always been good to me. It's my cousins who are awful. Uncle's *nice*."

I swallowed and flushed with rage as I saw the extent of her desolation. "Theodora," I murmured. "It will be all right."

"How?" she cried. "I need that money to buy cattle. To...to... purchase feed and new equipment. Hire hands. Fix the barn. I have nothing. How can a single woman run a ranch alone?" She swallowed a bubble of hysterical laughter. "I don't have a ranch. Just a bunch of worthless acres."

Caleb cleared his throat and shook his head. "Well, there I must disagree." He stared at me and then at Theodora. "Land is never worthless, and you have plenty of that, although it would be a shame for you to have to sell off acres." He paused, his gaze flitting to me before focusing on Theodora again. "You have water, Theo. Water that every ranch in this valley would pay dearly for."

I gaped at Caleb and shook my head. "No," I breathed. "Not the KBarT," I whispered as I saw Caleb nod. I couldn't count the number of times I'd been thankful for the water rights lease my father had signed ten years ago just before I fully took over running the ranch. Right after Mama died. I frowned, as something didn't make sense, but Caleb continued to speak.

Caleb tapped his fingers onto the papers on his desk and then tried to still his fidgeting. "Yes. And your water right's lease is up this spring."

I turned to stare at Theodora. "Just after your birthday." I sat in stunned silence as I realized why Caleb had been shocked for more than one reason last night. Our ranch thrived because we had secured water for the past decade from her ranch. Now, she could divert it or use it for her own fields. And I'd be stuck praying for rain. "Dammit," I hissed.

I forced myself to focus on her rather than my roiling thoughts. I listened as she continued to pepper Caleb with questions.

"So it doesn't matter what I do, the ranch is mine on February seventh?" she asked. "On my birthday." At his nod, she ducked her head. "But I can't go there beforehand?"

Caleb sighed. "Probably not. I don't know. Technically, it's your ranch, but your uncle is in charge of it until you're deemed an adult. Somehow, it was decided when you turned twenty-four was the appropriate time to consider you an adult." He shrugged. "Anyway, your uncle hasn't done much with it, so he shouldn't complain with you returning early, but you'd have to speak with him. I'd be happy to come with you as you contest the existence of that bogus codicil." His brown eyes gleamed with anticipation.

She nodded, her gaze sober. "How much money is left in the accounts?"

Caleb looked down and tapped on his notes. "A little over two hundred thousand. There's still a little there." He paused. "But far less than there should have been."

"How much was there when my father died?" she whispered, her eyes filled with anguish.

"Over two million, and it should have grown considerably since his death."

My eyes bulged at the number. I thought we had a good rainy-day fund, but her father must have been a very savvy investor.

"Can I stop him from taking any more money out?"

He smiled. "I've spouted my lawyerly speak to the bank already, and it should be safe. Hopefully." He stared at her. "I'm sorry, Theo."

"Me too," she whispered. She looked at me. "I'm sorry, Nolan. If I hadn't been such a fool and believed in that codicil, you wouldn't have had to meet me last night. I'm so sorry." She rose and ran from the room.

I followed her, watching as she rushed into the bathroom. With a sigh, I returned to Caleb's office and sat with a groan. My mind whirled at the implications for my ranch. I needed that water. I'd do anything to continue to have access to it.

I sensed Caleb watching me, and I glanced up, glowering at

him, as he seemed bemused. "What? What more could you possibly shock me with today?"

Caleb opened his mouth to speak but then stopped and smiled deferentially at Theodora as she reentered his office. He quirked an eyebrow, waiting for her to speak.

"You said probably," she breathed. "Probably I'd have to wait 'til my birthday to return to the ranch." She wrapped her arms around her belly and whispered. "What's the other option?"

Caleb glanced from her to me and back again. "You marry. And regain control of everything before your uncle has a chance to bleed you dry."

CHAPTER 4

NOLAN

"Dammit," I muttered. Shit, shit, shit, *shit!* I rose and paced the small space in front of his desk as I considered what Caleb suggested. I forced myself away from thoughts of a wedding night with Theodora and instead imagined informing my father of who I was marrying. His gaze was already filled with enough disappointment when he looked at me. I didn't need to add to it. I rubbed at the back of my neck as I considered Alessia, my only sibling still at the ranch. My breath caught at the fear she'd leave too.

"I can't," I breathed. "I can't marry her."

"Her?" Theodora asked in a hurt voice, now sitting crumpled in the chair again. "*Her?* As though I'm some faceless stranger?"

I took a deep breath and faced her, my chest tightening at the sight of tears silently coursing down her cheeks. "Theo," I whispered as I crouched down to be at her eye level. "There has to be someone else."

"Who?" she asked, her voice quivering as she fought a sob.

"You saw me last night. No one even noticed me. Even when I was exposed for all to see, I wasn't worth a second glance."

My breath caught as I remembered seeing her in all of her splendid, bare-chested glory. "That's not true," I rasped. "You're gorgeous." I grunted when she belted me on my chest.

"Don't lie to me!" she screamed. "I'm so tired of lies. Of deceit. Of..." Her voice broke. "I lost everything because I believed lies."

I pulled her into my arms, my already-shattered heart splintering further at her distress. "Theodora," I whispered, "everything will be all right." I wrapped my arms around her, attempting to ignore how right she felt in my arms. Every one of my senses rejoiced to hold her, to breathe in her scent, to be the one to soothe her.

Caleb cleared his throat, and I eased away, glaring at him over my shoulder. I wanted to smack the smirk off his lips, although I saw the deep concern lingering in his gaze. "If I may," he said.

I frowned at his words. "If you may what, Cay?" I reverted to my nickname for him.

He cleared his throat again, and I tensed at the hint of panic I saw on his face. "I'll marry you, Theodora."

I took a step in his direction, my fists clenched and eyes flashing with warning. My ire spiked as he merely watched me with amusement and challenge in his expression while he continued to sit behind his desk. *Bastard.* "Like hell you will!" I swallowed what more I would say, as I realized I'd already revealed too much with that snarl.

When Theodora spoke, I spun to her in shocked dismay. "You don't want me. He's willing to help me." She ignored me and focused on Caleb. "Are you serious?"

At his nod, I growled and lowered to my haunches in front of her again. "No, Theo, there has to be another way." As a tear tracked down her cheek, I swallowed what more I would have said. I glanced at my cousin. "There has to be another way," I whispered, my voice filled with pleading.

He shook his head. "I'm sorry, Nol."

He looked at Theo compassionately, and I felt like an ass because I wanted to beat the ever-living hell out of my cousin for making her stare at him like he could be her savior. What was wrong with me?

Caleb continued, "If and when you marry, Theo, you would regain the right to control your assets." He shrugged as he looked chagrined while nodding at her. "Well, you and your husband would. You should pray he has more scruples than your uncle."

I rose, facing away from both of them as every muscle in my body tensed. I imagined family dinners sitting across from Theo, seeing her smile at Caleb. Envisioned her big and round with his child. Why that should bother me as much as it did, I didn't understand. But on a deep instinctual level, it enraged me. Somehow, I knew that Theodora was meant to be mine. God help her, that meant she was stuck with me.

I took a deep breath and faced her. Sweat trickled down my spine, and I felt like I wanted to throw up, but I refused to let her marry Caleb. She was mine, dammit. "Theodora Miller, will you marry me?"

~

THEODORA

I sat in stunned silence after he blurted out his question, certain I couldn't have heard him correctly. He looked as angry as a caged tiger, and I wasn't certain how to respond. Had I even heard him correctly? Only Caleb's relieved chuckle proved I wasn't in a dream. "What?" I breathed, hating the flicker of hope I felt in my chest. Hope was such a fickle friend.

Ever since Caleb had said my solution was to marry, I had prayed that Nolan would offer for me. I hadn't expected him to categorically deny his willingness. I shivered as I considered all the times my family had made me feel *less* since my father had died. Less beautiful. Less intelligent. Less witty. Less wanted. Somehow, having their estimation of my lessness confirmed by Nolan had stung worse than anything they had done to me in the past. The death of hope was always a bitter thing to accept.

"You heard me," he snapped, flushing as I continued to stare at him as though he were an orangutan.

"You just said you couldn't marry me. You wouldn't marry me. Why now?"

His beautiful blue eyes flashed as he towered over me. "Because I'll be damned if any other man marries you but me," he bit out.

My breath caught at the fiery declaration and the barely restrained emotions in his gaze. I remembered something my father had said to me a few short months before he died as I cried on his shoulder over a boy whose name I couldn't even remember now. All I could remember was that the boy was flashy and always looking for attention. When I failed to give him what he needed, he looked to another for what he craved. My father had chided me while consoling me, murmuring, "Remember, my little snow princess, still waters run deep." When I stared at him in confusion, he rubbed tears from my cheek and spoke in a tender voice. "Don't look for the peacock. Look for the one who always does what's right, even when no one is looking. He's the one who'll stand by you through thick and thin."

Staring at Nolan, I had a sudden sense that Nolan was that man. Trusting in my father's advice and in everything he'd done and said in the past few hours, I nodded. "Yes, I'll marry you," I whispered. I broke eye contact and focused on my tightly laced fingers before I looked to Caleb who watched us with avid interest. For a moment, I'd forgotten we had a witness and I blushed scarlet. "I want it noted that my ranch remains mine."

Nolan snorted. "That ain't how this works, bella," he drawled. "If—*when*—we marry, what's mine is yours and what's yours is mine. Forever. I don't believe in that prenup crap Caleb likes to draw up and charge ransom money for. I don't believe in divorce." His eyes glowed with passionate conviction. "So, when you say yes, you mean it forever, or don't say it."

I shook and wrapped my arms around my waist. How could I say yes to a man I'd just met last night and mean forever? I didn't know if he was a good man, although I hoped he was. Although he had taken care of me last night, that didn't prove he'd be a good husband. I needed time.

Caleb tapped the tip of a pen against the papers on his desk, as though reading my thoughts. He murmured, "The one thing you don't have is time, Theo. You have to decide now." He flicked an irritated glance at his cousin. "Do you accept Nolan and his caveman views or not?"

That almost earned a smile, but I was so tied up in knots inside I could barely respond. I closed my eyes and imagined living on my ranch again. Entering the house I adored. Seeing pictures of my father and me. Looking out the big picture window, down the valley to the mountains in the distance. Home. I'd yearned for home for ten years. "Yes," I whispered and then repeated in a stronger voice. "Yes, I'll marry you, Nolan."

I opened my eyes just in time to see him swoop toward me and tug me up and into his arms. I gasped, then groaned as I felt his silky soft lips capture mine in a kiss. At first, it was sweet and gentle. When I groaned again and dug my fingers into his scalp, he nipped at my bottom lip, his tongue delving inside to duel with mine.

I heard him moan, and triumph and desire flooded through me. I wanted to crawl into his arms and feast on him for hours. I wanted to feel his hands all over me. I wanted to... I broke the kiss with a gasp and buried my face in his neck as I turned crimson. "Caleb's watching," I breathed, embarrassed. "What must he think?"

Nolan chuckled, the sound sending a shiver of delight through me. "That he was a fool to ever let you slip through his fingers." He kissed me softly one more time and then eased away. "Monday," he murmured.

"Monday?" I asked with a frown.

Caleb cleared his throat, and I looked over Nolan's shoulder to see him with his chair turned around so he was looking out the window of his office. "Are you finished?" he asked, wry humor in his tone.

"Yes," Nolan said, his fingers sliding over my cheek and eliciting another shiver. "For now."

Caleb swiveled and stared at us with amusement. "I can obtain the marriage license Monday morning. I'd suggest you marry soon afterward as word will spread quickly. You know how Mrs. Fredericks likes to gossip." He shrugged, as though accepting that as a usual occurrence.

"Who would marry us so quickly?" I asked, stunned and overwhelmed.

"If you want, I can perform the ceremony. I had a college friend whose minister was hospitalized with food poisoning so I became an ordained minister online in a matter of minutes. It's amazing how efficient the Internet is." He grinned and winked at me as Nolan rolled his eyes. "Think of me as Father Caleb."

I burst out laughing as I doubted he had many pure thoughts, and Nolan chuckled.

"Anyway, once you wed, I'll give you all the information you need to speak with the bank so you can change the passwords to the bank account, and I'll approach your uncle for the keys to your ranch." He looked at Nolan. "If you want my help."

"I'll want it," Nolan said. "A show of solidarity is never a bad thing." He eased me to sit again in my chair and settled beside me.

I looked from Nolan, who now sat clasping one of my hands, to Caleb. Any humor I had felt had faded, and I again felt overwhelmed by how quickly my life was changing. "That's it. We show up here, say a few words, and we're married?"

Chuckling, Caleb leaned back. "Yep. I've never understood the desire to beggar myself when it's really nothing more than a five-minute ceremony."

Nolan rolled his eyes and groaned. "That's because you don't have a sentimental bone in your body."

"No Italian blood in me," Caleb quipped. "Now, we need two witnesses. We can ask two of the secretaries. Or I can ask a few of my siblings to drop by. Or a few of your friends," he said, waving in my direction. "What would you prefer?"

"I don't care. I don't have a lot of friends," I said in a soft voice.

Nolan said, "Ask Cora and Quinn. If they're free, I'd prefer them to your secretaries."

Caleb nodded. "Yes, and they can keep a secret. Tara's the worst."

I frowned at the names flying around and Nolan explained, "They're Caleb's siblings. My cousins."

Caleb sat at the desk, writing down a few notes. When he spoke, all teasing was gone, and he stared at me solemnly. "You have to keep up the charade for a few more days, Theo. You have to have them believe you are weak and alone. If they suspect something's different, they could take the rest of what is rightfully yours."

I swallowed. "I understand." Pulling out my cell phone, I looked at Nolan. "Can I have your number?" I glanced at Caleb as he made a noise of disagreement. "I'll have to tell them something. I disappeared last night, and they'll wonder what happened to me." I blanched at the twenty-two new text messages from my cousins. The last one from Briar made me blanch. *Where the hell are you? How could you renege on your homage last night? We thought your father meant more to you than that you ungrateful little bitch. Willow and I expected you to be home by now. We'll plan another outing for you next weekend.*

I gasped, dropping my phone down as I fought panic. I wanted to stay here forever. To never go back to my uncle's house. To never see them again. Two more days seemed like an eternity.

I barely noticed when Nolan picked up my phone, stood, and handed it to Caleb, although I did notice he didn't seem as upset as I thought he would be. Focusing on Nolan as he stared at his cousin while he read the texts, I saw Nolan tense the more Caleb swore under his breath.

When Caleb read a particularly damning one out loud, Nolan swore and paced away.

"This is how they talk to you?" he rasped, staring at me with eyes lit with rage. For me.

I swallowed, momentarily overcome, focusing on his anger and concern. For me. *Me.* "If I'd answered the first text, it never would have escalated. I learned to placate them long ago." I sighed with relief when he pulled me out of my chair to hold me close, and I rested my head on his shoulder.

"You'll never have to suffer through their abuse again, Theo. You won't have to go out with them next weekend. We'll be married. You'll do what *you* want," he vowed.

"Promise?" I whispered as I tried, and failed, not to cling to him as his words were like a soothing balm to the aches in my soul.

He kissed my head before easing me away. "Promise."

Caleb tapped my phone on the desk. "In light of these texts, I think it best neither of us returns you to your uncle's home. I don't want to arouse suspicion."

I felt Nolan tense beside me before he nodded his agreement.

"Return to The Hill. There's a car service there. I'll arrange for it to bring you home," Caleb said as he picked up the phone. "I'll see you both here Monday at ten a.m."

~

I tiptoed into my uncle's house, uncertain as to my reception. It was after one in the afternoon, and I hadn't seen my cousins since last night. I had hoped they would be worried about me, but all of their texts were accusatory and hostile. Thankfully, they hadn't recognized Nolan.

Just as I was about to escape into my room, Briar gripped my arm and spun me around to face her. "Where have you been?" she demanded. "You snuck out last night rather than fulfill your side of the homage to your father."

I ducked my head as a decade's worth of bile and vitriol wanted to bubble up and burst forth. *Two more days. Two more days,* I chanted to myself as I took deep breaths. Soon, I'd be free. "I spent a little time with him. With the man who put his jacket on my shoulders."

She snorted and tossed back her black hair, her grey eyes lit with derision. "As if a man that gorgeous would even notice you. I bet Willow and I together couldn't satisfy that man."

I shivered at the thought of Nolan with them and prayed he'd never betray me with them. Anyone but them. I wasn't so naïve as to believe we'd have a fairytale marriage where he never strayed. Our marriage was based on necessity. He needed my water, and I needed him to help secure my funds from my uncle. Nothing more. Any passion we felt today would soon fade.

I grimaced as Briar screeched in my ear. "Yes, Briar?" I whispered as I scrunched over. Suddenly, playing the role of meek

41

little cousin wasn't all that difficult. I wanted her to ignore me so I could escape to my room and think about how my life had been upended in the past twenty-four hours.

"Where were you last night?" she asked, one hand on a curvy hip. Although she had no reason to preen in front of me, she believed she should always practice and relished any opportunity to make me feel dowdy and plain.

"I was with him. I fell asleep, and he let me stay at his cabin." I grimaced at the mention of the cabin, but Briar snorted and rolled her eyes.

"A likely story. He probably got a closer look at you and wanted nothing to do with you. You little parasite." She smiled. "Daddy only has to take care of you for a few more weeks and then you're on the streets."

I nodded, thinking about my uncle and what he'd done. My anger must have shone in my gaze because she gripped my chin to stare at me. I replaced anger with remorse, and she nodded with satisfaction.

After Briar sashayed away, I heaved out a sigh of relief and entered my tiny room. It held a twin bed that the door bumped into and a small dresser crammed into the space at the foot of the bed. There wasn't even room for a nightstand. I could almost touch two opposite walls with my outstretched arms, but the tiny space was mine.

Uncle had a small house, and I'd chosen this cramped space rather than having to share a room with either of my cousins. After dumping my bag on the floor, I ensured my door was shut and locked, and fell onto the hard mattress, instantly dreaming about the feather-soft bed from last night.

Was it all a dream? Was my life so miserable that I'd invented Nolan and Caleb?

I ran my fingers over my lips, remembering the feel of his lips on mine. I closed my eyes and breathed deeply, remembering his scent. Shivering, I heard his voice, that deep rich baritone. It hadn't been a dream.

As I lay on my side, I relived the moments I'd spent with him. Although he seemed sincere in his desire to marry me, I wondered if he could ever really care for me. His words from last night, "I'll hate you forever," ricocheted around my brain, and I curled up even tighter on my bed. What had I agreed to?

CHAPTER 5

NOLAN

The next day, I kept staring at the clock and wondering if the day would ever end. I wished Theo would call. Hearing her voice would ease a little of the panic I felt at what was to come tomorrow. How in God's name was I marrying tomorrow?

I'd never thought I'd marry. I'd thought I'd be the doting uncle who bought ice cream treats and took everyone fishing. The one who planned horseback pack trips and camping expeditions. My breath caught at the thought I could be a dad one day. Letting out that breath, I hoped I didn't fuck it up as badly as my dad had.

After I finished my chores and showered, I rested on my bed and gave in to temptation, pulling my cell phone out. As I listened to the phone ring, I was tempted to hang up. Why had they invented caller id? If I hung up, then Theo'd think I was a stalker or a freak. Now, I waited to see if she answered. And then find some way to leave a charming message if she didn't. This is why I never dated. Who was able to do this shit?

As I listened to ring after ring, I realized she wasn't going to answer, and I battled a deep disappointment. I needed to hear her voice. Just as I knew the call was going to voicemail, I heard a click. "Hello?"

Nothing but silence and a soft panting noise and then a click. I stared at the phone, wondering if she'd hung up on me, but it didn't say call ended. "Theo?" For some reason, I was whispering in my own bedroom.

"Nolan?" She was whispering too and then I heard music.

"Hi. I shouldn't have called. I'm sorry."

"No! Don't hang up."

I imagined her sage-green eyes pleading with me, and I settled back against my pillows. "I won't." I smiled, suddenly delighted by the intimacy of a phone call. Hearing her voice and having to imagine what she was doing was sexy as hell. "I wanted to hear your voice."

Dammit, why'd I say that? Now I sounded like a loser teenager, not a somewhat mature thirty-four-year-old worthy of marrying her.

"You did? That's so sweet. I've been trying to convince myself this isn't a dream. Hearing from you helps." She lowered her voice, and I felt chills down my spine at her sexy, throaty voice. "I'm hiding from my cousins in my bedroom."

"Were they horrible to you yesterday?" She sighed, and I wished I were beside her and I could hold her in my arms. How was I already this protective of her?

"Yes. They're angry I escaped with you. They think I owe them two nights of shame now."

"You owe them nothing." I unfisted my hand as I fought back my rage at the thought of her cousins attempting to shame her again. "You're free tomorrow, Theo." I said her name like *Teo*, and I heard her sigh again. I hoped it was from pleasure.

"I should ask you this in person, but I'll never have the

courage." A long exhale and then she cleared her throat. "Will you promise me something?"

"What?" I waited as the silence on the line was so long, I feared she'd hung up.

"Will you promise me you won't ever have an affair with either of my cousins?"

"What?" I sat up, wishing I could see her. I hung up, flipped through screens on my phone until I saw the app for a video call, and punched in her number. I saw it ringing and waited until she answered. "We can't have this conversation without me seeing you." I hated the embarrassment and shame I saw in her beautiful eyes. "What brought this on?"

She shrugged and raised a hand up to her face, covering her eyes.

"Theo, drop the hand. Please let me see you."

She did as I asked and met my eyes. "I saw Briar yesterday. She said she doubted I'd ever satisfy you and that she and Willow together wouldn't satisfy you."

I flushed red and had to bite back a string of swear words.

"I know this wasn't wanted by either of us, but can you promise me—"

When I shook my head, she deflated, and a tear trickled down her cheek. I raised my hand as though I could swipe it away. Damn this distance, even if it was only a matter of miles. I wanted her in my arms now. "Theo, stop." I waited until she looked at me again. "I promise I won't cheat on you with anyone. Ever." Her eyes flared with surprise. "I take my vows seriously."

"Forever is a long time."

I nodded, wondering if forever would be anywhere near long enough with this woman. "It is. And we'll fight. And make up. And have moments when we're bored. But I'll never cheat. I'll never make you feel second best. You'll always be the most important person in my life. You'll be *my wife*."

She stared at me in wonder. "I promise I won't cheat on you, either."

I grinned at her, letting out a deep breath of relief when she smiled at me. I laid back down and relaxed against the pillows. "Show me your room."

She pulled a face, but turned the phone around. "It's tiny, but it's mine." It took all of thirty seconds for me to see her minuscule bedroom with pictures of horses tacked to the wall.

"This is mine," I said, as I showed her my room with the pitched roof and a large window overlooking the ranch. It had a desk, a comfortable chair, and two dressers with a door leading to a Jack and Jill bathroom. It was all mine since only Alessia and my dad lived at home, and the third floor of the farmhouse was unoccupied except for me.

"You're so lucky." She was now lying down too, although it looked like her head was at the foot of her bed.

"I am. And tomorrow, you are too. You return to your ranch." I paused and then blurted out. "Why isn't your family better to you?" I winced as I knew she could ask me the same question if she knew me any better.

"You deserve to know," she whispered. "My uncle is my dad's brother. He hated the ranch as a boy, and when the ranch was left to both my dad and uncle, he insisted my dad buy him out. He wanted nothing to do with it."

"I don't understand."

"Land wasn't worth much when they were young. Not like it is today. He got what it was worth then, but it's worth a fortune now." She lowered her voice even more. "Uncle is in real estate now. Imagine what he could get for the land."

I paled. "You can't sell it, Theo. It's the best ranch land in the valley. Even better than mine."

She nodded. "I know." She fidgeted. "He thought my dad would leave him something. A parcel. I don't know, something. But my dad left it all to me, and saddled my uncle with caring for me. Uncle must have resented that. I always thought he liked me, but I was wrong. No one robs you blind if they like you."

"Theo, none of this is your fault. It's your uncle's." I winced. "Hell, it's even Caleb's or his dad's for not looking into it." I stared into her eyes. "Never yours."

"If I'd known I could end all of this earlier by marrying, I would have. I thought I had to wait until I was twenty-four. I'm so sorry for dragging you into this mess."

I shook my head, not wanting her to apologize to me again. "Do you care I'm ten years older than you?" I leaned up on an elbow, grinning down at her.

"No," she whispered, flushing. She cut off what she was going to say when there was a knock on her door. "I have to go. See you tomorrow."

She was gone before I could even say goodbye.

~

That evening, I rummaged in the fridge for something to eat. Ally, as Alessia was often called, was a fabulous cook, but she refused to cook for my dad and me every night. I didn't blame her. She worked hard and shouldn't feel the responsibility for feeding us too. However, as I stared into the empty fridge, I wondered if I'd missed my turn to go to the grocery store.

"Always did have a bottomless-pit stomach," my dad groused as he shuffled into the kitchen in search of another cup of coffee.

I grunted rather than reply, hoping to slink out without having to talk with him. I'd rather go hungry than have to share more than a few words a month with him. Instead, he stood in front of me, blocking one of my exits. I could push past him, but I knew it was better to hear him out than postpone whatever it was he wanted to say. "Yeah?"

"That's all you have to say after you didn't even commemorate the tenth anniversary?" His dark brown eyes shone with disgust, and his blond hair was shaggier than usual. My father was a giant of a man. Inches taller than I was at six feet five, he commanded the attention of everyone in a room by his mere presence. Before the death of my mama, he had earned their respect due to his kindness and willingness to do everything possible to help a neighbor. Everything had changed that day. Well, everything except his attitude toward me. That had been constant since I was a boy.

Whereas I had the look of my mother, with black hair and her blue eyes, he had straw-blond hair with eyes the color of chocolate. For ten years, I'd thought they'd been the color of bitter chocolate. "I commemorated it in my own way."

"You spat on her memory by refusing to go to the cemetery."

Taking a deep breath, I shook my head before pushing past him and walking to the other side of the kitchen, ensuring the huge island was between us. "No, I didn't. I went earlier in the day on my own. I didn't need to be there with a group. I talked to Mama by myself."

His eyes glowed with hatred as he looked at me. "Lie to yourself if you want, boy, but you weren't special to her. No need to start actin' like she had a soft spot for you now."

Staring at him, I felt like I was drowning in memories. In moments when he'd verbally torn a strip off me and Mama had always defended me. Where she'd found a way to ensure his cruelty didn't sting as badly as it should have. All I had was the memory of her love as a protection against him now, and after ten years, that protection was wearing thin. "Don't," I warned.

"Don't what? Speak the truth?" He snorted as he ran a hand over his jaw as though trying to figure out a way he could round the island and pummel me.

"Don't lie about how Mama was." My eyes glowed with love and devotion to her, and the memory of her love for me.

50

Huffing out a breath, he hitched out a hip and leaned against a counter. "Not that you asked, but a decent number of folks showed up for the memorial."

"Ally told me. Mama was well loved."

"Not by your siblings," he muttered. "They couldn't be bothered to return."

I stared at him, refusing to engage with him about my siblings. I knew they had scattered as soon as they were old enough, and I had no desire to talk about them with him. Although I wished I were closer to my six siblings who lived away from the ranch, too, I'd never admit that to him. Any perceived weakness was a weapon for my father.

He stood tall and moved to walk away.

"You've been holed up in your office on the computer a lot lately, Dad. If it's something for the ranch, you've never told me or Ally." When he continued to smirk at me, I glowered at him. "What are you doing?"

He smiled smugly at me and tilted his head as he looked me over as though he found me wanting in every way. "Why don't you try to figure it out?"

I felt my cheeks redden and bit back my urge to rail at him. At fate. Instead, I kept my voice as even as possible. "Tell me you aren't using the computer for porn, Dad."

"Porn?" He smirked at me and shook his head. "Why wouldn't I?" He shrugged. "But I've learned a lot of interesting things on that computer, and some have come in mighty handy lately."

He strolled off, leaving me puzzled as I rubbed at my now roiling stomach and aching heart.

~

THEODORA

Later that night, I rested in bed as I thought about my phone call with Nolan. I couldn't believe he'd called me. That he'd wanted to hear my voice. I'd wanted to tell him how sexy I thought his voice was, but I already felt like a silly schoolgirl. He didn't need to have any suspicions about me proved correct.

What would it be like tomorrow? Would it be as simple and as cold as Caleb had made it out to be? A five-minute ceremony without much emotion between the two of us as we said our vows?

Curling onto my side, I battled against a deep regret that I wouldn't have the wedding of my dreams. Although impossible, I'd always dreamed of my dad walking me down the aisle as Pachelbel's Canon played while friends and family watched. Considering I had few friends and no family who cherished me, that was a dream destined to remain unfulfilled.

I choked back a sob as the only part of that dream that mattered was my dad. I missed him so much, and he'd never be by my side again. I'd never hear him laugh or read something from the newspaper that he knew would entertain me or hear his wise advice ever again. He'd been gone ten years, but the missing him never ended.

Swiping at my tears, I focused on tomorrow. What would it be like to live on the ranch again? Nolan had his own ranch, so I doubted he'd want to move to mine. I couldn't kill the hope that he would because I longed to have a real marriage. A marriage where we wanted to spend time together.

Taking deep breaths, I tried to relax enough to sleep, although I feared it would remain elusive as I knew my life was about to be upended in a few short hours.

CHAPTER 6

NOLAN

I entered Caleb's office building a little before ten on Monday, battling doubts and sweating even though it was barely above freezing on a bitterly cold Montana winter day. Except for the few moments I'd spent talking with Theo on the phone, I'd worried every minute I was away from her that I was making the worst mistake of my life.

My father, not the most perceptive man since Mama's death ten years ago, had even noticed my unease. However, he'd only looked at me this morning, grunted, and returned to his computer to continue to search for God knows what. I didn't want to know, especially if he was watching porn.

God, how embarrassing would that be? My sixty-year-old dad watching porn? He hadn't denied it last night, and seemed to enjoy how uncomfortable I was.

I took a final swig of my coffee before I tucked the metal travel coffee cup proclaiming "We Have The Best Nuts In Town" into my jacket pocket. The owners of the local hardware store came up with a new outrageous tagline each year, and this was my favorite from two years ago. My sister Alessia preferred, "We're Here When You Have A Screw Loose."

I walked to Caleb's door and tapped on it. At his harried, "come in," I pushed it open and sauntered inside. When he glared at me in exasperation, I held my arms out at my sides. "What?"

"You couldn't even be bothered to dress up for your own wedding?" Caleb asked with a raised eyebrow. "You stink worse than a fresh pile of horse dung." His gaze flicked over my red-checkered flannel jacket with wool lining, stained jeans, and scuffed boots. "Nice wedding apparel."

I shrugged. "I run a ranch. What do you expect?" Suddenly wishing I had more coffee to drink, I fiddled with the cup's lid in my pocket. "Besides, if I showered and got dressed up on a Monday morning, Ally would have asked questions."

Staring at me with sorrow, Caleb nodded. "Yeah, but your dad wouldn't have, huh?"

I shrugged again, as though my dad's indifference didn't bother me. "She's not here yet?" At his roll of his eyes, I sat and then stood before sitting again. "I hope she's not late."

"It's not even ten, Nol," he muttered. "I just got back from getting the license. There's time." He set his pen down and stared at me. "You sure you know what you're doing?" His gaze was one of a fiercely protective older brother. Although we were nearly the same age, Caleb had always been my champion. He said the eleven-month age gap between us gifted him with wisdom I'd never have. Perhaps he was right.

"I sure as hell hope so," I muttered. I stood again and paced the small area before his desk. "What if we're miserable? What if we're not and then she dies?" I leaned a hip on his desk, and my shoulders sagged, finally meeting his gaze, now filled with compassion and concern. "What if she finds out the truth about me?"

∼

THEODORA

I stood, frozen in place with my hand raised to knock on the door as Nolan's plaintive question floated out to me. *"What if she finds out the truth about me?"* I canted forward, my breath catching, desperate to hear Caleb's answer. However, their voices were low murmurs, and I couldn't discern anything of value.

Taking a step away from the door, I tried to calm my racing thoughts. What about the truth was so awful that would prevent me from wanting to marry him? Did he torture puppies? Have ménage fantasies? Stalk his ex-girlfriend? Have a vicious temper and become abusive? My mind whirling, I thought I'd faint.

I gripped the doorjamb, suddenly wishing I hadn't agreed to this mad scheme. That I'd resigned myself to a few more weeks of misery at my uncle's house. Instead, here I was, about to link myself for life to a man I didn't even know. How had my life gone so topsy-turvy in a matter of a few days?

I heard a commotion down the hallway and firmed my shoulders, knocking briskly on the door. When Nolan opened the door, his eyes shining with relief at the sight of me, a small portion of my panic abated. However, I could still sense fear and uncertainty, and I knew, with an aching clarity, that our marriage was off to a rocky start.

"Nolan," I whispered, my voice shaking.

"You're here," he murmured, his deep voice evoking a shiver. At my nod, he pulled me close, hugging me. "Everything will be all right. I promise."

I felt him stiffen a second before he released me. "Cora, Quinn," he said to the people I suddenly realized were standing behind us. "Thanks for coming today."

I glanced over my shoulder, blanching at the sight of two

gorgeous women in fashionable jackets with scarves tied jaun-
tily around their necks. One had auburn hair while the other a
rich chestnut. They shared Caleb's eyes, and I realized they must
be his sisters and Nolan's cousins.

Following Nolan into Caleb's office, I ran a hand down my
skirt, wishing I had something other than my serviceable grey
wool. I'd worn black leather boots and my turquoise knit wool
sweater that always made me feel confident because it enhanced
my eyes. I fidgeted after taking off my coat as Nolan stilled,
staring at me. "Is everything all right?"

He shook his head, before reaching for my hand and giving
it a gentle squeeze. "Caleb's right. I should have dressed up." He
motioned to his work clothes. "Forgive me."

I squeezed his hand. "It doesn't matter what you're wearing,"
I whispered. "What matters is you're here."

"Speaking of that," one of the women who had followed us in
the room asked, "why exactly are we here?" She pointed to
herself and her sister.

Nolan winked at her. "You're here to witness my marriage."

I bit my lip as I saw his cousins' mouths drop open in shock
and edged closer to Nolan. When he appeared resolute in his
decision, a little more of my anxiety eased.

"Marriage," the chestnut-haired beauty gasped. "To her? Do
you even know her?"

"Do we know her?" the auburn-haired one asked. She looked
to be free-spirited with a nose ring and bright pink eye shadow.

"Cora, Quinn," Caleb said in a commanding voice that made
them bristle. I watched fascinated as the younger sisters swallowed the barrage of questions I instinctively knew they wanted
to unleash. Instead, Caleb gave them a quelling glance, and they
shifted in their stylish boots.

"I know her," Nolan said in a soft voice. "That's what
matters." He tugged at my hand and led me to stand by Caleb's
desk. "Let's get going."

I nodded. "I agree with Nolan. Let's marry and start our life together." I smiled as I felt him quiver at my words. Gripping his big hand with both of mine, I focused on Caleb and his solemn words.

Although this wasn't the wedding of my dreams—with the church pews filled with friends and family and my father walking me down the aisle—I promised myself I would remember this day. I wouldn't wish it away in my eagerness to regain my heritage. I sighed with pleasure as I realized Caleb wasn't saying only the bare bones of the required words. He spoke a few words that sounded like a blessing, urging us to turn to each other in times of doubt and to seek solace from each other from now on.

Soon, Nolan grabbed my hand and slipped a large ring onto my finger, pledging himself to me. I fisted my hand, not wanting his ring to fall off. When it was my turn to give him a ring, I looked at Caleb in defeat. I had nothing to give my new husband.

However, Caleb held out a ring and I grabbed it, slipping it on Nolan's finger, smiling at him when his breath caught as I caressed his hand while speaking my vows. I could spend days lost, staring into his eyes.

As I flung my hands up to cup Nolan's face to kiss him, the ring he'd given me flew off and I heard a muffled squeal. I giggled, and then sighed with pleasure as Nolan kissed me reverently.

"Later," he promised, raising his head. His blue eyes sparkled with mischief when he stared at his cousins standing behind us. "Did you catch the ring, Cora?"

"No, Quinn did," the chestnut-haired one, Cora, answered with a smile. "You really do like her," she breathed in wonder. "What will Alessia say when you come home with a bride?"

I saw Nolan attempt to conceal dread in his gaze, before he forced another lazy grin. "Who's to say he's not coming home with me?" I said in a throaty whisper, earning a startled gasp from Cora and Quinn and a bark of laughter from Caleb. Holding out my hand, I accepted the too large ring from Quinn and slipped it back on.

Meeting Nolan's fiery eyes, I shrugged. "I have a home now too."

He nodded, raising my fingers to kiss, and then urged me to sign the paperwork, formalizing our union.

~

I watched as Caleb pointed out to Nolan where to sign, surprised he had so much faith in his cousin that he didn't even read over the marriage contract before scribbling his signature. I took my time, reading each word. Nothing more than a wedding contract. Nothing less either. My hand shook and then I signed, underlining my name with a flourish.

I heard Nolan chuckle at that, and I met his amused scrutiny. "I see no reason to leave any doubt."

"You must have had none as you read the entire thing," he teased. He laughed as his two cousins pounced, giving him big, messy kisses, and then turned to me to offer handshakes.

"We'll have a family party soon," Quinn said. "Maybe that will be a way to entice the others to return."

"Quinn, leave it," Caleb barked. "Let them enjoy today, and we can plan something this spring or summer. When the weather's nice."

Cora leaned in, giving me the hint of a hug. "Congratulations and welcome to the family." She looked at Nolan. "You'll let us know when it's no longer a secret?" At his firm nod, she winked at him, waved goodbye to her brother, and steered her sister from the room.

"Thank God for Cora," Nolan muttered.

I ran a soothing hand down his arm, happy when he clasped

it as though it brought him comfort. A deep tranquility filled me today, and I believed nothing would be able to strip it from me. I had to trust I'd married a good man. His family adored him. I had to have faith that I'd soon adore him too.

"Now, to the uncle's?" Nolan asked.

"Do we have to?" I blurted out. "I'd hoped we'd go to my ranch and start putting the house to rights."

Caleb shook his head. "No, we must talk with him." He rose, snatching up the papers on his desk. "I'll have your license filed today and there will be no doubt it is legal." He looked at both of us with grim humor. "Soon, there will be no reason for Cora and Quinn to keep your secret."

"Just long enough for us to escape town and get to her ranch," Nolan said. He squeezed my hand. "Come. One more hurdle and you'll be home again."

I nodded, the dream of returning home filling me with hope. I ignored Nolan and Caleb's banter as Nolan helped me on with my jacket and then walked me down the hallway. "That's mine," I said as I pointed to my suitcase.

Nolan hefted it and led me outside to his truck, stowing it in the back of his double-cab truck. I wasn't used to being helped into vehicles as I'd had to fend for myself for so long, but I appreciated his assistance as I attempted to climb into the front cab wearing a skirt. I let out a gasp when he hefted me up and set me inside. I blushed as he ran a finger over my cheek.

"Just ask me next time, bella. I hate to see you strugglin' for no reason."

I sat, transfixed as I stared into his blue eyes. After I nodded at him, he chuckled and backed away, calling out that he'd meet Caleb at my uncle's office.

After he started the truck, I found myself unable to refrain from peppering him with questions. "Why weren't any of your siblings present?" I asked. "You mentioned seven or eight." I flushed at the acknowledgment that I'd paid such close attention to what he'd said the night we'd met.

"Seven," he murmured. "Most have flown the nest, as I suppose they should do." He sighed. "Few ever want to come home."

I heard a deep remorse in his voice. "Why?" I whispered.

"The ranch is mainly mine. I need help running it, but the day-to-day decisions are mine. I've done a good enough job of it," he said, his voice laced with pride.

I nodded as the LBarM was the most prosperous ranch in the region, if not the state. "They resent you?"

"No, they hate my father," he said. "My mama held us together. When she died, we started to splinter. There's little that will bind us together again."

I stared out the window, my belief that nothing could pierce my tranquility today already being tested. "They'll hate me too." At his silence, I knitted my hands together. "I'll cause you to lose your siblings."

He huffed out a breath, although I didn't hear any humor lacing the sound. "I've already lost them, Theo. They aren't coming back, and they sure as hell don't care about what happens to me. They left me to my fate years ago."

I gaped at him, confused and disquieted as he parked the truck outside my uncle's office. Suddenly, I wished this was all a dream. How had I agreed to marry a complete stranger?

∾

NOLAN

What a fucking moron, I swore to myself. Why not just tell her everything so she can run to the hills now? I silently fumed as I opened her door and lifted her out. Her skirt made it hard for her to maneuver, and I appreciated the fleeting moment I had to hold her in my arms. Taking a deep breath of her scent calmed me as I set her down, ready to face her uncle.

I stood beside her as she pushed open the office door and softly spoke to the secretary. When I heard the secretary try to fob Theo off for later in the week, I saw red. Thankfully, Caleb gripped my arm and shook his head.

"I think you'll see we're the eleven o'clock appointment," he said in his officious lawyer voice. "We're right on time."

The secretary looked down and then looked up at the three of us. "Oh, how silly of me to have overlooked that appointment."

"Overlooked, my ass," I muttered as I followed Theo to her uncle's office. I watched as he smiled with feigned interest and snuck a peek at his watch when she entered. Probably hoping for an early lunch.

Caleb shut the door behind us, urging Theo to sit. I sat beside her. He found a small table to perch on and he beamed at her uncle. "Uncle Bradley, it's so wonderful to finally meet you."

"Who are you to be calling me Uncle Bradley?" Bradley Miller demanded. His bushy eyebrows furrowed as he stacked his hands on the desk in front of him. He wore a tan suit that made him look washed out, and the harsh glare from the overhead lights made the bald spot on his head shine. "There's no love lost between me and the Doyles."

"Ah, so you know who I am." Holding a hand to his chest, Caleb smiled broadly and said, "Just so there's no confusion, I'm Caleb Doyle, of *D, D and Son*. I just became family today."

"That's impossible," Bradley Miller sputtered. "Theo?" he asked as he focused on my wife. "Who are these men and what are they playing at?"

"He's Caleb Doyle, my lawyer," she said in a low voice. "This is Nolan Burke." She froze as her uncle rose, pounding his desk with his fists.

"Get out! Get out now! You have no right to be in my office

and I will not speak with you." His brown eyes bulged with disbelief when none of us moved to obey his command. He seemed particularly surprised at Theo's disobedience. "Theodora," he growled.

"Is this how you've treated her for the past ten years?" I asked in a soft voice. "Ordering her about and expecting blind obedience?" I shook my head. "No wonder you were able to trick her into believing your baseless lies about a codicil to her father's will." I frowned when I saw confusion rather than cunning in his gaze.

"I don't know what you're talking about, young man," her uncle said. "I do know that I've been working diligently for the past few years to save what remains of her inheritance. No thanks to you and yours!"

I cast a quick glance at Caleb who shook his head in confusion. "Explain."

He shook his head, focusing on Theo. "Why are you here with these men?" he demanded.

"I married Nolan this morning. I know all about the fake codicil. I know all about you stealing money from the ranch account."

He blanched and shook his head. "No, Theo, you know nothing!" he rasped. "Please tell me you're not truly married to him. He's a vicious, manipulative bastard. Your life will be hell. By the time you're free of him, you'll have nothing. Nothing, Theo."

I squeezed her hand, hating the quiver of fear I felt in her. "As opposed to you?" I asked. "Tell us where the money's gone if you're so honorable."

He glared at me. "I don't know. I've been trying to figure out who's stealing it, but I can't."

Caleb snorted and rolled his eyes. "A likely story. Did you look to your daughters? They live a rich lifestyle without doing any hard work."

Miller's jaw ticked and his cheeks flushed. "Don't you dare insinuate that my daughters have been anything but good to their cousin these past ten years."

I heard Theo gasp in shock at his comment, and I burst out laughing. "You're kidding me, right? You claim to know nothing about the codicil to the will that says Theo has to agree to a ritualized humiliation every year on the anniversary of her father's death. Do you want to know what that's entailed?"

"Nolan, no," Theo whispered.

I ignored her, incensed that her uncle hadn't protected her. That he hadn't seen how vile his daughters were. "They force her to sit with her tits on display at a bar for thirty minutes, reveling in any and all abuse she receives. That's how we met."

Miller's eyes widened even farther, and he sat back in his chair. "It's not for dinner?" he whispered.

I saw Theo shake her head as tears slipped down her cheeks and landed on her chest. I suddenly felt like the bastard my father always said I was for hurting her. "Theo, I'm sorry," I breathed.

When her uncle chuckled, I focused on him again. He sat, comfortable in his chair, staring at me with contempt.

"Oh, aren't you a smooth one. Putting on the performance of a lifetime, feigning that you care about a damsel in distress. Did you act like you didn't know who she was so she trusted you even more? Did you act like you had no idea about the contracts?"

"Contracts?" I asked, casting a quick glance in Caleb's direction. When I saw Caleb glaring at Theo's uncle as though he wanted to commit murder, I knew I was only going to be in more trouble with her soon.

"Oh, you are good at acting the innocent," Miller said as he leaned forward and rested his forearms on the desk. "Her father kills your mother, in an innocent, horrific accident. But that's not good enough for your family, is it? Someone has to pay. Someone has to take the blame."

"Not Theo," I said in a hard voice.

"No," her uncle said, looking confused. "Her father. Thankfully, I was able to squash your own father's pathetic attempt at spreading the rumor he was drunk. Jake never drank."

"How do you know?" I demanded, a tinge of desperation in my voice.

"My father was in AA since I was six," Theo whispered beside me. "He hadn't touched a drop since my mother left us."

I sat, deflated at her words. Stunned, I gaped at her uncle who stared at me with a triumphant gleam in his eye. Suddenly, I knew my day was going to turn to pure shit.

"But no, your family, the blessed Burkes, had to have someone to blame. Someone had to pay for their loss," Miller went on. "What about what my niece lost? She lost just as much!"

"Black ice is a bitch," Caleb muttered, and I glared at him. I had no interest in his attempt at levity.

"We did nothing to her," I snapped, praying I spoke the truth.

"Nothing?" her uncle said as he slammed his fist onto his desk. "Your father said that if we didn't give you water rights for a decade, he'd sue and turn Theo's life into a living hell. He stipulated she was never to set foot on the ranch again until she was an adult, and that we could never have any contact with you."

"Cay?" I whispered.

He looked miserable as he met my tormented gaze. "I had nothing to do with this. It was my father who wrote everything up."

I winced as he didn't deny knowing about the contract, the horrible stipulations, and how bad it made me look. My God, had I really hated her for all these years when she should have been the one to despise me?

"How much were the rights for?" Theo whispered.

"A dollar a year."

"A dollar?" she gasped. "You've become rich and prospered for the past decade while I was forced to live in exile from my home?" She stared at me in horror.

I gripped her face, staring deeply into her eyes. "Listen to me, Theo." I swallowed as I attempted to still my racing heart and the panic that threatened to overwhelm me. "I knew nothing about this. Nothing!" I looked into her eyes, my breath quickening when I saw doubt and mistrust. "I promise you."

"What are your promises worth?" she whispered. "I don't know you well enough to know what to believe." She pulled back, freeing herself from my hold as she glanced at her uncle.

"Theo, you've acted like a fool and been played by a pair of charlatans. We'll get this marriage annulled. There's no reason to continue with this farce."

Theo looked at her hands gripped tightly together on her lap. "You said in that agreement with the Burkes that I could have returned when I was an adult. I've been an adult for years. Father wanted me to go to college, but I graduated two years ago." She looked at her uncle with grave disappointment. "Why was I never allowed back?"

"It's not out of guardianship until you are twenty-four. That's when I consider you an adult," her uncle sputtered.

She stared at him, her gorgeous green eyes dulled with pain. "So I should live years of my life in a town where I'm an object of pity, without friends, with cousins who hate me, in a room the size of a closet rather than at my own home on a *ranch*?" She shook her head in confusion. "It makes no sense, Uncle."

"Who the hell would want to live on a ranch when you could live in town? I saved you from a life toiling away on that godforsaken land. Don't be such a damn simpleton like your father," her uncle snapped at her, his bitterness about the ranch leaking out. "Divorce him, and everything will be fine again," he demanded.

I sat, my fingers digging into my thighs as I waited for her response. I knew, no matter what I said, I had to give Theo the freedom to answer. I needed her to make her own choice.

"No," she breathed. "I won't divorce him. When I said my vows, I meant them. The 'for worse' part of our marriage just happened to come a little sooner than I would have liked."

She stood and I rose, flanking her. "Goodbye, Uncle."

She left the room with Caleb and me behind her, ignoring her uncle's bellows of, "Theo!"

CHAPTER 7

NOLAN

We rattled down the bumpy lane to Theo's ranch, and I realized I owed Caleb yet another favor. He'd had someone plow out the drive. I swore as we hit a particularly teeth-rattling pothole, wincing as I had no desire to blow out a tire this far from anywhere. With my luck, we'd be out of cell range and then we'd freeze to death on our first day of marriage.

We pulled up at her ranch house, and I shifted to park but kept the truck running as it was pumping out heat on this freezing January day. We'd be fortunate if it was only five below. "Wait." I grabbed her arm as she moved to hop out of the truck. I hated the scornful look on her face and the way she jerked away from my touch. How had everything changed so quickly?

She sat there for a minute, eyebrows raised, and chin jutted forward. "What?" she demanded. "Why do I have to wait?"

"You don't know what the inside is like. It could be a mess. No one's been in there for a decade."

"Don't tell me what to do. It's not like this whole thing wasn't planned by you and your cousin," she snapped, flinging the door open. She winced at the brutal slap of frigid air and tugged her scarf more tightly around her neck before hopping down.

I turned my truck off and raced after her as she clomped through snow drifts in an attempt to reach the stairs leading to the front door. "Dammit! I'm not the villain in all this!" I screamed.

"Are you kidding me?" she yelled as she stopped three steps above me. "You conveniently forgot to mention the minor issue of blackmailing me and my estate so that you'd have cheap water for a decade. And adding the little proviso that I remain far from the ranch?" She scratched at her chin in a mockery of someone in deep thought. "Somehow I think you're full of shit!"

She turned around to resume her climb up the stairs, but her foot caught on a patch of snow hardened into ice and tripped. Losing her balance, she had nothing to grab onto, and I saw her reach for the banister, but all she grasped was handfuls of snow.

"Theo!" I roared as I leapt forward, catching her at the last minute as she tumbled backward. I grunted at the impact and at feeling her in my arms again. "Jesus, woman, don't scare me like that again." I shook as I held her close, swiping snow off her face and hat. "Are you all right? Did you hurt anything?"

She squirmed and struggled. "Let me go. Don't touch me. I can't stand you!"

"Seriously?" I snapped. "Fine." I took a step away and released her, watching her fall into a snowbank. Rather than pleasure, guilt swamped me as she emerged, sputtering and miserable, covered head to toe in snow. When she burst into tears, I felt like the worst bully. "Theo," I whispered. "I'm sorry."

She sat in her prim skirt and heavy parka, shivering as she sobbed. "Why can't anything ever go right?" she whispered.

I groaned and hauled her up, patting off the worst of the snow. "This will go right, I promise you. Our marriage will be something good. You'll see."

"We're already fighting." A tear was caught on her eyelash, making it sparkle. "How can that be a good omen?"

"Fighting doesn't mean we're doomed to fail," I whispered. "Fighting can lead to really good make-up sex." I chuckled when she flushed. "Come, let's see if there's any hope for your house tonight." I ignored her protests and carried her up the stairs, carefully stepping around the spot that had caused her to trip and topple backward.

I set her down, hating to feel her shivering from the cold and swearing at myself for being such an asshole as to dump her into the snow. When she finally opened the doors to her house, we entered. I sniffed, expecting a musty scent of a long empty place. Instead, it smelled like furniture polish and air freshener. "Who would come in here?" I asked.

She shook her head. "I don't know."

She shucked her boots and outerwear, and I smiled at seeing her thick woolen socks. My smile faded as I watched her wander through the rooms, her fingers reverently touching pieces of furniture. She paused in different places, her gaze distant, as though reliving a precious memory. When she turned the corner into the great room, I heard her gasp.

I raced toward her, wondering what could have happened. "Theo," I panted as I rounded the corner. She stood with her hands over her heart as she stared at a table full of pictures. Tears streamed down her face as a shaking hand reached out to trace over one of the framed photographs. In it, a much younger Theo stood beside her father with his arm wrapped over her shoulders as they held fishing poles.

Leaving her to her memories, I looked around the large room with cathedral ceilings. This well-built log home had a great room with enormous windows facing an expansive view down the valley. Along one wall was a huge stone fireplace. To the other side of the great room was the kitchen and dining area, and I saw a hallway that I assumed led to bedrooms. Although winter, it wasn't cold. No dust had accumulated on the fine antiques and other furniture in the room. Who had taken care of this house?

I wandered to the large window and stared down the valley. To the right, I could just make out the entrance to my ranch. Our home was over a ridge, so I'd never paid much attention to this home, other than to admire it the few times I saw it. Now, this is where my wife wanted to live. *My wife*, I thought with a deep panic.

I turned to face her, my eyes roving over the room as I realized she was absent. She had disappeared without making a sound. After glancing into the empty kitchen and dining room area, I headed down the hallway. The first room was the master bedroom, empty and curiously devoid of the personal touches present in the great room. I poked my head into another room and frowned. This must have been her father's room. Much smaller than the master bedroom, it had a cozy feel to it with a thick woolen blanket on the bed and a comfortable chair in the corner to curl up in to read late at night.

I approached the next room, my breath catching at her highlighted in the last burst of sunlight as she laid with her arms out on what must have been her childhood bed. Her hair was loose around her, sparkling red and blonde in the sun's rays. How could I ever have thought of this beautiful woman as a mouse?

The light pink and purple comforter she rested on was covered in unicorns, and my heart stuttered to imagine how her life had changed ten years ago. I'd been devastated when I lost Mama, but I'd been a man in my twenties. She'd only been thirteen. I'd had my siblings, until they'd abandoned the ranch, one by one, leaving only Alessia behind. And I'd always had Caleb.

She, my sweet Theo…she'd had a featherbrained uncle and her viper cousins.

"Theo," I whispered, kneeling beside her bed and placing a hand on her calf. "Bella," I breathed. "I'm so glad you're home."

Her hand dropped to trace over mine. "How is it so clean?" Her soft voice was filled with wonder. "It's as though I just left to go to that stupid party at my friend's house." Her breath caught. "If I'd just stayed home that night. If I hadn't…" She closed her eyes as tears leaked out. "I never would have lost all of this. I'd still have my dad."

I held her hand, my thumb caressing her soft skin. "None of it was your fault. It was never your fault, bella." I sat by the bed, taking comfort in the fact I could hold her hand and that there was a momentary truce between us. I wished we could simply forget the ugliness from the visit to her uncle's office, but I knew we'd have to face that at some point. For now, I would take the peace that filled my soul. I knew how fleeting it was, and I savored it.

∾

THEODORA

I rested on my old bed, memories of my life before the accident overwhelming me. Seeing my dad's room—clean and as though in expectation of his arrival at any moment—had been a dagger to my heart. Now, resting on my old comforter, remembering my thirteen-year-old self, I pleaded with time to let me go back. To change just one decision.

Nolan sat beside me, his presence comforting. I never knew holding someone's hand in silence and understanding could bring so much solace, but it was a balm to my tender heart. I felt bruised and battered and unable to argue about what I'd learned at my uncle's office.

Turning my head, I buried my face in my pillow, unable to face another betrayal. Not today. Today I'd wanted to celebrate my triumphant return home. Instead, all I felt was a deep sorrow and an all-consuming remorse.

I didn't know how long we sat like that in silence, but by the time I opened my eyes, darkness had fallen, and long shadows filled my room. I shifted, stiff and achy. "Nolan?" I whispered.

"Bella," he murmured, his soft, deep voice reassuring me in ways I didn't even know I needed reassuring. "Do you want supper?"

I felt him kiss my fingers and melted even farther into the bed. "Yes, but we don't have any food." I was unable to stifle my groan of regret when he released my hand and stood up. When he leaned over me with his hands on either side of my shoulders, I battled a desire to swipe at the locks of hair that had fallen over his forehead. Somehow, everything and nothing had changed during our quiet interlude together.

"Let me see. Rest, my bella," he murmured, kissing my nose before he eased away.

I listened to his soft footsteps as he departed, and I curled onto my side, hugging the hand he'd kissed to my chest. "I'm acting worse than my thirteen-year-old self over him."

Dozing and daydreaming, I had no idea how much time passed before he returned and urged me to rise. When he saw me shiver, he left and came back with my suitcase from the back of his pickup and nodded to it.

"Put on dry clothes. I should have brought this in earlier for you so your clothes were warmer. I'm sorry." His blue eyes gleamed with sincerity as he nodded and slipped away. "I'll be in the great room."

Shivering, I wondered what the night had in store for us.

NOLAN

C aleb, in all of his organizational wonder, had had an intern shop and leave bags of food in the back of my truck. Thankfully, we had plenty of food to get us through the next few weeks if we wanted. The furnace seemed to be in good condition and pumping out heat, although I needed to search around outside to see if there was any firewood. I'd love to curl up with Theo in my arms before that fireplace in the great room.

Just as I was finishing up making us sandwiches, she emerged from the back part of the house in flannel pajamas and fuzzy socks. I grinned at her. She'd never looked more adorable. Or so young. I could envision her, running around the house as her father cooked and she told him about her day. Doing homework on the table near the kitchen, shouting out questions to her dad as he hummed or whistled. Lip syncing songs as she improvised dance routines. All the things my sisters had done that drove me crazy but endeared them to me in ways I could never fully describe. With an aching clarity, I realized she was a woman who could make every place she went a home.

"I've made sandwiches," I said, clearing the gruffness from my voice. "I can heat up some soup if you prefer."

She shook her head. "No, sandwiches are fine." She smiled as I motioned for her to sit at the table and set a plate with a sandwich, cut up carrots, and a cookie in front of her. "You make me feel like a little girl."

I shrugged and flushed. "It was what was easy. I find I'm in the mood for easy tonight." I picked up a note and handed it to her. "I saw this when I started to prepare supper."

I watched as she read it, a smile playing over her features. "What?" I whispered, taken with her subtle beauty.

"Your cousin is a remarkable man. He had a key to the house. Or his father did as my lawyer. I'm not sure why." She shrugged as she waved her arm around. "He arranged for someone to come and clean all day yesterday and to ensure fresh sheets were on the bed."

I smiled. "That's Caleb. Always caring for us." When her delighted blush faded and she looked away, focusing on the simple meal in front of her, I stared at her in confusion. "What?" I grimaced at barking out the same question, but I needed to know what she was thinking.

She bit her lip, her finger flipping a carrot piece over and over. "I have to talk with you." She kept her eyes downcast.

"Spit it out, Theo. I hate attempts to make me guess or feel like shit because I'm not a mind reader."

She gasped and raised her eyes to meet mine. The confusion and embarrassment I saw nearly gutted me. "Whatever it is, you can tell me. No matter what your uncle said today, you can trust me, Theo."

She nodded. "I don't understand our tangled history, Nolan. I don't understand what role you played and what you knew."

I sat across from her, itching to reach for her hand but settling for playing with the food on the plate in front of me. I watched as she nibbled at her sandwich. "I didn't play any role. I had no idea about that contract, Theo. I promise."

She bit her lip and stared at the space between us as though weighing whether or not to believe me. After a few more bites of her sandwich, she whispered, "I don't know who to believe. My uncle has never been a horrible person."

I made a scoffing nose as I took a large bite of my sandwich. When she cocked an eyebrow, I swallowed and muttered, "He didn't protect you from your cousins. He didn't care enough to ensure your inheritance is intact. If he knew money was missing, he never reported it."

She bowed her head. "True, but he's never been mean to me. And he said he was trying to figure it out." She shook her head when I opened my mouth to argue. "No, Nolan. I need time. Time to get my bearings."

"Time?" I asked. "What does that mean?" I set down my sandwich, suddenly no longer ravenous, and I never turned down food. Was she going to ruin what we could have by allowing doubt and fear to sully what I knew was growing between us? Dammit, didn't she feel this too?

"No kissing or anything more until I know…"

"Until you know that I'm not a mean, double-crossing bastard?" I asked, my eyes flashing with anger as I rose and paced away from her. "We're married, Theo. *Married.*"

She nodded. "Yes. In name only." I watched as she took a deep breath and watched me intently, as though waiting to see how I'd react. When I swore under my breath and ran my hands through my hair but didn't approach, she relaxed. "I want more time before it's more than just in name only."

I took a step toward her before forcing myself to freeze in place. "Do you want it to be more?" I stared deeply into her mesmerizing eyes. "Or did you only want your ranch?" At the shake of her head, I rasped, "Do you want *me* at all?"

A tear trickled down her cheek, and I felt a small piece of my heart break.

After an interminable silence, she whispered, her sage-green eyes snaring me more completely than any trap I'd ever encountered. "Yes, I want you, Nolan. But not yet. Not yet."

~

THEODORA

L ater that evening, I ventured out of my bedroom. I had no desire to continue to face my memories alone. As I entered the great room, I stilled to find Nolan sitting on the couch, peering into the roaring fire as though he attempting to unravel the web we found ourselves in.

"Do you mind if I join you?" I whispered.

His body jerked at my voice, and I realized he'd truly had no idea I had entered the room. "Theo," he whispered in that different way I'd never heard before.

"Why do you say my name like that?" I asked as I moved to the opposite end of the couch, curling up and pulling a throw blanket over me.

He shook his head, his beautiful lips curving up in a hint of a smile. My breath caught at the promise of passion in his blue eyes, burning brightly. However, he remained at his end of the couch, his hands far away from me. I suddenly wished I hadn't been so honest earlier. This was our wedding night after all.

"I hope there's a reason for you to know someday," he said in a soft voice. "Will you always hide underneath blankets with me?" He quirked an arrogant brow, and I longed to rub my finger over it and smooth the wrinkle away. "I'll let you in on a little secret—I already know what's hidden beneath."

Flushing beet red, I tugged the blanket up higher, while my foot kicked out to bash into his leg. I should have known better as that just made him laugh. "More's the pity for you," I mumbled.

"Oh, no, Theodora," he rumbled in that low sexy voice that made my stomach turn over. *It's hunger, it's hunger*, I chanted to myself although I knew it was all Nolan. "I'm the lucky bastard who's seen what you attempt to hide from the world." He leaned in my direction, and I felt short of breath at his vehement sincerity. His mouth tilted up in a teasing smile. "Tempt me again."

I felt myself falling into his amazing eyes, my breath emerging in pants as the blanket fell around me. I was confused, aroused and—yes, dammit—tempted. But who was this man who was my husband? Could I trust him? "I want to," I admitted on a breathy sigh. "But I'm not ready for more. For everything."

His eyes flashed with triumph, and I groaned as he moved up, bracing himself over me on his muscular arms. Unable to stop myself, I ran my hand up and down his flexing arms, feeling them flinch with my soft touch. "You're so strong."

He chuckled, his head dipping so his nose nuzzled my neck. "I work on a ranch. I don't need a gym."

I barely understood anything as I arched up into his touch. Why was it that a simple glance from him could turn me to fire? Why couldn't I have felt this way about my other, sensible, boring boyfriends?

Any thought fled as he continued to touch me softly, reverently with just his lips. His touch made me feel like molten lava, and I yearned for it. Gasping, I tilted my head, giving him better access, raising my hands to cling to him. I needed an anchor in this world that was suddenly topsy-turvy.

"Theo," he rasped, saying it in his special way that sounded like *teo*. "I want to kiss you."

Running my hands through his hair and over his shoulders, I lifted up, nipping at his jaw and then his lower lip. "Yes, please God, yes." I didn't have the chance to say anything more as he swooped forward, pressing me back as his mouth descended and devoured mine.

I'd thought the kiss on Saturday was passionate. That was a kiss between a nun and priest compared to today. His tongue delved into my mouth, wreaking havoc and setting all of my nerves on edge. Our tongues dueled, and I was lost. All I could feel was him. Him surrounding me. Him making me feel desired.

Truly wanted by a man for the first time in my life.

His arms had relaxed, and he rested a good portion of himself over me. Rather than feel hemmed in, I tilted and shimmied against him, reveling at the feel of all that hard muscle against my softness. When I arched my belly and felt the hard ridge of him, he groaned and jerked his head away, thrusting his head back with his eyes closed as he pressed his hips into mine.

"Jesus and all the saints," he whispered. "You'll be the death of me, woman." He took a few deep panting breaths as he looked down at me. "I can think of no better way to go."

Rather than dive back in for another kiss, he ran soft fingertips over my cheek, smoothing away strands of hair as he gazed deeply into my eyes. "You have a witch's eyes," he whispered. "I'd do anything to see them glow as they do now." Leaning forward, he kissed me gently. "You are worth so much more than a quick fuck on a couch, my Theo."

Groaning with what sounded like regret, he pushed himself off me and moved to his side of the couch. Tugging at my blanket, he pulled half of it off me so it covered his legs. "Hey, that's not fair, it's mine!" I pulled at it, but he was far stronger than me, and I knew we'd simply end up tearing it in half.

When I rested back in a huff, he chuckled. "If you want to stay warm, come snuggle up beside me." His eyebrow was raised in challenge again.

I crawled toward him, falling against his side in a clumsy manner. I'd always wished I'd been graceful, to no avail. When he chuckled, I attempted to wriggle away from him, but one of his strong arms held me in place, and he kissed the top of my head.

"No, stay here. Please," he whispered. "This is what I dreamed of. Holding you in my arms after sharing passion with you and watching the fire." He tipped his head down, his smile filled with rueful humor. "Although I'd prefer more passion, I understand your desire to wait. I can be a patient man, Theo."

My brow furrowed as I attempted to discern what he said. I stared into his eyes after that kiss, a muddled mess. "What?"

"I'm saying you'll have to make the first move when you

decide it's time for us to make love," he whispered, holding me closer as I shivered. "For now, let's enjoy this."

I pressed my head against his strong chest and focused on the flames and the quiet sounds of life on the ranch. The wind blowing outside, the howl of a wolf in the distance, and the crackle of the wood all combined to lull me into a peace I hadn't known in years. Too soon, I drifted off to sleep, calm and happy. Any panic from earlier in the day had eased, and I was content, exactly where I was.

CHAPTER 8

NOLAN

The following morning, after leaving Theodora snuggled under a mound of blankets in her bed and with a kiss to her forehead, I departed for my ranch. I needed to check in with my men and ensure that everything could run smoothly for a few days while I helped Theo and adjusted to my new marriage. At my racing heart, I sat in my truck for a minute. Marriage. What the hell was I doing, married to anyone?

I closed my eyes as panic enveloped me. She thought she liked me now, but soon she would despise me. She'd wish she'd chosen a better man. That she'd opted for Caleb rather than me. I was only good for my brute strength.

With a sigh, I started up my truck and headed for home for a few hours, hoping that Theo would still be in bed and receptive to another kiss when I returned. Thoughts of Theo and of holding her in my arms all night long filled my mind on my ride home. I never could have imagined simply holding a woman would have brought me so much pleasure.

As I pulled up in front of the barn, I saw my father in the

doorway, sipping a cup of coffee as he looked me over. Shit. Word must be out already. "Hi, Dad," I called out as I hopped out and approached. Nodding to his cup of coffee, I smiled. "Any more of that?"

"You want to act like you didn't just make the biggest mistake of your life?" He shook his head. "Or are you just relieved you found a woman who'd take you on? She must be as big of an idiot as you are."

I always told myself that I wasn't hurt by my dad's comments, although some still managed to pierce the shield around my heart. His insulting Theo was another matter. "Don't say a word against her. She's a fine woman."

"A fine half-wit to have saddled herself with you." He stared at me. "Well, boy, who'd you marry? All Mr. Franks would say is that he'd heard it from Ms. Jacobs who'd heard it from Sally who'd heard it from that lady at the clerk's office that you'd married. Who is it?"

I sighed at the ways of the town we lived in. Although growing, certain things never changed in Burnside Creek. Deciding nothing would sweeten this bitter pill, I stood tall and met my father's challenging stare. "Theodora Miller."

My father dropped his coffee mug and gripped me by my jacket, thrusting me against the wall, my head slamming against the wood with an unceremonious thud. I kicked at him, but he wouldn't release me. Ranch hands approached, but they'd long since learned to leave my father and me to our fights. Unless it looked like one of us was going to kill the other.

"Like hell you did," he snarled. "You were never to meet her."

I shrugged. "Well, I married her," I snapped. "She was desperate and so was I."

His chuckle was mirthless as he released me and looked me over with derision and pity. "Of course you were. What woman would want anything to do with you if she knew what you were?"

"Dad, leave it," I hissed.

"You married the woman you should have hated forever. Her family's the reason your mother died. How could you?"

I ducked my head, my eyes closed as I rubbed at my temple. "Dad, don't."

"You're no son of mine," he rasped. "But then, you never were. And you never wanted to be."

He glared at me as I pushed past him, ignoring the pitying looks from my stalwart ranch hands, and slammed into the office. With a groan, I saw Alessia already there, poring over books and reports. "Ally," I muttered.

"He's been waiting for you for hours," she murmured, looking me over, her brown eyes sparkling with concern. Where my father's were a cold, bitter chocolate, Ally's were milk chocolate—warm and inviting and always filled with humor. "Good night?"

"Don't start," I said, although I couldn't help chuckle. Ally, the sibling closest to me in age, always found a way to make me laugh. I sat with a groan and dropped my head into my hands. I flinched when she slapped me on my head and glared at her. "Ow! What was that for?"

"For not inviting me to the wedding! How could you invite Cora and Quinn and not me?"

I hated the hurt I saw on her face and sighed. "Because I knew you'd object when you heard who I was marrying." At the worry creeping into her gaze, I whispered, "Theodora Miller."

She paled and collapsed back into her chair. "You married that woman? After what her father did?"

"You don't understand, Ally."

Her cheeks flushed, and she stared at me like I was a complete stranger. "You're right. I don't. Make me. Make me understand why you'd marry the daughter of the man who killed our mother. Why you'd even go near her." Her lips quivered. "Her family ruined our lives that night."

I nodded, aware of how much we had lost when my mother died. Everything had changed. The ranch. Our family. Everything. The only constant for me had been Ally's loyalty and love. I suddenly panicked at the thought of losing both.

"Ally, her father wasn't drunk. He was in AA. He hadn't had a drink in years." When she snorted and rolled her eyes, I whispered, "Caleb confirmed it. He's known for a long time but couldn't say anything. He's her lawyer too. His father before him."

"Caleb?" she whispered, a hand to her chest as though she'd just been doubly betrayed. "He knew and said nothing?"

I closed my eyes in silent misery. "I think he understood we needed someone to hate." I firmed my shoulders and shook my head as my gaze glinted with determination. "But that person isn't Theo. And it's not her father." The echo of the agony we'd lived through shone in my eyes. "It was icy and a terrible accident. We should never have felt as though we had a vendetta out for them."

"If we had a vendetta we would have ruined them."

I tilted my head to the side as I studied her. A whisper of unease traveled down my spine, but I ignored it. Alessia was loyal, but not reckless. She'd never do anything to endanger our ranch. "We need water, Ally." At her confused stare, I pointed in the direction of Theo's ranch. "That water pact we signed ends in a few weeks."

When Ally continued to stare at me in confusion, I rubbed a hand over my face. "Theo has water. It's from her land. By marrying her we're guaranteed water forever."

"So you married her out of desperation? Greed?" My sister shook her head at me. "Do I even know you?"

"Don't say that, Ally. Please." I stared at her as panic filled me that I was going to lose the one sibling who had remained and always supported me. I wouldn't be able to run the ranch without her. "Don't leave."

Her head snapped up at my barely audible entreaty. "I'll never leave." She cupped my face. "You're stuck with me, Nol." Kissing my head she swiped at my hair and backed away to sit at her chair again.

"Agree to meet her before you despise her. Please." I hated that all I seemed to do today was beg. "Be the Alessia you've always been. Not like Dad. Be like Mama."

Her eyes shone with momentary shame and she nodded. "I'll meet her, but I can't promise I'll like her."

I sighed, knowing I could ask for no more. I prayed my sister and my wife would become friends because I didn't know what I'd do if they were enemies.

∼

THEODORA

That evening after supper, I entered the living room expecting to find the room empty. Nolan had been a bit distant during supper, and I worried he was second-guessing this marriage. Instead, he waited for me on the sofa, opening his arms wide so I could settle against his broad chest. With a groan, I relaxed into him as I breathed in deeply of his scent that always calmed me.

"What's the matter, Theo?" His hands ran over my arms, and I relaxed further against him. I was becoming addicted to his caresses.

"I'm worried you're already regretting our marriage." I bit at my lip after speaking, worried I'd been rash. When he huffed out a breath and his arms tightened around me, my anxiety ratcheted up.

Kissing my head, he murmured, "I'm sorry. I never meant to act like an ass tonight." He sighed, the arm wrapped around my waist holding me even tighter. "When I'm thinking over a problem, I brood, and I know that can't be easy to be around." He kissed my head again, the soft caress soothing me. "I don't regret our marriage, bella, although my family wasn't pleased about it today."

With a moan, I pushed away from him and sat up so that I faced him. "They were angry?"

His blue eyes were filled with regret. "My father was. But he's always angry. He's been angry for a decade." When I flinched, he ran a hand over my arm as though to take the sting out of his words. "Alessia was confused and disappointed."

"She thought you could do better."

He chuckled and shook his head. "No, Theo, I think she was mostly disappointed I didn't invite her to the wedding, although she was perplexed about why I married you."

"Water," I whispered.

His eyes flared with heat as he looked at me. "We both know it was for more than water or a ranch." He waited for me to protest or agree. When I remained quiet, he held his hand out, inviting me to rest against him again. When I did, he groaned in pleasure.

"Can we take a little time to get to know each other, like we would if we were dating?" His hands seemed incapable of not stroking over me, and I relished the thought he loved touching me as much as I loved his touch. "I know you want to take things slow, but I'd like to get to know my wife. Learn what you like, dislike. What makes you happy." He paused. "What makes you smile."

"I am afraid the more we learn about each other, the more we'll realize we shouldn't be together."

"Never, Theo." He sighed as he rested his chin atop my head. "Never. We were always meant to meet."

"Tell me about your family."

He chuckled, and I could feel him settle back into the couch. "I have seven siblings, but only Alessia lives at the ranch. The rest wanted to live on their own. After Mama died…" He paused and a long silence ensued. The wood in the fire popped, and coyotes yipped in the distance. "After Mama died, the ranch wasn't the same. It wasn't welcoming and warm—a place where everyone wanted to gather and spend time."

"So your siblings left you to keep it running while they had their freedom."

"I suppose that's one way of looking at it. They wanted to go to college or explore. I couldn't blame them. They traveled to Europe and moved to big cities. Did things I could only imagine." He shrugged. "Sofia and Carmella are in Seattle." He paused as though thinking about his sisters. "Reid and Giulia are in San Francisco, although Giulia spent years in Paris."

"And the other two?" I perched on his chest, watching as his stare was distant as he thought about his siblings.

"I don't know. I don't hear from them." His voice held an old sorrow, and I stroked a hand over his shoulder as though to ease the burden of his lack of knowledge about them. "I don't begrudge them for leaving. They would have been miserable here."

"Always the older brother," I teased as I tried another tactic to ease the ache I suspected he felt, although I couldn't imagine how hard it must have been for him watching his siblings depart. "You must have wonderful reunions when they return for holidays."

"We've never been all together at one time since Mama's funeral." His voice sounded distant before he cleared his throat. "We will be, soon. Perhaps this summer I'll invite them home to celebrate our wedding."

I murmured my assent, my mind racing that he truly had been abandoned to run the ranch by his siblings. Only Alessia had shown him any loyalty. Nolan had been almost as alone as I had in the years since the accident. Yet another bond formed through mutual understanding.

Soon, our conversation turned to lighter memories, and we laughed and teased each other. I relished this time and admitted Nolan was correct. Not only did we need to wait before we made love; we needed time for courtship. Smiling at the old-fashioned word, it somehow seemed appropriate.

∼

A few days later, Nolan returned home early from the ranch. Winter days were short in Montana, and he managed to arrive while there was still daylight. I peeked out the window to see him looking at the barn with his hands on his trim hips. Gazing at him, I marveled that such a man was my husband. Tall, broad-shouldered, and handsome as sin, he was also proving to be loyal, dedicated, smart, and funny.

I ran to the coat peg, tugged on all of my outerwear and a heavy pair of boots, and raced outside to join him. "Nolan!" I waved at him as I clomped down the stairs, gripping the railing so I didn't slip on the icy spots.

He turned at my voice, smiling widely. "*Teo.* You didn't have to come outside."

"I wanted to." Breathing in deeply, I closed my eyes as the crisp winter air filled my lungs. The fresh scent of pine trees tinged with the hint of wood smoke teased my senses. I loved this time of year. "What were you staring at?"

He grimaced. "Your barn. It needs work or it won't last."

I spun to stare at the gorgeous building erected by my ancestors. Was it my grandparents or my great-grandparents? It towered over the house, its red paint chipped and faded to grey with missing shingles and a sagging center beam. "Can we save it?" I held a hand to my heart as I dreaded his answer.

This was the place I'd spun out my dreams as a child. Where I played hide-and-seek and created mystical faraway lands in the hayloft. Where I was Rapunzel, locked in the tower—well, at least until my dad called me in to dinner. Where I'd had my first kiss. The initials of everyone who ever worked the ranch were carved into the wood of one doorway, silently marking the passage of time on the ranch. Without the barn, how would this be my ranch?

"Nolan?" I whispered, my throat thick with fear as the silence lengthened.

He nodded as he continued to stare at it, his eyes squinting against the bright sunlight glinting off the snow. "It'll take a lot of work, and I should see if I can't try to prop up the main beam." He nodded again as he grinned at me. "She'll make it through winter and then we'll have her looking pretty as a picture again, Theo. Although we might have to buy every bucket of red paint in the state of Montana."

I squealed with delight, throwing myself into his arms and catching him off guard. He stumbled backward, into the snow with me on top of him. "Oh my God, I'm so sorry." I expected him to push me up and sputter as he glowered at me.

Instead, he hooted with laughter as he held me tight. "Seems you want to make snow angels." He ran a finger down my cheek and ensured my hat and scarf were still keeping me warm. "I've never made a two-person snow angel." He clasped my hand and said, "Hook your boots onto mine."

I rested completely on top of him as he moved his arms up and down and opened and closed his legs. I should have felt ridiculous. I should have insisted he let me roll to the side to make my own. Instead, I relaxed and felt cherished, enjoying this unexpected moment with him.

I tucked my head against his chest, listening to the soft beats of his heart and the scraping noise of his clothes moving over snow, the sound rhythmic and almost like a lullaby. I'd never felt safer. Or happier. This was better than any dream I'd ever spun in the princess-tower hayloft.

"Don't fall asleep, bella," he whispered. "I have no wish to freeze."

I mumbled my protest as I shimmied around on top of him, stilling when I heard him groan that I was killing him.

"God, you know how to torture a man. Torture *me*." He stopped his snow angel making, raising his hands to wrap them around me and keep me from moving. Sighing with pleasure, he held me as close as our heavy winter coats allowed. "This is almost as good as being on our couch with a fire roaring. Although I can't feel my ass any more."

I giggled and kissed his jaw. "You're incorrigible."

He smiled, kissing my head as he sat up, helping me to step back and away so I wouldn't ruin our snow angel. He followed me up, groaning as he patted at his legs and butt. "I might never feel it again." He looked at me with a lascivious grin. "You could pat it and make it feel better." His blue eyes were lit with merriment and a dare.

I tilted my chin up and strolled toward him, ignoring my slight trip in the snow that almost made me faceplant at his feet, and placed one hand on his chest for balance as I reached down to pat at his bum. "There. Better?"

"Hell no," he rasped as he tugged me to him and lowered his head. "Now I'm on fire."

I gasped as he stopped inches away from my lips, his breath fanning over my cheeks. I breathed in the scents of coffee and mint, and I stood on my toes, brushing my lips against his. "Kiss me, Nolan. Warm me up."

Groaning, he pulled me even closer, his lips settling on mine softly until I opened to him. Then he gave a growl of triumph as his tongue stroked inside, setting me on fire. My hands rose, knocking his hat off as I tangled my fingers in his hair, holding on tight as I wished the layers separating us melted as easily as snow. God, how I ached for this man.

He broke the kiss, panting heavily, peppering kisses down

my neck as he pushed my scarf out of the way. When I whimpered and shivered, he stopped, his hands gripping my hips so hard I wondered if I'd find bruises tomorrow. "You make me crazy, bella."

"I want you," I gasped and arched back as he nibbled his way up my neck, giving him access to as much of me as possible.

"I can't wait until we can skinny-dip in the creek and run naked through the fields this summer." He eased away, his eyes shining with mischief and promise. "You blush now, but by the time the fields are green and lush, you'll want that as much as I do, and you won't be so modest with me."

A portion of my pleasure fled as I imagined him doing something similar with a nameless woman, curvy and beautiful and confident in all the ways I wasn't. I stiffened and dropped my arms, as I tugged my gloves back on, attempting to step away from him. However, his hold on my hips tightened and he matched my attempts to move away. When I dared to look into his eyes, I saw his beautiful blue eyes were clouded with worry.

"What did I say, bella, to make you sad?" He ran a gloved finger over my cheek. "To make you doubt?"

I shook my head. "I'm foolish." When he waited, I sighed and gathered my courage. "I wondered how many women you've done that with. How many you've cavorted with in the fields." I waved my hand around and flushed furiously as I lost my courage to speak plainly about his romantic liaisons.

A sly smile bloomed at the old-fashioned word, and his eyes were now filled with mischief. "Well, my bella, I can guarantee you'll be the first woman I'll cavort with. Here or on my land. I know I'll enjoy every moment with you." Suddenly, he was serious, and he cupped my face, so I looked deeply into his eyes. I had the sense he was afraid I'd miss how sincere he was. "I've had a few girlfriends, Theo. I won't lie. But they were short lived and always in town. No one ever came to the ranch. No one ever saw what my ranch means to me. No one ever cared to."

"Why?" I whispered as I raised a hand to run through his hair, wishing I didn't have gloves on as I wanted to feel the silky strands on my skin. "Without seeing you on the land, either here or at your ranch, it's impossible to know you."

"No one ever wanted to know me. They wanted a handsome cowboy with a successful ranch. Who cared about the man?"

Taking a step so I was chest to chest with him, I whispered, "I do."

He nodded, his blue eyes lit with a fervency I'd never seen before. "I know. And that makes you precious."

He lowered his head and kissed me softly. Slowly. Almost reverently. Somehow it was more passionate than anything we'd ever shared, and I felt vulnerable and exposed even though I was covered in layers of coats and sweaters. I whimpered when he broke the kiss, wishing he'd kiss me like this forever.

"Come, bella. I don't want you to freeze."

Those first days after our marriage set the tone for the next two weeks. Although we didn't spend another afternoon together because Nolan was too busy at his ranch, we spent every evening together. I cooked supper, he cleaned, and we talked about everything but our marriage and the history our families shared. Instead, he told me about his siblings, spread all over the country. He made me laugh with tales about the antics he, Caleb, and a friend named Chase had pulled when they were in high school. Best of all, he listened—with no judgment—as I talked about life with my cousins. He seemed to understand the importance of finding a way to survive hardship. I realized that was something we shared, and it added to our growing bond.

After supper, we snuggled on the couch, where I invariably fell asleep on him. And by that I meant on top of him. He was more comfortable than the bed at Caleb's cabin at The Hill. It was as though his scent, which I could never get enough of, put a spell on me, lulling me to sleep. Every morning, I woke in my bed with a sense that I'd been held all night long. Even though I smelled him on the pillow next to mine, I never woke while he lay beside me, and nothing more ever happened between us. Not even a kiss.

Although my body yearned for more, I was thankful we were taking the time to get to know each other. Rather than rushing in, I was learning who he was and learning to trust him. In every conversation we shared, in every laugh and story and the growing sense of togetherness, I knew we both had yet to fully bare our deepest secrets. The doubts and fear that I was merely a means to an end for him to secure water rights for his precious ranch were slowly easing, but they lingered. I'd yet to learn any deep, dark secrets of his, and I'd begun to suspect almost nothing he told me would change how I felt about him.

Sighing, I flipped through the mail. Two weeks wed and only a few kisses with my husband who looked like a cowboy god. What kind of simpleton was I? I should jump his bones tonight and move our relationship forward. I needed to take a leap of faith and trust I wouldn't be crushed so cruelly again.

I stared out the front window of the great room with the mail forgotten in my hands, not focusing on the grey storm clouds moving with speed across the sky, hiding the mountain peaks in the distance. The wind howled and a storm threatened. Instead, I wondered if I had the courage to don sexy clothes and push our relationship to the next level. I was ninety-nine percent sure he wanted that, too, but that one percent doubt froze me with indecisiveness.

Sighing again, I focused once more on the mail, pausing as I saw a letter in my uncle's handwriting. Ripping it open, I scanned what he wrote, and then flipped the page to read what he'd attached. I gasped, falling to my knees, a deep sense of betrayal filling me.

How could Nolan have lied to me? Why, after all the time we'd spent together and the hours I'd spent in his arms, wouldn't he have had the decency to tell me the truth? A tear slipped out and I rubbed at it angrily. He wasn't worth my tears. I was better off without him.

My traitorous heart insisted I read the letter again. And again. Each time, I felt a little more of my faith in what we'd been building die. I knew that I'd not be able to fight my tears for long as anguish filled my soul.

This, this was why I'd held myself back from Nolan. I knew I couldn't trust him. Somehow, I'd known. My eyes flew to the direction of the kitchen door as it opened, and he called out to me. In that moment, I wished he had chosen to never come home.

~

NOLAN

"Theo?" I called out as I entered her house. I forced myself not to say "our" although I'd already called it our house too many times to count in my mind. This house felt more like home to me than anywhere I'd ever been. All because she was here.

Slipping off my jacket, hat, scarf, and boots, I rubbed my hands together and moved to the great room to start the fire. Although I had no doubt that my wife could ably start a fire, she seemed to appreciate me building one each night for us. I stilled when I saw her on her knees staring out the large windows with her arms wrapped around her belly. "*Teo*? Are you all right?"

"Stop calling me that," she said in a low, dead voice as she pushed herself to stand, swaying slightly before she caught her balance. She flinched when I took a step closer to her, so I froze a few feet away from her. "Say my name right. For once, give me the respect of saying my name correctly."

I stilled, uncertain what to do. This wasn't the usual response to my returning home after a long day. Generally, she smiled or kissed my cheek and urged me to take a shower and relax as she finished supper. I sniffed, realizing nothing was cooking. "What happened?" I hoped my steady voice would soothe her. Instead, it infuriated her.

She spun to glare at me, her glorious brown hair twirling around her as her beautiful eyes swam with tears and indignation. "How can you ask me that after what you've done?" She took a step closer, her hands around herself.

I sensed if I touched her, she would explode like a powder keg. She vibrated with pent-up energy. Instead of reaching for her and soothing her as I desired, I stuffed my hands in my pockets and feigned a nonchalance I didn't feel. I shook my head and shrugged. "Why don't you explain what you think I've done?"

"Oh, aren't you smooth? The smooth-talking cowboy. So handsome and charming that no one looks below the surface. No one sees all that's lacking because they're too blinded by your handsome face. I was too stupid to see what a fool I was when I agreed to your proposal."

Ignoring her softly spoken words, which cut me worse than anything my father had ever said, I raised my hands up in an attempt to show I wanted peace, but that only seemed to enrage her further. "We both got what we wanted."

"How dare you act like the innocent?" she shrieked, her hand lashing out to hit mine. "How dare you, after...after all you did?"

I took a step back and shook my head. "Can you explain to me exactly what you believe I've done?"

She held up a sheet of paper, and my blood turned cold.

"This. You signed this paper. How could you act as though you knew nothing about it?" A tear trickled down her cheek as she stared at me with absolute betrayal. "All this time we've spent together, have you laughed at me for being so naïve and gullible? For believing that you wanted me?" She stared at me as though I were a defiler. "Why couldn't you just be honest and admit the water rights were what you desired?"

"What does it say?" I asked.

"Here!" she screamed, thrusting it at me.

I grunted as she slammed it against my chest, and I glanced over the paper, blanching when I saw my signature at the bottom of it. "I don't understand," I whispered.

"Oh, right. You have no recollection of how your signature is at the bottom of the agreement between your ranch and my uncle, granting you water rights for a dollar a year and exiling me from my ranch?" She rolled her eyes and spun away, her shoulders hunched. "Or do you do this sort of contract so frequently that what you've done to me's not even memorable?"

I stared at the sheet of paper as an icy foreboding filled me. "I...I don't know what to say," I whispered in a hesitant voice.

She screamed and twirled to face me. "How dare you act as though this isn't important?" She pushed at my chest. "How could I *ever* trust you now?"

"Theo, please," I pleaded.

"Get out!" she yelled. "Get out of my house!"

I froze. "This is *our* house. We're married," I said in a low voice. "Remember, what's mine is yours and what's yours is mine."

"It's all been built on lies. Lies!" She held a hand to her heart, and her breath was scratchy as she tried to breathe deeply. However, she seemed unable to catch her breath and she fell to her knees. "Lies," she whispered as her voice broke.

"Theo, please."

"Leave, Nolan. Leave me alone."

I backed away, holding the sheet of paper in my hand. What had I done? As I looked at my sobbing wife, a searing agony and an equal amount of confusion filled me. My heart broke as I stared at my wife crying her heart out, even as my blood boiled as I realized I'd been duped. Again.

CHAPTER 9

NOLAN

The next week was a living hell. Theo barely acknowledged me and I rarely saw her. She didn't come out of her room until after I'd left, and she was back in her room when I returned at night. I was now sleeping in the master bedroom. I didn't dare enter her father's room. Although the bed was comfortable enough, I missed sleeping with Theo in my arms.

Today, I worked in the barn, eager to do anything to burn off the restless energy thrumming through me. Yesterday had been Theo's birthday. I'd gone into town and bought her a cake and flowers. I would have cooked her dinner, but she avoided me the entire day. This morning, I found the cake and flowers in the trash. Slamming the hammer against a board, I swore at the futility of it all. There was nothing I could do to erase my name from that contract.

I set the hammer down as I rubbed at my fingers to prevent them from freezing. Dammit, I missed Theo. I missed her smiles and the hesitant hope blooming in her gaze. I missed the way she trusted me and snuggled against me. I missed the laughter and stories. I missed everything. How had a woman I'd known for such a short period of time gotten under my skin so quickly?

Trying to ignore the ache in my heart as I looked around the run-down barn, I focused on the work I needed to do so Theo could have a functional ranch again. Three of my trusted ranch hands had come over to help, grumbling that they were giving up precious poker time, and we'd replaced a sagging beam and rotted boards. Looking up at the roof, I suspected that would need to be replaced this summer too.

Now, I was working alone, repairing stalls. I'd sent my hands home, to do their own work and to keep an eye on our cattle. Calving season would start soon, and I'd need to return as soon as it did. It was one of the busiest seasons of the year on the ranch, and I'd be away from Theo for at least a month. I wondered if she'd even notice my absence.

This past week had been a preview of what it would be like away from her, and I hated it. The main difference would be I'd spend all of my time at my ranch. I always slept in the office in the barn on a small cot, available at all times to help whenever needed. It was exhausting work, but essential for our ranch for it to continue to thrive.

During those first two weeks of our marriage, I had envisioned Theo visiting me. Bringing me meals or thermoses of hot chocolate. Sitting with her on my cot as I fought sleep and relished in her quiet companionship. Leaning against her as I dozed, lulled into a sense that all was right in my world because she was close. Now, this would be like every other calving year. An exercise in tenacity and endurance with little to lighten the load.

"So, this is where you come every day to hide," Alessia said as she entered.

I set the hammer down and shoved my hands in my pockets, grimacing as they tingled and pricked as they slowly warmed up. "Ally. What's the matter? Has the calving season already begun?"

She shook her head, taking in the subtle decay, but also the promise in the space. "This would be a good horse barn," she murmured, walking over to one of the stalls and running her hand over the top of its wall. "It's a bit run-down, but the bones are good."

I nodded. "I had the same thought. The ranch will be twice as big now, with secure water. We can expand like you've always dreamed." I saw a flash of hope in my sister's eyes and smiled at her.

"I won't agree to anything Theo doesn't want to do," Alessia said, shaking her head as though to clear it of what could be. "I don't even know her yet." She gave me a searching glance and frowned. "What's happened, Nol? You look awful."

I rubbed under my eyes and shrugged. I knew better than to lie to her. She always saw through my bullshit and loved me anyway. "Why'd you lie to me? Ten years ago?" I asked in a low voice. "Why?"

She shook her head and approached me to rest her hand on my forearm, giving it a gentle squeeze. "I've never lied to you, Nol. What we have wouldn't work if you can't trust me."

"I know," I whispered. I pulled out the sheet of paper that Theo had thrust at me a week ago, handing it to my sister. "Can you explain that to me?"

I watched her reading, paling as she read it.

Her shock-filled gaze met mine. "How were you ever given this contract?" she asked in a breathless voice. "This was the last contract Dad did before you took over the ranch. You should never have signed it." She read it again. "And this wasn't the contract he had me review or that Caleb's dad drew up. We were supposed to pay more than one dollar and we sure as hell weren't banishing her."

I looked deeply into her eyes and saw no cunning. I had to

trust her, for if I didn't, I had no one. "I don't know what happened. It was after Mama died, and we were devastated. I didn't think you'd trick me, but..." I waved my hand at the copy of the contract in her hand. "Somehow I signed that."

She read it again. "This contract is why we've never struggled for water while everyone else has suffered during droughts and why it's been so cheap for us. I always wondered, but never looked into it." She sighed as she rubbed at her head and paced in front of me. "This is why she hates you now?"

I nodded, my jaw clenching together.

Alessia came to a halt, her hands on her hips as she stared at me. "Surely, after you explained, she forgave you." Her eyes narrowed as my jaw ticked when I clamped it shut tight. "You didn't explain, did you?" At my swift shake of my head, she folded the paper and thrust it at me again before pacing away.

"I can't," I whispered.

"Come on, Nolan!" she yelled. "If she's a halfway decent person she won't care."

I fought panic at telling Theo my deepest shame. "No, Ally, leave it be."

She walked toward me. "Do you really think you'll be able to hide this from her?"

I heard a gasp and spun to see Theo watching us with a look of betrayal in her gaze. Her hair was tamed in a braid, and she was bundled up against the cold, a turquoise scarf covering her cheeks, which only enhanced the beauty of her eyes. "Theo, listen."

"You don't even bother to hide your meetings with your lover?" She looked around as though searching for a bedroll. "Couldn't you have had your rendezvous at your ranch?"

"Theo!" I bellowed as she spun on her heel and stormed away. "Dammit." I slapped my hands against my thighs, grimacing at the sting. Shoving them back in my pockets, I glared at my sister as she grinned at me.

"She has you tied in knots the way Aunt Jackie does Uncle Craig. It's good to see." Her eyes lit with teasing as she spoke of Caleb's parents who still acted like newlyweds even though they'd been married nearly forty years. She sobered as she studied me. "You have to tell her, Nolan. She's your wife, and she should know."

I rubbed at my head. "Perhaps." I knew Alessia was right, but I dreaded seeing the pitying look on Theo's face. In knowing, deep inside, that Theo would wish she'd chosen anyone but me as her husband.

I nodded as Alessia gripped my arm and slipped out of the barn, leaving me deep in thought. Would I only know two weeks of harmony in my marriage? Would everything be stress and strife from now on?

~

THEODORA

I waited in the unheated basement, staring outside at the parked trucks, waiting for that woman to leave. I clung to my anger so I didn't have to examine all the other emotions roiling through me. How dare this woman track down my husband on my ranch?

How dare that woman believe she could seduce my husband on my land? I huffed out a breath and looked to the barn, debating if I should march in there again to interrupt them. Letting out another deep breath, I marveled that I hadn't had a panic attack since the first night I'd met Nolan. Somehow, I felt steady and secure with Nolan, even with all the discord between us, and I'd be damned if some other woman was going to tempt my husband away from me. Even if I was irate with him for lying to me.

When I saw her walking out of the barn, her gait relaxed and graceful, I wanted to scream. Of course Nolan would be attracted to this beautiful woman with long legs and a curvy figure that not even an overstuffed winter jacket could hide. "Stay away from my husband!" I screeched as I barreled out of the basement, skidding on a patch of ice. I grabbed at a shrub, barely preventing myself from going ass over teakettle.

When she giggled, I glared at her. "Who are you?"

"Why don't you ask your husband?" she suggested, her expression hopeful. She held a hand over her eyebrows and squinted at me, as the day was bright with the sun glinting off the snow. Unfortunately, the sun did little to warm the day up as it was barely zero. And that was before the breeze blew.

"Tell me," I demanded, shivering.

"I'm his sister. Alessia." She grinned at me as I gaped at her. "I have just as much reason to not like you, although Nolan's tried to rid me of my ten-year prejudice against you," she said with an impish smile. "Can you do me a favor? Can you never again suggest I'm having an affair with my own brother? Ick!"

I giggled at her disgruntlement, shocked that my anger fled so quickly and at the affinity I felt with her open friendliness. "You're truly Alessia? The only sibling that remained on the ranch?"

"He told you about us," she murmured. "Yes, I stayed. I had to. For him." She looked at me as though she expected me to comprehend the undertone of what she hinted at.

"I don't understand."

Alessia sighed and scratched at her head. "You think everything is black and white because that's what you read on a piece of paper." She paused, as though carefully considering her words. "All I can say is that not everything is as obvious or as straightforward as we'd like. There's plenty you don't understand."

I watched as she gave me a little wave and then drove away. Rather than return to the house, I marched back in the direction of the barn. Sliding the door shut behind me, I approached my husband, who stared at me with cautious optimism. "How could you, Nolan?"

He dropped the hammer and put his hands on his trim hips. I forced myself to only gaze into his eyes and to ignore that he seemed even more handsome and muscular than the day we married, three weeks ago. "What have I done now?"

I took another step toward him. "You let me make a fool of myself! That was your sister."

He chuckled and shrugged. "Yeah, I don't think she liked envisioning herself as my lover." He made a gagging sound. "Yuck." His blue eyes twinkled as they looked at me. "Whereas you..." he murmured.

I stood with my shoulders back as I confronted him. "What about me? I'm a wife who doesn't even merit a birthday card."

He flushed and bridged the last bit of space separating us, striding to stand in front of me. "And you're so ungrateful, you tossed what I did get you into the trash!"

I blushed and ducked my head. "I'm sorry," I whispered. "I regretted it almost immediately, but I couldn't salvage the cake. The flowers are on the table in an heirloom vase." I wrapped my arms around my waist. "I feel so alone." I shivered as his fingers gave a whisper-soft caress to my neck before trailing up to my jaw and cheek. My head tilted back of its own volition, and I stared into his passion-filled blue eyes.

"You're only alone because you've chosen to be," he whispered.

I looked up, mesmerized by the look in his eyes. Like he was awed that he stood in front of me and was able to touch me. Like there was nowhere else he wanted to be. I took a shaky breath, reached my hands up between us, and ran my fingers over his scruff. He hadn't shaved today. I trembled when he turned into my touch, as though he craved any contact with me as much as I did with him.

"I've missed you," I breathed.

"God, Theo, please," he begged, his head dropping so our noses touched, but still he refrained from kissing me.

I took a deep breath and gave his head a soft tug as I stood on my toes, arching up to kiss him. From the start, it was a lush, deep, hungry kiss. A kiss to make up for days apart. I groaned as he wrapped his arms around me, spun us, and pressed me against the barn wall.

Our tongues dueled, and I ran my fingers through his hair, delighting when he groaned and pressed against me, eager for more. When his nimble fingers unzipped my jacket, I shivered, but then gasped as his hands snaked under my sensible flannel shirt to my sexy lingerie.

"God almighty, woman, are you trying to kill me?" he muttered as his lips skimmed over my neck and down to my jaw, nibbling and setting every place he touched on fire.

I gasped and arched into him, desperate for more of his touch. "Don't stop. Please don't stop, Nolan," I panted out, my fingers digging into his jacket and wishing I was touching his bare shoulders instead. When his thumb and finger tweaked my nipple, I gasped and curved into him. "More."

With a satisfied chuckle, he pushed my shirt up and ducked his head, swooping down to suck on a nipple.

"Nolan!" I wrapped my arms around his neck and lifted one leg to sling over his hip, pressing into him. Why did I have so many clothes on? I felt like I was in an inferno. Or I was the inferno, about to go up in flames.

Shivering as he nipped at one peak, his fingers continued to caress one nipple as his mouth moved to my other breast. Sucking and nibbling, he feasted on me as his free hand stroked over my belly, making it quiver and jump.

Just as I began a prayer for him to unzip my jeans, he gave a final nip to my breast and backed away. Rising to stand in front of me, his chest rose and fell like a bellows, and he yanked me to him as he crushed me tightly against him.

"Nolan," I whispered.

"No," he murmured. "Give me a minute." I felt as he shuddered as he held me, pressing his hard length against me and burying his face in my loosened hair. "God, you always smell like a summer garden. If your eyes didn't seduce me, your scent would. And then you'd give me heart failure with your luscious curves and silky skin. What did I possibly do in this life to deserve you?"

I flushed with delight at what he said, melting against him, any stirrings of embarrassment forgotten as his beautiful words in his deep voice washed over me. I dug my hands under his jacket, yearning to feel closer to him. "We don't have to stop," I whispered, kissing his ear. "Come inside with me. Make love with me."

He raised his head, gazing deeply into my eyes. His cheeks were flushed, and eyes passion glazed. "You have no idea how much I want to throw you over my shoulder and do just that."

"Do it," I whispered. "I dare you."

His thumb rubbed over my mouth and then caressed my cheek. "I don't want you to hate me, Theo. I couldn't bear it."

At the sound of a throat clearing behind me, I screeched and tugged at my shirt, shimmying until it covered me. Nolan remained in front of me, hiding me from view.

I saw him glance over his shoulder and swear.

He spun, but kept his back in front of me, sheltering me from any curious eyes. "What?" he barked.

"Sorry, boss, but it seems the season's started earlier than we'd like," a gruff voice said. "It's time."

As I ran a hand over Nolan's back, I felt him shiver.

"Dammit. Fine. I'll be there soon. Thanks, Buck."

After I heard footsteps walking away and a truck start up, Nolan turned to stare at me, his expression filled with regret.

"I'll have to take a rain check, darlin'. Calving season's started. I won't be home much for the next month or so."

"Month?" I whispered. "Won't you come home to sleep?" I motioned in the direction of his man who'd just left. "He could take the night shift."

"Yeah, he could, as could any of my men. But we have a big operation, and we'll all be exhausted soon enough. I can't ask them to work hard while I'm off with my bride." He bent forward, kissing me gently. "No matter how much I want to be."

Gripping his arm to prevent him from leaving me, I stared into his eyes. "There's still so much I don't understand," I whispered. "Will you ever explain it to me?"

He swallowed before giving a single jerk of his head. "Yes. After calving season, I promise. There's still a chance for you to annul this marriage. I shouldn't steal that from you."

He kissed me once more before spinning and racing from the barn, leaving me breathless and stunned. Why would I want an annulment?

CHAPTER 10

NOLAN

Three weeks later, March had begun even if it still felt like the height of winter in Montana. We were nearing the end of the busiest part of the calving season, although it would continue for another two months. After another few weeks, I knew I should be able to return home. To Theo.

I'd barely seen her since our passionate encounter in the barn the day after her birthday. My mind was almost always filled with visions of her—unless I found a way to distract myself. This evening, I rested in the office with only a lamp lit on my desk, listening to an audiobook. I lay on my cot in the dimly lit room with my eyes closed, my hands crossed over my belly, as I was immersed in a world of dragons and knights and mad sorcerers.

"Is that what you dream of?" a soft voice called out.

I jerked up, hitting pause on the remote for the small stereo. "Theo," I whispered. "What are you doing here?"

She shrugged and edged into the room, shutting the door behind her to keep in the room's heat. Although it was March, it wasn't much warmer than the day we'd kissed in February. "My husband is never home so I thought I'd visit him." She bit her lip as she stared at me, remaining in shadow. "I should have ignored my silly impulse."

"No!" I said as I heaved off the bed. "Come here. I never know when I'll be called again to help or sent out to search for a cow and her calf." I yawned as I patted the spot beside me on the cot.

Approaching me, I saw her taking in the map of the ranch tacked on the wall behind me. She glanced at my desk, devoid of almost all papers, and then at Alessia's, looking like a paper hurricane had just occurred. "Come," I coaxed, holding my hand out.

"You're tired. I shouldn't bother you," she protested.

With a tug, I urged her to sit beside me. Dropping my head to that sexy place where her neck met her shoulder, I breathed deeply. "Ah, paradise," I sighed, kissing her there.

An overwhelming lassitude filled me, and I leaned against her, feeling relaxed and at peace. Her arm snaked around my middle, and I felt myself slipping toward sleep. "What did you do today?" I whispered.

She kissed my head and ran a hand over my overlong hair. "I looked through old boxes and packed things up to take to the thrift shop. I doubt there's much my dad had that would interest you."

"Keep something to remember him by," I murmured. "I was devastated when I realized all of my Mama's stuff had been removed."

"I miss him so much." She pressed against me at her whispered confession. "I wish I'd been a better daughter."

"Oh, Theo, how can you doubt?" I murmured as I held her against me. "He raced to you because he loved you more than anyone."

"If I hadn't been so stupid and selfish…" She broke off as her breath hitched, and tears coursed down her cheeks. "My dad would have approved of you. A strong, loyal, capable man."

"Thank you." Her words soothed an ache deep inside I hadn't known needed healing. I breathed in deeply and tumbled to the side, bringing her with me as she stifled a shriek. "Rest with me," I said as I held her in my arms.

I felt her shift as she shucked her jacket and then she was curled around me. "God, I've missed holding you." I kissed her forehead and ran my hands over her back.

She arched into me. "I've missed you, too, Nolan." She gasped as my hands roved over her back underneath her sweater. "I hate being in the house alone."

"Why?" I traced a hand up and down her spine, delighting in her quivering at my soft touch. I marveled at how responsive she was and lamented that I was in the middle of calving season. Dreams of a proper honeymoon with my bride would have to wait.

"I get lost in memories," she whispered. "I never realized how much I miss my dad until I'm alone in the house. Everything reminds me of him, and I wish…" She pressed against me. "I wish I hadn't been a stupid girl."

"Hush, darlin'," I murmured. "I know you were never stupid."

"You don't know that," she whispered as she clung to me. "For now, I want to enjoy this short time with you."

I sighed, pressing my face into her hair. "When you were a girl, what was your dream?"

Her fingers rubbed over my chest, and I felt her relax in my arms at my question. "That's easy. I wanted to live on the ranch with my husband and children." She lifted her head and flushed as she met my gaze and admitted the rest of her dream to me. "But I didn't want to raise cattle. I wanted to breed horses. My father said it would be expensive, but that he'd do what he could to ensure my dream came true."

I sobered. "Now that dream's been stolen by your family," I

whispered, seeing the grief she tried to conceal in her eyes. At her nod, I cupped her face with one of my large hands. "It will take time, but we can make it come true." At the flash of delight on her face, I grinned at her.

The door burst open and I groaned. "Devon, knock!"

"Sorry, boss," he muttered. "Ray left the fence open for a minute and two cows wandered out who are about to drop. We need to find 'em in this cold."

I nodded. "I'll be right there." I helped Theo stand and sighed as she gazed at me with longing. "I'll come home as soon as I can, Theo, but it will still be a few weeks." I flushed and felt like a goddamn teenager. "Can I call you? I miss your voice."

A soft flush bloomed and she smiled up at me, her green eyes enchanting me. "Call me as often as you can. I love your voice." Standing on her toes, she kissed me softly. "Come home as soon as you can. I miss you."

I watched her leave, hope and fear battling for supremacy inside of me.

THEODORA

I left Nolan's office, warm and reassured. Although I hadn't seen him in weeks, our kiss in the barn had fueled my dreams and my hopes. With a sigh, I tugged my jacket back on, wrapping my scarf around my neck. As I approached the truck Nolan had left at the ranch for me to use, I stifled a shriek as a man emerged from the shadows.

I clung to the belief that if I yelled loudly, someone would help me. "Who are you?" I stared at the tall man with broad shoulders who stepped into a patch of light. His blond hair glimmered like a beacon, although I couldn't see his eyes.

"I'm your father-in-law. I thought I would have merited a visit from you by now."

His venomous tone pierced the bubble of joy that had enveloped me after being in Nolan's arms, and I wrapped my arms around myself as I took a step away. "I follow my husband's lead. He did not think it was wise."

Chuckling, he made a tsking sound. "Wise? Wise?" Matching my backward step, he stalked me. "How unfortunate for you not to realize that you should never use that word with my son."

Glaring at him, I frowned. "How can you say that? He operates the most successful ranch in the area."

"And you know nothing." He nodded as I quivered at his ferocious tone. "You've been here weeks and you think you know my son? Know his secrets?" He scoffed. "You're a fool and you'll be sorely disappointed when he proves himself a disappointment to you too."

I stiffened. "I won't be disappointed in him. Although I can't say the same for his family." I spun on my heel, hoping to put space between me and his horrible father.

I gasped when his strong hand latched onto mine, twirling me to face him again. I could now see his bitter gaze, and the hatred and anguish within terrified me. "Let me go!"

"Oh, I will. Just as my son will. You're not worth keeping." He hurled my arm away, snickering when I stumbled.

I wrenched the truck door open, slamming down the lock so he couldn't follow me inside. After I was halfway down the drive, I pulled over to rest my head against the steering wheel, as I shook from my interaction with my father-in-law. I tried to ignore the doubts his father had sowed, but I couldn't help wondering if Nolan would find a way to let me go. If I wouldn't end up alone and heartbroken. All my dreams had been for a happy, large, loving family. How would that be possible if all of his family hated and resented me as much as his father did?

~

T he next evening, I rested on the couch hugging a pillow as I stared into the fire and wished for Nolan's arms around me. I'd fought my desire to travel to his ranch again to snuggle up against him, telling myself he needed time to rest. That he'd be out working. That he didn't need a needy wife clinging to him.

Ugh. I wished we hadn't been interrupted in the barn and everything was different between us. I longed to know that he felt at least a portion of what I did. If I was the only one burning up with desire, then life was truly cruel.

When my phone rang, I cringed. It would be one of my cousins calling to taunt me. Or berate me for betraying the family. I'd ignored their calls the past few weeks, and I knew they were only getting angrier with my disinterest in them. Glancing at the number with no intention of answering, I gasped when I saw Nolan's name and hit the button to talk. "Yes?"

"Theo?" Nolan asked. "Are you all right? You sound breathless."

Flushing beet red, I lay back down on the sofa. "I hadn't expected to hear from you." Tingles traveled up and down my spine as he chuckled. God, he even sounded sexy as sin.

"Tell me about your day, bella," he murmured, and I imagined him resting on his cot. Although separated by a few miles, I felt an intimacy between us.

"Oh, it was more of the same. I went through more boxes. Prepared things for charity. Dreamed about my—our—barn."

"Hmm," he mumbled in his deep sexy voice. "What do you dream?"

"That it's repaired with a sound roof and fresh red paint. Filled with horses with foals born every year." I sighed. "I majored in Equine Studies at Western and took business classes as well."

"Damn, I never knew I was marrying such a smart woman," he teased.

I relaxed as he didn't seem upset at my college degree. Too many men I'd met had been upset I was more educated than they were. "It's what I love."

"And that's what counts."

I sank into the sofa, soothed and aroused by his quiet confidence and encouragement of me. "How was your day?" I heard him yawn and imagined him quivering with it as he did when I was in his arms.

"Oh, just like you. More of the same. Chasing cattle around who want to hide away to give birth." He groaned. "God, I hate this time of year. I wish I never had to do it again, but there are times, like last night when I was out at two a.m. and the air was so cold I thought it would freeze my nose, but so clear too, that the sky looked like it was a river of stars." He yawned. "I can't help but stop and marvel at the beauty, even though I'm freezing my ass off."

"For my sake, I hope you didn't freeze anything off." I bit my lip as I realized I was more flirtatious than I'd meant. At his bark of laughter, I curled on my side and felt like my teenage self again, flirting with a boy I was hopelessly charmed by. How had I come full circle?

"I promise, bella, nothin' froze off."

I knew if he'd been sitting by me, he would have winked, and I was suddenly thankful for our slow, tortured courtship. "I miss you." I covered my face with my palm at my blurted words, wishing to call them back. When I heard his sharp inhale, I almost hung up, but forced myself to remain on the line.

"Damn, Theo, I miss you too. I promise, I'll come home as soon as I can."

"Call me," I whispered, hating the pleading in my voice, but I couldn't hide it. I was a wife, dammit—his wife—and I needed some affection from him.

"Every day." His soft, solemn words eased the tension thrumming through me. "Every day I'll call and hear your gorgeous voice and let you drive me wild as I think of you at home on our couch in front of the fire without me."

My breath stuttered out of me, my hand now clenched against my chest. "That's where I am. What I'm doing." I swallowed. "Instead of hugging you, I'm hugging a pillow."

"Good." His voice was now thick with desire and humor. "No pillow can ever compete with me."

I heard a commotion on his end and knew our conversation would end. "Stay warm. I don't want any of you freezing."

"Don't worry about that, Theo. The thought of you has made me an inferno. Ciao, bella."

I rested on my side with a stupid smile on my face, staring into the fire, until I drifted to sleep.

∾

A few days later, I was tired of going through boxes and confronting memories of my past. Of sitting by myself as I wished I'd acted differently. How many times could I ask myself, *"How could you be so stupid?"* when I thought about my thirteen-year-old self before I went insane?

With an aggrieved huff, I rose and slapped my hands against my thighs, rubbing dirt off my faded, well-worn jeans. I knew my cousins would call them rags, but I loved them. They were comfortable, and I'd mourn them when I had to finally throw them into the dust bin. After a few more minutes wandering the house aimlessly, I decided to go into town for groceries. Anything to fill the time.

Rumbling down the long driveway in the truck, I already felt lighter as I stared over my land. *Our land*, my mind whispered, as I already thought of this ranch as both mine and Nolan's. Although still snow covered, I envisioned it green in spring and then golden in summer, with the late summer light shimmering off it. Nolan and I would ride through it, or walk, hand in hand. The work would be ceaseless, but it would be ours.

I shook my head as the truck bumped over the cattle grate, and I slowed to turn onto the main road into town. I pushed thoughts of my too-tempting husband from my mind. I was successful for about thirty seconds. How could I stop thinking about the most magnetic man I'd ever met? Besides, he was an enigma. He was gorgeous, smart, funny, and considerate, and yet he thought I should want someone else? Why would he believe I wanted an annulment? How could I ever want someone else after the phone calls we shared, never mind the kisses?

Every night he called, and every night I felt more and more linked to him. Last night he'd teased me about Alessia, and rather than be upset, his teasing had taken away any pain from that day. We laughed, flirted, and skirted a very fine line between propriety and indiscretion with our banter. Every night I hung up aching for him.

Forcing my thoughts from Nolan, I thought about his father, Jameson. Why did his own father talk about him with such scorn? I shivered as I thought about Jameson gripping my arm and hoped I never had to see that man alone again.

As I entered Burnside Creek, I saw the library near the town square and made a mental note to pick up a book before leaving town. After parking near the café—having decided to have an impromptu lunch in town—I hopped out and pulled my wool hat lower over my head. Although March, it was still freezing. Nolan loved my turquoise scarf, and I wore it today, thinking of him and wishing he were here with me. It felt like everyone was staring at me. Did they approve or disapprove? With a shake of my head, I told myself it didn't matter. But deep inside, it did.

Just as I was about to enter the Lupine Café with its large glass front windows covered in drawings proclaiming they had the best coffee, sandwiches, and huckleberry pie in town, the door opened, smacking me in my shin. Gasping in pain, I jumped back a step, hopping on one foot as I glared up at the person who'd hurt me. "Willow." Any hope of an apology fled as I stared into her gleeful gaze.

"Oh, look who it is. The gold digger."

"Gold digger?" I stood on both feet, wincing as I put pressure on my injured leg. "Are you sure you know what that means?"

Briar sidled out, her black hair shiny as it cascaded over her shoulder in a braid. "Oh, we know what it means. It's a woman so desperate for what isn't hers, she'll do anything to get it." She looked me up and down and then smirked. "Although it's obvious he still doesn't find you desirable enough."

I'd never been good at deflecting their mean comments or hiding my pain when they hurt me. If I had, maybe they'd have stopped hurting me as it wouldn't have been as much fun. Cursing as my cheeks flushed red with humiliation, she crowed with delight.

"I told you, Willow."

"I hate it when you're right," Willow said as she sashayed a step closer to me, ensuring her hips swayed in case a man within fifty miles was looking in her direction. "But then, betting over pathetic Theo was never worth more than fifty cents."

Just then a hand landed on my shoulder and gave it a gentle squeeze. "Have I missed a family reunion?" Closing my eyes in relief, I relaxed as I realized Caleb must have seen us and had taken pity on me.

When he squeezed my shoulder again, I stood a little taller and opened my eyes to stare at my cousins with disbelief as they simpered and preened for Caleb. I shouldn't be surprised, but they never failed to shock me. "Willow and Briar…" I paused as I could think of nothing kind to say.

"Oh, I know all about who they are and what they do," Caleb said, his voice laced with menace. "Come, Theo. I'm so glad you made it into town for lunch with me today. I can't wait to catch up with my favorite cousin." He glared at them as he shook his head. "Alone."

He waited for them to depart, ignoring their grumbles and glances filled with entreaty to be invited and then urged me with a soft press into my back to enter the café. He smiled at Marla, the longtime owner of the Lupine, and we sat at a booth away from the door, but still near a window. "A little privacy at least."

"How are you here?" I asked after we ordered our drinks from our waitress.

Caleb shrugged. "I get tired of staring at contracts all day, and I just happened to wander outside today for a breath of fresh air. And there you were, confronting those two harpies." He stared at me in concern. "I saw you limping. Are you okay?"

"I didn't see them coming out and they whacked the door into my shin. I'll be fine."

His jaw ticked and he shook his head. "Nolan will be pissed."

"Why? By the time he returns home, there'll be no bruise and there's no reason for him to know about it." I shrugged and smiled blandly at the waitress whose eyes gleamed with far too much interest as she set down our drinks.

"Thank you, Sue," Caleb said. "I'm so glad Bert is doing better." When she stood bolt upright and scurried away, Caleb chuckled before taking a sip of his coffee. Meeting my curious gaze, he winked at me. "Helps to be the most trusted lawyer in town. Keeps everyone honest and quiet when you want them to stay out of your business because you already know theirs."

A genuine smile bloomed as I fully appreciated his cunning. "I hope you're always on my side."

He sobered as he stared at me. "I will be because you're married to Nolan. You're like a sister to me, Theo. Never forget that." His blue eyes blazed with sincerity.

My throat thickened and I had trouble speaking. "Thank you."

After our sandwiches were delivered, I nibbled on mine while Caleb devoured his. He nodded at my food and frowned. "Aren't you hungry?"

I groaned and my shoulders slumped. "Every time I see my cousins, I'm reminded of everything I'm not." When he raised his eyebrow and nodded for me to continue, I sighed in defeat. "Beautiful. Sought after. Curvy in all the right places." I looked down at my comfortable jeans and felt like a frump.

Caleb burst out laughing and I frowned as he laughed so hard he started to cough. "Oh, Jesus, you're serious," he wailed as he grabbed his paper napkin to wipe at his face. "Holy shit." He swiped at his cheeks and shook his head. "I need to have lunch with you more often if I can laugh like that." He smiled at me tenderly as I glared at him.

How dared he laugh at me and how I feel?

Gripping my hand, he shook his head. "Theo, you have it ass end backward. And forgive me for laughing, but this week's been crap...and I hate them...and for you not to see..." He sighed and shook his head. "I didn't mean to hurt your feelings."

"Why did you laugh?"

"You're everything they'll never be. Truly beautiful. They use makeup and clothes and hair products. I don't know. All those things women spend money on that make them look good. But it doesn't help if you have the soul of the devil. And they do." His blue eyes shone with sincerity. "Why do you think they hate you so much?"

"Because I have a ranch and they don't?"

He nodded. "Partly. Mainly because they're selfish bi...uh, women, but also because they look at you and see you don't need all that stuff to shine. You have an inner glow that no amount of makeup can create. You are beautiful as you are, Theo. Nolan saw it and was drawn to you from that first moment. I knew when I entered the cabin that night at The Hill that he was a goner for you."

"But you were going to marry me!"

He shrugged. "A good lawyerly tactic to push my cousin to act." He sobered. "I would have married you, Theo, to save you from them. And we would have been happy."

I bit my lip and grinned. "But not nearly as happy as I am with Nolan."

"Ouch," he said as he held a hand to his chest as if I'd just stabbed him, although I saw the humor in his gaze. "I deserved that." He looked straight into my eyes. "Forgive me? I never meant to laugh at you. It's just what you said was so ludicrous. Those cousins of yours are like a papier-mâché doll of a beautiful woman compared to what a truly gorgeous woman is."

I sat back, stunned by his words. "Thank you." I was no longer concerned about my cousins and what they thought of me. They were truly in my past. Suddenly, I was starving, and I dug into my lunch.

Caleb took another sip of his coffee as he watched me eat. "How's Nol?"

I shrugged after I swallowed down a bite of my BLT. "Working too hard. The only way he seems to relax is by listening to audiobooks." I frowned. "I find them more work than reading, but he must be so tired after all that physical labor that he enjoys listening with his eyes closed."

"Something like that," Caleb murmured cryptically. "Have you met Jameson yet?"

Shivering, I nodded as I pushed away the last few fries. At Caleb's quirk of his eyebrow, I nodded and watched him gobble them down. "Once. He seemed to think I'd rue the day I married Nolan. How can he be so mean?"

"Easily." Caleb's jaw twitched. "He's been an ornery old goat for as long as I can remember." He sighed as he rolled his shoulders. "He's my mother's brother, but I always felt closer to Evelina, Nol's mom. She was a fine woman."

I blushed. "I'm sorry."

Shaking his head, he shrugged. "You didn't kill her, Theo. Fate. Black ice. Faulty brakes?" He shrugged again. "Rail at all of them. Not at yourself. You lost as much, or more, as any of the rest of us." He looked at his watch and slurped down another sip of coffee. "I have to run." He pulled out a few bills and threw them on the table. "Don't fool yourself, Theo. This interlude without Nolan won't last, nor does he want it to. I know he's eager to return to you."

I flushed at his words, praying they were true.

~

NOLAN

I rested on the cot, wishing for Theo. Wishing I smelled her elusive scent that calmed me and reminded me of days when I wasn't told what a failure I was. God, I missed Theo and I was so damn tired. Why did we have to have a calving season every year?

Yawning, I stretched and then relaxed again, forcing myself to sleep the few hours I had before I was called out to help with a birth or to search for a missing cow. Every year I promised myself we'd have a better system. Every year, something always went wrong. I should know better than to believe I could outsmart nature or the will of a huge beast.

March was proving to be almost as cold as February and a brutal month for calving. Although the days were slightly longer, we'd still lost more calves than we'd like and we had to be vigilant. I'd hoped to have returned home by now to be with

Theo, but I knew that wouldn't be a reality for a while. For too long.

When the door opened, I groaned with relief and opened my arm. "Theo," I breathed. "I'm so glad you're here. I need to hold you."

I thought I heard a snicker, but that didn't make sense. Theo loved her time with me. Didn't she?

"Although I thought about cuddling up to you to freak you out, I just can't," Caleb said as he chuckled. "Besides, the weight of both of us would ruin that cot of yours and then you'd spend the rest of calving season on the floor."

I groaned and rubbed at my face. "What are you doing here? Can't you leave me in peace?" I rested a hand beneath my bent elbow as I propped myself up and stared at him through bleary eyes. If I couldn't see my wife, I didn't want to see anyone.

Caleb pulled out a chair and sat near my cot as he looked around the office. "Some things never change. Alessia's still a slob."

"She's not a slob." I yawned again, my whole body shaking. "She thrives in chaos.'"

Caleb snorted as he stared at her desk. "Call it what you want, that's a disaster." He focused on me, and I froze. He rarely visited the ranch during calving season, and he generally came with pizza and thermoses of coffee to bolster my spirit and my flagging energy.

"What's happened?" I forced myself to sit up although I yearned for sleep. I was getting too old for this crap. How was I only thirty-four? I felt ninety.

"Imagine how tired you'll be when you have a child and you're in the middle of a calving season."

"Stop looking so gleeful." I rose, stomping around the room as I attempted to wake up. Somehow, I knew I needed to be wide awake for whatever he had to say. He had the air of a lawyer about him, rather than that of my best friend and cousin. "Spit it out, Cay."

"I saw Theo today. She went into town for groceries." He met my stare of *"who gives a shit?"* with raised eyebrows.

"I'm sure it was more enjoyable than wrangling cows in a pool of mud."

"I wouldn't be so sure of that." When I frowned, he nodded. "I interrupted a conversation between her and her cousins. They enjoyed bruising her shin with the door and then bruising her spirit with their spite."

"Bitches." When he grunted his agreement, I smiled. Whatever happened in this world, I knew I had Caleb at my back. Thank God. "What did you do?"

"I took Theo to lunch and made sure her cousins knew they weren't wanted." With a sigh, he rested his hands over his strong chest and shook his head as he stared at me with disappointment. "How can you not have told her by now?"

I blanched, stumbling in my pacing. I leaned against my desk and gripped its edge as I stared at the floor rather than see the disapproval on his face. "You don't understand. She likes me now. I think she even believes she could love me right now." I took a deep breath. "When she knows who she married, everything will change."

"Trust her, Nol." Caleb waited until I met his gaze, now filled with compassion. He'd lived through the hell of my childhood, standing beside me the entire time. He'd never forsaken me. "Trust that not everyone leaves."

I nodded, my shoulders stooped. "It's not easy to believe when almost everyone in my life has." I didn't say it aloud, but I knew he was tallying up everyone just as I was. My mama. All of my siblings except for Alessia. Our best friend, Chase. Only Alessia and Caleb had remained. I still marveled I had ever earned their loyalty.

Why should Theo feel that for me after only a few short

months? Ally and Caleb were my blood and with that came some expectations.

"Trust in her," Caleb murmured. "Your instincts weren't wrong."

I nodded.

"She met Jameson."

I stood bolt upright, my hands fisting and immediately ready for battle. "What? When? What did he do to her?" The thought that my precious Theo had met my bastard of a father alone nearly made me insane.

Shaking his head, Caleb rubbed at his chin as he made a motion for me to calm down. "I don't know what he said or did, but he spooked her. He knows better than to hurt her. Besides, you're his favorite punching bag."

"Does she know?" My small burst of adrenaline faded, and I collapsed against my desk again. "I'm too tired for this shit, but I hate the thought of anything upsetting Theo."

Caleb smirked. "And that's the third thing you have to admit to her. Why you say her name the way you do."

He left, and I frowned at his abrupt departure. A moment later, he reentered with two pizzas and two thermoses. Groaning with relief, I grabbed a pizza and sniffed as I yanked the top open. Extra cheese, extra pepperoni, mushrooms, black olives, and peppers. "Extra everything," I said with a reverent sigh as I breathed in the greasy aroma. Caleb had always teased me as a kid. Now, he always got me one of my own, and for him, he got a loaded veggie crap one that tasted like cardboard. I taunted him that he could work out on the ranch rather than at the pansy gym and eat real food, but he preferred flirting with the other patrons too much. I knew he loved living in town too much to ever risk getting stuck on a ranch again.

"Your hands have already devoured all the others I brought for them."

"Thanks, Cay, you're the best." We tapped our thermoses

together as he told me about gossip from town while we ate our fill. When he left, less than an hour later, I collapsed onto my cot, full and worried. Caleb was right. I had three secrets to reveal to Theo. Would she still want me after she learned the whole truth?

～

"What are you doing?" I demanded as I stared at my father as he picked at the lock to my office door. He didn't even have the decency to look embarrassed at being caught. "You know you're not allowed in there."

"I have every right to go in there. That was my office for decades!" He bellowed in my face, and I was so tired I wanted to shrug and say I didn't care.

But I did. If he had access to my office, Caleb could spend the rest of his career cleaning up my father's messes and still die with unfinished business. Leaning against the wall so I didn't fall over from my fatigue, I gazed at him with blatant loathing. "What do you want?"

"I want to know what my children are hiding from me!" He rattled the doorknob and kicked at the door. "I'm your father. You should respect me!"

Adrenaline surged through me, giving me a spurt of energy. "Now you want me to respect you? You want me to think of you as good old Dad?" I said those last words in a singsong voice as though we were living in a fifties sitcom, mocking him and our reality. "You know that's not how it was or how it will ever be. *You* ensured we lived in this fucked-up reality."

"Your mother—"

"Don't you dare blame Mama for your inability to be a good, decent man." I stood tall with my hands in fists. "She was nothing like you."

Leaning toward me, he gave a huff of disgust. "Do you really believe that bull crap—that your mama would be delighted with your choice of bride?" He shrugged. "But then, she never did have high expectations for you. She'd delight in the fact anyone was willing to marry you."

I attempted to ignore his barbs, as my father never fought fair. "Stay away from Theo, Dad."

"Or what?"

"Or I'll toss you off this ranch without a second thought."

He stilled, his smirk frozen as he detected the sincerity of my words. "You'd throw me out? Your own father?"

I shrugged. "You know as well as I do you've never taken to that role with me. What difference would it make?" I met his dark glower. "Stay away from my wife, and you'll have a home. Otherwise, I don't care what happens to you."

I watched as he stormed past me and stomped down the stairs, sighing with relief to have a few hours to rest before I had to go out again. Pushing thoughts of my father aside, I envisioned Theo and holding her in my arms again. Soon, I promised myself.

~

THEODORA

March was almost over and Nolan had yet to return. I cooked supper every night for two, praying I'd have someone to share it with. When he didn't come home, I froze his portion or ate it for lunch the next day. At this rate, I'd grow sick of my own cooking.

With a sigh, I stared into the fire, admitting the truth. I missed him. I *yearned* for him. Did I really care what he was hiding from me? Groaning, I fell back onto the couch as I hugged a pillow, wishing my arms were instead around Nolan.

I did. I knew I did. But at this moment, I'd take a few hours in his arms rather than the unvarnished truth. I wanted to be held by him and reminded of how good it had felt to be in his presence. Stolen minutes on his cot were lovely, but I could never fully relax as I knew at any moment a ranch hand could barge in and interrupt us. I wanted time on this couch for us to cuddle like we used to. Or for us to find passion in our bedroom. Finally.

My phone rang and I snatched it up. "Nolan!"

"Hi, bella, were you expecting someone else?" he teased as I heard him laugh softly. "This is our phone date time."

"No," I breathed out, although a fine tension thrummed through me. I heard him moving around and imagined him settling onto his uncomfortable cot, resting his head on one of his arms.

"Can I ask you something?" At my soft sound of assent, he spoke in a quiet voice like one used not to scare off a child or wounded animal. "Why didn't you tell me about meeting my dad?"

"Oh," I gasped, a breath of air gushing out of me. "I wanted to forget him." I swallowed as I watched the fire. "I didn't want to cause any trouble."

"Why? Because you think you're not worth it?" He made a noise of disgust. "That's crap and you know it, Theo. You're my wife, and if he thinks he has the right to talk with you, he's an idiot." He exhaled. "What happened?"

"He taunted me and held my arm and—"

"He manhandled you?" Nolan roared and I heard a clunk, which I imagined were his boots hitting the floor. "He dared to touch you?"

"Nolan, please." I stopped, uncertain what to say.

"Please, what, Theo?" he asked. When a long silence dragged on over the phone, he whispered, "Please ignore the fact my dad's an asshole and dared to scare you? Please ignore the fact my first loyalty is to you? Please ignore the fact you didn't care to share this with me?"

"Nolan..." I took a deep breath. "I never want to come between you and your family."

"You didn't, bella. He did." He let out another deep breath. "If I were there right now..."

I flinched and tilted my head up, imagining the argument we'd have. "What?"

"I'd kiss you senseless so you'd understand."

His deep, sexy voice washed over me, and I shivered. "I don't understand."

"I'd love you so hard you'd never have any doubt about my priorities."

"Nolan," I breathed, suddenly feeling a molten heat in my veins.

"What are you wearing, bella?"

"A flimsy nightshirt."

He sighed and groaned. "Damn, I bet your curves are all soft and just waiting for me to caress and kiss them."

I waited for him to say more, but he remained quiet. "What would you do, Nolan?" I whispered in a breathy voice, pulling a blanket over me and cocooning myself in a little world just for us. "What would you do to me?"

"Oh, *Teo*, what wouldn't I do?" His voice had dropped an octave, provoking a shiver in me. "I'd slip my hands under that flimsy shirt of yours and finally feel the lush beauty of your breasts. They've taunted me with their perfection for long enough. I'd nibble and taste you until you were writhing and screaming my name."

"Nolan," I gasped, arching back into the couch as though he were in fact playing with my breasts.

"Then, I'd leave a trail of kisses down your belly. Your beautiful, perfect, silky soft belly. You'd wriggle and moan as I flicked my tongue in and out of your belly button." He paused, and I swore I heard a smile in his voice. "Should I stop?"

"Nolan!" I curled onto my side, desperate for him to be with me now. Not days or weeks from now. But *now*.

He chuckled. "I'll take that as a no." His voice lowered to a near whisper, and I was spellbound. "My fingers would trace over your inner thighs, tickling and teasing you. Feeling how wet you were for me." He swallowed, and he finally gave a sign he was affected by our conversation. His breath emerged in a rush, and he groaned. "Damn, you'll feel so good."

"God, why aren't you here with me?" I moaned.

"Shit."

I heard the phone clatter to the floor and the sound of the door opening and then a crash. Everything was a bit muffled, but I waited for him to return, calming ever so slightly although I was on the knife edge of coming just from his words.

"Theo?" His breath emerged in harsh pants. "Shit, shit, shit. I have to go."

"No," I moaned as I buried my face into a pillow. "Not before the good part." I'd lost my modesty somewhere along the way.

Chuckling, he blew me a kiss. "Oh, darlin' that will only be the appetizer when we're finally together. Miss you, bella."

Groaning, I disconnected and dropped my phone down beside me. How long was calving season? The wait to make love with my husband was about to kill me.

The next evening after an uneventful day, I rested on the couch and counted down the moments until Nolan called. I was worse than Pavlov's dog, waiting to hear from him. God, maybe tonight he'd talk dirty to me again and we wouldn't be interrupted. I rested my head against the couch and took a deep breath as I tried to still the anticipation thrumming through me.

I heard a door slam and bolted from the couch, tripping on the throw blanket. Racing to the window I looked out but couldn't see anyone. He was home! I ran to the door, wishing I had on something sexier than my comfy sweats and oversized sweatshirt, but in this moment I didn't really care. All that mattered was that, in a second, I'd be in his arms.

Flinging the door open, I faltered back a step at the sight of four women standing in front of me. "But...why?"

"So happy to see you again too," muttered one in the back I remembered was Cora.

"No, I'm sorry. Forgive me." I waved them inside as I was suddenly close to tears. Alessia was the last one to enter, and I ignored her pitying look as I shut the door, staring at it a long moment as I tried to compose myself. Nothing worked as a sob escaped.

"Theo," Alessia whispered, running a hand down my back. "Do you want us to go? We thought we'd surprise you with a girls' night. We were having one and then we thought of you here, all alone while Nolan works."

"No." I tried not to stammer, but it was futile as I couldn't control my sobs. "I'm happy you're here."

"Yes, I sob uncontrollably when I'm ecstatic," a wry voice said.

"Shut up, Tar." And a smacking noise was heard.

That made me giggle as it was all so surreal. Here I was, finally having a girls' night at age twenty-four, and I was crying over a man. How had some things remained constant? "I'm emotional." I turned and faced them, uncaring that they saw my puffy, red eyes and runny nose. "I'm Theo. Theodora."

"We know who you are," Cora said as she rolled her eyes. "In case you've forgotten, I'm Caleb's sister, Cora." She held a hand to her chest as her hazel eyes gleamed with amusement. "She's

Quinn." She pointed to the woman I remembered from my wedding day, a stunning woman whose auburn hair fell in waves around her oval face. Today she wore bright yellow eyeshadow, and her light blue nose ring sparkled in the kitchen light. Quinn waved at me.

"And I'm Tara," the other sister said, with a broad smile and mischief in her gorgeous cognac-colored eyes only partially hidden behind a pair of wire-rimmed glasses. Her red hair and alabaster skin were striking, and I only had a moment to stare at her before she pulled me in for a hug. "I can see why Nolan is smitten with you."

I flushed at her frank assessment of me, although I knew I was nowhere near as gorgeous as any of Nolan's family members.

"Stop mothering her, Tara," Cora said.

"I have the snacks." Alessia led the way into the great room.

"And I have the booze." Quinn set down a heavy bag, looking around. "Wow, this is gorgeous. I can see why Nolan doesn't want to live at the LBarM anymore."

"God, Quinn. He doesn't want to live there because Theo's here." Alessia shook her head at her cousin as though she were a child in need of a lesson. After setting out paper plates and napkins, she pulled out bread, cheese, a fruit and vegetable tray, nuts, and bite-sized brownies.

"Do you always eat like this on girls' night?" I blurted out, flushing when they stared at me.

"No, some nights we actually eat. Tonight, it's just nibbles," Tara said as she plopped down on the floor and grabbed a carrot to dip in hummus. "Who wants wine?"

I watched in wonder as glasses were passed around and conversation flowed with ease. There was teasing, laughter, and no one seemed upset when a story stopped and restarted twenty minutes later—like when the mention of the color red reminded

Quinn of the story about Flynn's prized rooster who'd escaped and raced all over town.

"Flynn?" I asked as I settled by the side of the table, nibbling on a slice of baguette with the most delicious cheese I'd ever eaten. If this was girls' night fare, sign me up.

"Oh, he's an annoying guy I've known since I was a girl. He lives near me, and his rooster's always roaming around free. I help him catch it when I have a chance."

I stared at her and her feigned indifference for a moment, but no one else seemed to think anything of her explanation. Soon, the conversation had turned to Alessia and her latest horrible first date.

Sighing, Alessia swirled her pinot grigio around, staring into it as though she could find a reason for the latest debacle. "Can you imagine inviting your mom to sit at the table next to us so she could give tips on what to say?" She groaned. "I had such high hopes of meeting someone who wasn't a cowboy."

"You should have found your true love when you went away to college," Quinn said.

Alessia gave a weak smile and shrugged. "Considering I didn't finish my degree..."

Tara rolled her eyes as she settled near me, relaxed and at ease. "We know that was because Aunt Evelina died right near the start of winter semester your senior year."

Alessia nodded and then shrugged. "I still wish I could find someone who liked to talk about something other than ranches or fishing. I love working on the ranch, but..." Her gaze became distant.

"Maybe you just haven't met the right cowboy yet," I murmured, flushing as everyone stared at me with avid interest, and Alessia smirked at me. "You have to admit Nolan's pretty great." I attempted to appear nonchalant, but I knew I was coming off as a lovesick bride, alone too long without her husband home.

"He's the best, but I wouldn't want to marry him," Cora said. "He's overbearing and overprotective and stifling."

"Nolan?" I sat in stunned silence. "I've never felt that way. He's generous and warm and encourages me. I feel safe with him."

Tara leaned forward. "Do tell more."

I froze, belatedly remembering either Caleb or Nolan muttering she couldn't keep a secret. "Nothing. There's nothing more to say."

"Come on, you guys!" Tara glared at her sisters and cousin. "Stop spreading rumors. I might tell Mom things, but that doesn't mean I can't keep a secret." She failed to hide the hurt in her gaze. "I could have been trusted not to talk about your wedding for a day."

I looked at her with remorse. "I'm sorry. I had no idea."

"Don't blame Theo," Alessia said. "Besides, I wasn't invited either, and it was my own brother getting married."

I ducked my head, suddenly feeling like I'd made everything worse by sticking up for Nolan, but I couldn't help it when it seemed like they were attacking him.

Cora let out an irritated huff. She seemed to be the most volatile sister, and I remember Nolan saying she held onto a grudge the best. "If you're left out of the family party this summer, *then* you should complain." She smiled at me. "It was a nice ceremony, but nothing like the church weddings we're used to. Be thankful you didn't have to prepare for one of those."

Quinn groaned as she refilled all our glasses while Tara fought with the bottle opener, squealing joyfully at the "pop" as the cork burst free. "Can you imagine what Mom will have to say when any of us finally marry?"

"I think that's why Caleb's remained a bachelor," Tara said as she finished topping off our drinks. She pushed up her glasses then she sipped at her wine. "He doesn't want to deal with Mom."

"No, he remains a bachelor because he's never recovered from Valeria."

"Valeria?" I repeated, enjoying the exotic sounding name on my tongue as I repeated it silently a few times.

"Never say that name to Caleb. He'll skewer you in the way he knows best. With words. And then you'll wonder how you're walking around when you're bleeding internally and why no one can see your wound." Cora spoke, but all the sisters nodded, while Alessia frowned at the validity of the statement.

"How awful." I tried to imagine the Caleb I'd only begun to know as the man who would act that way, and then I remembered his subtle warning to the waitress at the café. In that moment, I knew he'd be capable of such a thing.

"As for Nolan, he suffers in silence, accepting Jameson's punishment." Tara shook her head.

"As though he has to make up for the sins of the past generation," Quinn muttered.

Alessia shot me a worried glance, murmuring, "That's enough!" But the sisters kept talking. The wine, the warmth from the fire, and the camaraderie they felt had loosened their tongues, and I was eager to hear all they would share. Thankfully, I hadn't had much to drink yet, and I wasn't sitting here a muddleheaded mess.

"Uncle Jameson's always been a beast, hasn't he?" Quinn muttered as Cora scolded her. Raising a hand up she stared at her sister in defiance. "Tell me one time he was nice when it wasn't to Alessia or to Aunt Evelina." At the deafening silence, she nodded. "Exactly. A beast."

"You know Mom says he's suffered a lot." Cora bit her lip at the feeble excuse.

"No one's suffered like Nolan. Living under the weight of Uncle's expectations even though he's not his son." Tara snorted. "I'd have told him where to shove it. Or kicked him off my ranch. Why is Nolan so damn good?" She rested her head against the couch, her eyes closed and already half-asleep. "Wake me when it's time for chocolate."

"It's always time for chocolate." Quinn picked up a bite of brownie and moaned with delight. "We need red wine to fully enjoy the flavor." She chugged her glass of white and searched around in the bag, clanging bottles, until she found what she was looking for. "Ah, a yummy bottle of cabernet sauvignon." She glanced at me, growing more bleary-eyed by the second. "You haven't had enough to drink yet. Drink with me."

I tried to protest, my mind spinning with what I thought I understood. Alessia relaxed incrementally as the conversation moved from Nolan to chocolate to wine, so I knew I hadn't misunderstood. Nolan wasn't Jameson's son. That's why the older man resented him. Hated me. With a huff of relief, I held out my empty glass for Quinn to fill, eager to toast anything they wanted as I said a silent prayer of thanksgiving that the man I adored was truly not related to a man I feared and despised.

CHAPTER 11

THEODORA

I dozed, curled on the couch hugging a pillow as I stared into the fire. It was nearly April, but the evenings and nights were still cold in Montana, and I was still alone. I smiled, as I knew there would be evenings in July where I'd enjoy a warm fire.

The girls' night gathering a few nights ago had been wonderful. I'd enjoyed their company, their subtle initiation into the family and their close-knit group, and the sense that I was wanted for me, not just because I was Nolan's wife. They had helped with the loneliness for one night, although I still puzzled over the information that had been shared after many bottles of wine had been opened.

I longed to know the truth. To have no more secrets between Nolan and me. However, more than anything, I ached for Nolan's presence in my life again. He'd been away nearly two months now, and I yearned for more than a few stolen moments, cuddled together on his cot in his office. Although I had visited him every few days since that first visit, it wasn't the same as having him home. The phone calls helped too, but nothing was enough. I needed him in my arms in a place where we wouldn't be interrupted.

I missed discussing my day with him and hearing about his. I missed how he always focused on me, truly interested in my thoughts and ideas. I missed the times when no words were needed, and I rested in his arms, feeling truly at peace with the world. We hadn't had an evening like that since I had read the letter from my uncle.

I felt myself slipping into a semidream state, and I curled up against the warm pillow. Warm pillow? I sniffed, sighing with pleasure as the pillow smelled like Nolan. A hint of spicy bay rum, horses, and man.

I woke with a start, my head jerking up to see Nolan had inched himself under me before falling asleep. He'd let a beard grow—although he'd kept it from becoming shaggy—and he looked even more handsome with the black facial hair. "Nolan," I breathed.

Crawling more fully over him, I draped myself on him, holding him tight as though afraid he'd disappear. Like a wonderful dream that faded under dawn's bright rays. Tugging the blanket up to cover both of us, I snuggled in.

"Stop wriggling," he murmured, his hand rising to caress my head and then down my back to tickle the bare flesh of my lower spine. "God, you feel like heaven."

"So do you." I kissed the underside of his jaw. "Welcome home, husband."

Groaning, his hold on me tightened. "Don't start something you don't want to finish," he said, his eyes flashing a warning. "I've been dreaming of you for weeks, Theo. I'm out of my mind with wanting you."

The fire provided the only light in the room and cast him in half shadow. His eyes glinted with pent-up passion, and I shivered, realizing it was meant for me. He truly wanted *me*. Shifting, I groaned as I pressed into him. How was it possible that he felt even more muscular than he had when we were first married?

"I want you, Nolan," I whispered, my hands playing through his hair and scraping through his beard. I watched, wonder-struck, as his eyes closed with pleasure at my whisper-soft touches. "There's so much I don't understand. I worry…"

He kissed my palm, nipping the tender flesh and earning a startled yelp of surprise. He smiled when he saw the love bite aroused and excited me. "I promised you I'd tell you everything, and I will." Taking a deep breath, he gazed deeply into my eyes. "Do you trust me enough to make love with me before you hear my sorry tale?"

If my eyes were those of a witch, his were a sorcerer's as they held me captive. Garnering all of my strength, I closed my own and rested my forehead against his as I thought. Although fully rational thought wasn't possible as I rested on him like a cat, I had a better chance when I wasn't gazing into his eyes. We'd been married more than two months. Too many secrets remained between us. Could I trust him?

I thought of my life before him and of my life now. Except for the years I spent studying at college, I had known little happiness and no love since my father had died. Since meeting Nolan, I had laughed, felt joy, and known sorrow. The faint but persistent belief that what we had would bloom into something strong and beautiful had taken root. Not even my uncle's letter had killed that hardy bud.

"I trust you," I whispered, opening my eyes and seeing the shock and delight in his gaze. "I still want to know everything you're hiding from me. I want to know why you said what you did to Caleb on our wedding day." At his confused look, I whispered, "I overheard you talking, just as I was about to enter." Lowering my head, I rubbed my cheek against his beard, shivering at the sensation. "But it can wait."

"It can wait?" His fingers roved up and down my sides.

"Later."

He groaned, his arms banding around me. "God, yes, later," he rasped. "Now, we find out if all my dirty talk will come true." His strong hands dug through my practical braid, freeing my hair until it flowed over my shoulders and over him.

Giggling, I reared back as his beard tickled my neck.

"Ticklish?" he asked with an impish smile.

"Yes," I sighed as I turned my neck to give his lips better access as they worked over my sensitive skin. "I love the feel of your beard."

"Good," he whispered. "I have no desire to shave it off." He nibbled at my earlobe before pushing me up. Rising with a grace I envied, he tugged at my hand. "Come, wife."

I nodded, following him to our bedroom. When we arrived, a burst of shyness enveloped me, and I tugged at my shirt that had risen up to expose my midriff.

Nolan looked at me, opening his arms to pull me close. I felt him shudder as I pressed against him. His heart beat an erratic tattoo against my ear, and my hands flexed and stroked over the powerful muscles of his back, making them jump and quiver. I marveled I could provoke such a reaction in this man.

"Nolan," I breathed, edging away and biting my lip as I flushed.

"Kiss me, bella," he whispered, dropping his head to brush his lips over mine. "Don't doubt what you feel. What I feel." His hands ran up my sides to cup my breasts. "Don't doubt how much I adore your body and you."

I groaned, opening to his kiss and then gasping as he thrust his tongue inside. Soon I was lost to his touch, to the feel of his mouth on mine, to the passion rising between us. I tugged at his shirt, lifting it so I could run my hands over his muscled chest, delighting when his muscles jumped at my feather-soft touch.

When his marauding hands stroked over my belly, I gasped

and arched back, pushing my chest against his. He broke the kiss, running his lips over my neck, and I loved the contrast of his soft lips and the scrape of his whiskers. "Nolan."

Crying out as his fingers pinched my nipples and then stroked over them softly, I raised my hands to cup his head as he ducked down to follow his fingers. I obeyed his silent command and lifted my arms for my T-shirt to be pulled over my head and tossed aside. When my bra fell to the floor and his lips latched onto my bare breast, I stifled a scream.

"Jesus, you have perfect tits," he rasped as he laved one nipple, before sucking and giving it a soft bite that elicited a moan. He released it with a soft *pop,* his lips traversing the valley between my breasts to move to the other nipple to give it the same treatment. "I loved your tits from the moment I saw them." He ran his lips around and around my nipple before pulling it into his mouth while his fingers fondled and tormented the other sensitized one.

Oh my God, I'd never felt anything like this. A molten passion boiling through my veins—all I could do was feel. "Please," I gasped. "Don't stop."

"Hell, no," he murmured, a trace of humor in his voice. Soon, he'd peeled my pants and panties off, kissing my belly and hips as he freed me of my clothes. Nolan eased me backward and I felt the cool sheets of the bed beneath me. Resting on my back with no thought of finding a blanket or sheet to cover myself, I focused on him, stripping away his pants. My breath caught at the sight of him naked for the first time. His cock was huge, and I felt a flutter of panic. How would that fit in me?

"Don't think. Feel," he murmured as he crawled over me, enveloping me in his scent and warmth. One hand ran over me, while his chest pressed against mine and our tongues dueled. His cock nudged my inner thigh, and I gasped at the promise of what was to come. I was overwhelmed by him, and I relished the sensation.

When he ran a whisper-soft caress over the skin of my inner thigh, I jerked. "Nolan," I gasped, unable to say anything more. I'd been rendered nearly mute as my breath heaved in and out of me.

When he pressed fingers firmly against my clit, stroking and discovering the places that made me squirm, I clung to his shoulders. When he lowered his head, sucking and biting a nipple, I arched up, groaning as I felt everything tighten and then convulse. Wave after wave of pleasure ripped through me, and my nails clawed into his skin.

"Bella," he rasped, his tone reverent, one finger dipping inside me, enhancing my pleasure.

I clung to him, panting and boneless as aftershocks rippled. "I need you. I want you. Please."

I felt the hot tip of him nudging my entrance, but he stopped, and I was desperate for him. I tilted up my hips, encouraging him, willing to beg. "Don't hold back."

With a groan, he inched his hips forward, and I moaned at the feel of him burrowing inside me. He was huge, cramming me so full it was almost painful. With a gasp, I arched my back, shimmied my hips, and then cried out in ecstasy. This was glorious. "More."

He pulled back and slammed forward. Each time, he was less restrained, until he grunted and I cried out, my legs wrapped tight around his waist with my feet on his ass. "More!" I screamed.

All I could feel was him hammering inside of me, my body accepting each powerful thrust and the absolute pleasure each evoked. I screamed, convulsing around him, waves and waves of pleasure cascading through me, even stronger than the last.

I held on tight as he lost all control, plunging without restraint into me again and again. When he froze, stiffening above me, I clenched my inner muscles, holding on tight as he spilled deep inside of me. His strong arms holding him up shook, and I loved knowing he was as undone by our passion as I.

"Jesus," he whispered, his warm breath panting against my neck. "Give me a second."

I kept my arms and legs wrapped around him until my muscles quivered and then they fell away from him. When he toppled to my side, I felt a momentary sense of loss until he hauled me against him, resting my head on his shoulder.

When I felt him kiss my head and run his hands down my back, I relaxed. "When can we do that again?"

He chuckled, the sound echoing in my ear against his chest. "Soon, bella, soon. Give me a few moments to enjoy holding you."

I sighed, replete as I rested against him.

~

NOLAN

I caught my breath as I lay on my back with Theo in my arms, staring at the ceiling in her childhood bedroom. Thankfully, the unicorn bedspread had been replaced, but the bed was too small for us. Tomorrow, I'd broach the idea of moving us to the larger master bedroom. I could imagine soaking in the large master bathtub with her.

"You seem pleased with yourself," she whispered as her hand roved over my chest. She'd fallen asleep and just woken up, not long after our first bout of lovemaking. I couldn't wait for our second. And third. And hundredth. I felt her smile, and I silently laughed, my chest moving up and down and causing her to jiggle on top of me.

"I am." I kissed her nose. "I'm the most brilliant man because I married you." I saw her eyes widen in disbelief before pleasure and delight filled her gaze. "I knew you were beautiful, but I never dared hope you'd be as passionate as you are."

"Only with you," she whispered, resting her head on my chest as her fingers played through my chest hair. I shivered as she flicked my nipple and then winced when she hit a ticklish spot.

"Good because there'll be no other besides me forever more." I knew we'd talked about this on the phone the day before we married, but after the passion we'd just shared, this was so much more real. Rather than seeing defiance or disappointment in her gaze, I saw relief.

"Good. As long as that extends to you."

I cupped her head, kissing her hair. "I honor my vows." I felt her relax in my arms and closed my eyes, hoping to have a catnap before making love with her again. "Bella, we never talked about birth control." I smiled as she blushed.

"I have an IUD," she whispered shyly. "We're fine."

"One day, I won't want to be fine. One day, I'll want children with you." I saw the delight in her expressive eyes and sighed with pleasure, determined to let her rest in my arms now that any doubt about us having a family had been eased.

However, my wife had other plans.

"Nolan, why does your father resent you so much?"

I sighed. "All relationships in families are complicated. Ours more than others." I closed my eyes as I thought of him. "I hate talking about him with you in our bed after making love, but I promise you I'll tell you all about him one day soon."

"Does he resent you because you're handsome, intelligent, and inspire loyalty?"

My breath caught at her description of me, and I was momentarily tongue-tied. I remembered this feeling of not finding words and staring at people as though I were the village idiot. I thought I'd outgrown it when I was a teenager, but somehow my wife could evoke such strong emotions in me she stripped me of my ability to speak. Finding my words, I choked out, "No. He doesn't see me that way."

She huffed out a breath and perched her head on her hands propped on my chest, staring up at me. "Then he's a fool, for you are all those things and so much more."

"More?" I teased, hoping to lighten the mood. Anytime I thought of my father, I wanted to do battle with someone. I'd much rather make love with my beautiful wife again.

She smiled at me impishly, and I wondered how I was ever so fortunate to have her become mine.

"Yes, more." Her bewitching eyes glowed with mischief. "More handsome. More intriguing. More sexy. More..." she said and then sighed in a dramatic fashion.

I tickled her, delighting when she arched back and squealed, toppling off me. Soon we were both panting, and I was leaning over her again. "You're more too," I whispered as I brushed my lips over hers in a featherlight kiss but didn't kiss her deeply as I knew she desired. "More friendly and kind and lovable and..." I shook my head. "There aren't words for what you are."

"Nolan," she breathed, wrapping her arms around my neck. "Love me again."

She didn't have to ask me twice, and I lost myself to the passion I found in her arms.

CHAPTER 12

THEODORA

Two days later, I sat at the kitchen table, poring over bids for roofing the barn. I sighed with frustration as I knew I should logically choose the cheapest option, but I wasn't sure if the cheapest contractor had the best reputation and if the work would be done to last for years. I didn't want to pay a small fortune and then have to repeat the work in a short time. I smiled as Nolan entered the kitchen and pointed at the small mound of papers in front of me. "Care to help?"

I thought I saw a flicker of panic cross his face, but just as quickly he seemed curious.

"What are you working on?" he asked as he took a sip of coffee.

"I put the word out I'm looking to roof the barn, and I received bids. I don't know who to choose." I paused, waiting for him to join me at the table and to start looking through the papers. When he remained leaning against the counter, I forced a look of unconcern as I fought disappointment. "I shouldn't have bothered you."

"No, bother me," he said with a quick smile. "Tell me about them."

Sighing with frustration, I held up a few of the pieces of paper that held the bids. "It'd be much quicker if you just read them and told me what you think." I stared at him as he paled and set down his coffee cup. "Nolan?"

He stood, staring at the floor for a long moment before he whispered, "I can't."

I frowned. "If you don't want to, just tell me. You don't have to act like you're interested."

Flushing, his fingers tapped at his thigh in a nervous pattern. "I want to help you, Theo. I can't." He stared at me with bleak panic as he waved at the mound of papers in front of me. "I can't read."

A stunned silence enveloped the room as I sat with my hands resting on the small mountain of papers. "Why not?" I finally asked in a soft voice. "You went to school."

He let out a humorless chuckle. "I'm too much of an idiot. They passed me out of charity."

I rose and moved toward him, instinctively understanding he was trying to protect a deep wound. I'd done that enough times to understand the tactic. "You are not an idiot. You run a ranch. A very profitable ranch." I shook my head in confusion. "How?"

"Alessia," he whispered. "And Caleb. And before him his dad. They work on the contracts and ensure there's nothing hidden in them that I shouldn't sign. Alessia does all the paperwork. She quit school after Mama died and I began to run the ranch. I've never had to face doing this alone."

"That's why her desk looked like a tornado had struck," I whispered. "Why you listen to audiobooks. Why you signed the marriage contract without reading it." At the resigned look in his eyes, I murmured, "Why there was no birthday card."

"I can sign my name, but I can't write a flowery message. Nothing that could express how I feel." His hand gripped the back of his neck as he flushed with agitation. "Hell, I wouldn't even know if what I bought you would offend or please you. I look at words and the letters become all jumbled. All I get is a headache."

"Why?"

I shrugged. "I've heard the word dyslexia tossed around, so maybe that's it or part of the reason. I don't know. My dad, Jameson, refused any extra testing or help for me. Said I was making it all up and trying to get attention I didn't deserve. Mama tried, but nothing ever made sense in my head. So I got further and further behind. And then I figured out ways to game the system or took classes from teachers who pitied me and who'd pass me so I could be with my friends."

I paled as I stared at him, finally comprehending the full depth of what he said. "You truly didn't know about the contract for the water rights?" At the shake of his head, I whispered, "What happened?"

"I don't know. Alessia doesn't either. She'd just returned to the ranch. It was the last contract my dad did before I took over the ranch, and I never should have signed it. According to Alessia, it wasn't the one that Caleb's dad drew up. We were never to pay so little for your water or banish you." I swallowed. "My father must have tricked me. Tricked all of us." I sighed. "He used to try to do that when I was younger. Now, he's never allowed near the office so he can't attempt anything devious. There's little he won't try to get the ranch from me."

I pressed against his chest, ignoring the fact he didn't hold me tight. Instead, I held on even tighter to him, breathing in his scent and feeling the steady beat of his heart. "His inability to see what an amazing person you are is his shortcoming. Not yours. He should have loved you, no matter what." I kissed the underside of his jaw, scraping my lips against his stubble, my fingers now meandering up his body to cling to his strong shoulders. "It's his lack. Never yours, my love."

I gasped as his arms banded around me, squeezing all the air from me.

"Why don't you think less of me?" he asked, his forehead pressed to mine and his blue eyes bright with unspoken fears. "I think less of me."

"No," I whispered. "You won't make me." My fingers traced over his cheek, and I nipped at his jaw.

"Is it passion?" His hands pressed down my body until they cupped my ass and hauled me even closer to him. "Is that all you want?"

I wriggled and pushed at him until there was a little space between us, although we still stood close enough that we shared the same air. "No!" I frowned as I looked at him, my heart cracking as he attempted to cling to every defense that had protected him for years. "Don't do this, Nolan." I cupped his cheeks and swayed forward and back, desiring every moment of physical contact with him, but also knowing now was not the time to get lost in mindless passion.

"You wanted your ranch. You have it," he said.

"And you wanted my water," I whispered in a soft voice. "Haven't things changed in the past few months? In the past few days?" I shivered, as I'd never considered myself all that brave. However, I knew I never wanted my husband to fill his mind with lies.

Marshaling all my courage, I took a deep breath and stared deeply into his guarded gaze. "I never thought I'd meet a man like you." I pressed my fingers to his lips to prevent him from making a disparaging remark and shook my head. "Kind, generous, funny." I nodded when he stared at me in disbelief. "You're dedicated to your ranch and your family, and I never thought to be fortunate enough to have your loyalty extend to me."

"It does," he whispered, kissing my fingers. "It always will."

My eyes filled and I smiled at him. "How can you not see how remarkable that is to me? When I look at you, I see a man living the life he was meant to. A life he loves." My eyes shone as I fought tears. "I love you so much and I'm so proud of you."

I shook my head when I knew he wanted to speak. "Your dad is a mean man and nothing like you. I'm only sorry you had to suffer all those years listening to his lies. For they were lies, my love. Lies."

He stared at me in stunned disbelief. "How can you say you love me?"

"I say it because it's true, my darling." When he remained silent, I smiled at him, unable to stop running my hands over his shoulders, chest, and back. "I was visited a few nights ago for girls' night. They drink an astounding amount of wine." I shared a smile with him. "And friendship and good food and gossip." I felt him tense and wrapped my arms around him. "Quinn and Tara spoke of their Uncle Jameson and what a mean man he is. Was."

He nodded, his expression shattered. "He is mean. Especially to me."

Cupping his face, I stared deeply into his gaze, waiting for him to say more. When he was silent, I didn't press for him to tell me more than he was ready to. I didn't need my suspicions confirmed. "Then he's a fool for not rejoicing in you." I kissed him, breaking the kiss when he failed to respond. Instead, I rested my head on his chest, refusing to let him go.

He let out a stuttering breath. "I can't read," he said in a broken voice. "I was too stupid to learn. You deserve a better man. A whole man."

I held him tight. "No! Never stupid. Never stupid." I held him so tight I wondered how he could breathe. "Your father should have done everything he could to ensure you received the help you needed to thrive. Due to his pride and his insecurity, he denied you what you needed. That is his crime as a parent. His failing as a man. Never yours, my love."

I paused, hoping he'd say or do something. Instead, a thick silence settled over us. I whispered, "There is no better man for me than you."

I gasped again as he yanked me tight, holding me in his arms as he shuddered. "You're not alone now, Nolan."

~

NOLAN

I clung to Theo, needing her more than I'd ever needed anything or anyone in my life. "I need you, Theodora," I whispered, feeling her shiver at my words and the way I said her name. My lips nipped and kissed up her neck to her jaw before marauding over her cheek to her lips. Delving inside, my tongue swept over hers, and I angled my head to kiss her deeper.

My hands dropped, yanking on her flannel shirt, unheeding when I ripped the buttons off and sent them pinging across the floor. Her tiny gasps and shivers only made my blood boil hotter. I had to have her. I needed her panting and moaning and writhing for me. *Me.* The man who should never have been good enough for her. The man she said she loved.

My heart stuttered at the thought as I broke the kiss, biting her lower lip gently as my hands freed her breasts. Dipping down, I picked her up, setting her on the counter, pressing into the vee her legs made. With a groan, I thrust against her, gently nibbling at her neck before lowering my mouth to her breasts.

"Nolan!" she cried, her head falling back and bumping into a cabinet as she arched into me while I nipped and sucked at one nipple. I loved her breasts. I had since the first moment I'd seen them, and I moved from one to the next and back again, enjoying her whimpers and attempts to get even closer to me.

With a delighted chuckle, I ripped off my shirt, pushed my jeans and underwear to my knees, and pulled her jeans and panties off, uncaring that they dangled off one foot. All that mattered was that she was bared to me.

"God, you're beautiful," I whispered as I ran my hands down her breasts, belly, and to her pussy. I found her clit, rubbing over it softly and then with a little more pressure.

"Nolan! Please, oh God," Theo cried as she wriggled and arched and pressed so hard into my hand she nearly fell off the counter.

Chuckling, I picked her up, moaning when she wrapped her legs around my waist, her wet center all too close to my dick.

"On the floor. On the floor. Oh my god, I need you," Theo panted over and over. "Please, Nolan. No playing, just love me now."

"Oh, I'll love you now," I whispered as I settled her onto the floor and eased down between her legs as I kissed the inside of one thigh and then the other. "I'll love you tomorrow," I murmured as I gave a teasing lick to her nub. "I'll love you forever," I breathed as I got to work, focusing when she rocked her hips. I grunted with delight when she latched onto my hair, tugging as she writhed in an attempt to chase her pleasure. When I filled her with a finger and then another, she screamed my name and quaked as I felt her body ripple and clasp.

God, how I adored her. How I wanted her. As I kissed her once more, reverently, I knew it was more than a mindless fuck I wanted. I wanted to love her and cherish her. She knew my darkest truth and hadn't shunned me.

I stared up at her, watching her breasts heave as she tried to catch her breath, flushed and satisfied with her messy hair and witch's eyes captivating me, and I knew I was a lucky bastard. "I need you," I whispered, groaning with appreciation and delight as she opened her arms and tilted her hips to welcome me in.

"Heaven," I gasped as I pressed inside. "You always feel like heaven." I moaned as she wrapped around me, her arms clinging to my shoulders and her legs wrapped around my waist, her softness and wetness welcoming me. I grunted as she gripped me tight, and she met every one of my deep thrusts with a pant of eagerness. My Theo didn't shy away from passion; she met it headlong and with absolute abandon.

Her eyes held me captive, seducing me as much as the hot confines of her body, the promise within beckoning to me. With a gasp, she arched her head back, her mouth open, as her nails dug into my back and her heels into my ass as she screamed her pleasure, rippling around me.

There was nothing better in this world than watching and feeling my wife find her pleasure. "Theo!" I bellowed, quivering and quaking as I fell forward into her arms, letting myself go and losing myself to her.

When I finally roused myself, I moved to heave off her with a muttered apology.

"No, stay," she whispered. "I love the feel of you."

Pressing up on my arms, I took my weight off of her and gazed down at her, unable to feel anything but an overwhelming joy and a rekindling of passion to realize we were still joined. "Theodora," I whispered. "How I love you."

Her eyes filled, and she nodded and ran a hand through my hair. "You don't have to say it just because I did."

I frowned, pressing my hips forward and causing her breath to catch. Leaning in, I kissed her lips, brushing my nose over her face as I breathed in her fragrance. "I know," I whispered, backing away enough to see her face.

Confusion, doubt, and then relief flitted across her face as she looked deeply into my eyes. "You know?"

I nodded, unable to hide my enchanted smile. "I know. I won't ever lie to you, Theodora. I promise. Not even a lie of omission." I nodded as she acknowledged what I'd failed to tell her until tonight. Waiting, I gazed deeply into her eyes. I could spend a lifetime staring into them.

With a hint of awe in her voice, she whispered, "If you said it, you mean it." I nodded, brushing a thumb over her cheek. "You love me?" A tear leaked out, and I stroked it away. "Me?"

Brushing my nose over hers, I whispered, "Of course I do. You're loyal, generous, and kind. You accept and rejoice in what is. You see me," I paused as my throat thickened and I was momentarily unable to speak. I cleared my throat, but my voice remained raspy. "You see *me*, and find the good, not the failings. You inspire me every day, Theodora."

She stared at me for what felt like forever, the doubt replaced by an unfettered joy. Taking a shaky breath, she whispered, "Will you ever tell me why you say my name the way you do?"

I ducked my head. "Ah, another thing I have to admit to you." I flushed. "You'll think I'm even stranger than I am."

"Trust me," she murmured, sighing with pleasure as I rolled so she lay sprawled on my chest. Although the kitchen floor wasn't the most comfortable place for a romantic interlude, any place with Theo in my arms was paradise to me.

I rested for a few moments with one of my arms tucked up under my head, the other playing with her hair as I felt her fingers tracing over my chest, as light as butterfly wings. These quiet moments with her were precious. "Thank you," I whispered. I met her questioning look and smiled. "For these moments when words aren't needed."

She smiled, a mischievous womanly smile, and I sighed with pleasure. My woman was happy and all was right in the world.

"Theodora," I murmured, her name rolling off my tongue. "I know I don't say your name right."

Theo kissed my chest and whispered, "It feels like it's the way it should always have been spoken."

"My mama was Italian. I learned a little from her, although

that irritated my father. He thought we were in Montana and what use would we have for Italian here?"

"Have you ever wanted to travel there?"

"Yes," I breathed. "But I know I never will." I peered down at her. "I adore you."

She smiled and flushed, arching up to kiss me. "I adore you too."

"No, that's what I'm saying when I say your name the way I do. I adore you." When she gaped at me in stunned silence, I flushed. "At first, it was a sort of joke, but I soon realized I spoke the truth. I've adored you for a long time."

"It's why my name sounds so different," she breathed.

I nodded. "It's *ti adoro*, not *ti adora*, so it's always a little different. And your nickname, Theo." I flushed. "I call you *Teo*."

"Why is that embarrassing?"

"Well, it's a man's name, but it means divine gift. I've always thought it appropriate for you." I smiled as she snuggled against me.

"I love it, although when we travel to Italy, you'll have to call me something other than Teo."

"Don't worry, bella." I kissed her shoulder. "No one would ever mistake you for a man."

She giggled and squealed as I tickled her sides right by her breasts. I wrapped my arms around her, holding her close. I sighed with pleasure as she kissed my neck and snuggled closer to me. "Do you mind moving to our bed? This floor isn't as comfortable as I thought it would be."

She giggled, kissing me before pushing away from me. "Let's go to bed, Nolan."

After we stood, I wrapped my arms around her, my hands roving over her silky skin. "How was I ever lucky enough to find you?"

"I don't know." She pressed against my chest. "Ti adoro, Nolan. Ti adoro."

My heart stuttered at her attempt to use Italian. I knew she accepted me as I was, not as she wished I were, and I'd never felt more at peace. Wrapping my arms around her, I said a silent prayer of thanksgiving Theo's cousins pushed her to stand beside me that evening. They'd given me the greatest gift.

∼

"Will you help me?" I asked Theo as she entered the kitchen a few mornings later. I handed her a cup of coffee with three sugars and cream, just how she loved to drink it. Tilting my head down, I sighed with pleasure as I kissed her softly. "Morning, bella."

She mumbled a greeting as she pressed herself against me, careful not to tip her full mug of hot coffee over my back. "Morning, my love," she murmured as she kissed my chest. "I missed you in bed."

Groaning, I set her coffee aside before cupping her face and giving her the good morning kiss I'd yearned to. My mouth angled over hers, but with softness and reverence. The all-consuming hunger was held at bay for the moment. "I always miss you."

She flushed with delight and pressed against me. "What does bella mean?"

"Beautiful." Running my hands through the mass of her hair, I grinned at her. "You've always been beautiful to me, *Teo*, even when you thought you were overshadowed by your cousins."

"Incorrigible," she mumbled as she pressed harder against me, her arms wrapping around me with all their might. "I... thank you." She peered up at me and saw my confused expression. Reaching up, she ran a finger over the wrinkle in my brow, the delight in her alluring eyes making my breath catch. "I've always felt beautiful with you."

"Good." My breath ratcheted out of me and I closed my eyes.

"God, all I want to do is take you back to bed, but I do need your help."

She smiled—her siren's call smile—and backed away, lifting her coffee mug to her lips. Momentarily mesmerized by watching her, I had to tear my gaze away from her for a moment to gather my scattered thoughts. "Alessia said there were some irregularities in the books." I motioned to the computer on the desk. "She uses some fancy program on the computer."

My breath caught as she appeared captivated by what I asked. "You want me to help with your ranch?" She nearly bounced with joy at the thought. "I'd begun to fear I'd never use the degree I earned at Western." She shrugged as I stared at her, stupefied. "The one thing I know my dad insisted on in his will was that I had to go to college."

"How can you bear to be with me?" I asked, flushing as I thought of all she'd learned and all I couldn't offer her. I closed my eyes as I willed myself to be different, better, smarter than I was. I knew it was futile and I'd only give myself a migraine. But, God, how I wished I could be something more.

Stiffening, I felt her hands cup my face, her fingers tracing through the beard I'd yet to shave off. I shivered as her lips fluttered over my jaw. "I love you," she said in a low, fervent voice. "You, Nolan, as you are. Not as you wish you were."

Her voice faded away and my eyes opened, against my will, as I yearned to believe that I'd not been a fool to love her. To trust in her. To have faith that fate could be kind this time. "I have demons," I rasped. "This isn't easy for me."

She smiled, kissing my cheek. "I know. Someday, you'll see yourself as I see you. And you'll understand why I love you as much as I do."

Mesmerized by the sincerity in her eyes, I gave a tiny jerk of my head. "Just as you'll see yourself as I see you." I smiled, half self-deprecating, half-teasing. "We'll be so self-aware of how amazing we are that everyone around us will be sick of us."

She giggled, wrapping her arms around me. "Trust in us. Trust in this, please, Nolan."

I shuddered, holding her tight. She was my lifeline and I would never let her go. "I promise." Burying my face in her hair, I whispered, "Will you put that fancy university degree to use and see if you can figure out what's going on at my ranch?"

She backed away, her gaze filled with concern. "Is someone stealing money from you?"

Shaking my head, I flushed. "No, the opposite. There's too much there. It's as though we've been overpaid for a few years. It makes no sense."

She looked to the computer and then to me. "Alessia doesn't mind me helping?"

I chuckled. "She said it would be a relief. Working on the books is her least favorite activity on the ranch. She'd rather be riding out with the men or working with our horses." My eyes closed for a moment as she kissed me softly before spinning to open the laptop.

"This isn't safe, you know," she said, holding up a sticky note that had been placed on the keyboard.

"Alessia wanted you to have the password. She'll change it again when you're done." I nodded. "Precautions to prevent my father, Jameson, from meddling." I watched as she focused on the information in front of her, fascinated with her ability to tune out everything occurring around her. I left her to work, moving to the great room to build a fire and listen to an audiobook as I waited to hear what she would discover.

~

THEODORA

I pored over the accounts, puzzling at the inconsistencies. Alessia was correct. Somehow the ranch had more money in its bank account than it should. I noted eight equal disbursements each quarter, remembering that Nolan had seven siblings. It seemed that even though his siblings, except for Alessia, didn't live on the ranch, that he still supported them. The ranch must belong to all of them.

After nearly four hours, I sighed and stretched, groaning. The quiet murmur of an audiobook played in the living area, and I moved toward it. When I found Nolan stretched out on the sofa, I sighed with pleasure. "Mind if I join you?"

He shook his head and raised a hand up to me to invite me down to join him, switching the audiobook off with a remote. "Of course not." When I had settled against him, he wrapped an arm around my waist and murmured with contentment.

We lay like that for at least half an hour. "I can't make heads or tails of what I'm finding." His arm around my waist stiffened, and he buried his head in my hair.

"I feared that would be the case."

"Is there any chance one of your other siblings could be funneling money back into the ranch?"

He let out an unamused huff of air. "Why would they do that? They've enjoyed living off the ranch for too long to actually believe they have to work for any of it."

Running a hand over his arm, I was surprised by the bitterness in his tone as he spoke of his siblings. "Nolan, what aren't you telling me?"

He pulled me tighter against him. "Too much. I'll explain it all soon. I promise."

"I trust you," I whispered and felt him relax incrementally behind me. When he remained quiet, I asked in a soft voice, "What will you do now?"

The fire crackled and popped and threw heat and light into

the room. "I'll speak with Caleb. He has a lot of friends from law school. I'll see if he can figure this out."

Rolling over, I faced him. "Whatever you find, tell me. Please." When he nodded, I rested against him, determined that no one would steal this joy I had just found.

CHAPTER 13

THEODORA

I ran errands in town, thankful Nolan continued to leave a ranch truck for me to use. Although I relished my time on the ranch, I liked knowing I had the freedom to travel into town when I needed to. I wanted to shop for groceries and check out the price of lumber. I wouldn't do anything without speaking with Nolan, but I wanted to try to start pricing how much repairs would cost.

As I walked along the sidewalk in Burnside Creek near the town square, my spirit felt light, and I was eager to finish in town so I could return to the ranch. Every day, it was the home I'd always remembered. Sharing it with Nolan was the greatest gift, and I woke most days marveling at my good fortune.

As I looked around downtown, it appeared the townsfolk were eager for the end of winter and the arrival of the warmer weather too. A few business owners had put out hardy potted plants, although there was still the threat of frost. On this sunny late April day, the café and coffee shop had set up tables outside to entice more customers, and almost everyone was smiling and in a cheery mood as they walked along the main street of down-town. I tilted my head up to the sun, relishing the feel of the gentle rays on my skin. After the long, cold winter, I'd forgotten the simple joy of being warmed by the sun again.

"You should take care that you don't burn, Theodora."

I jerked at the sound of my uncle's voice. Opening my eyes, I faced him. He looked as he always had, although he seemed a bit more somber as he stared at me. "Uncle."

"You look surprisingly well for a woman who's betrayed her family and the memory of one she claimed to love."

Flushing, I glared at him. "I've betrayed no one." I glanced around, thankful we were on a quiet block near the park and no townsfolk lingered who would listen in on our conversation. "Why can't you admit what you've done?"

He smirked at me. "All I did, Theo darling, was care for my brother's ungrateful brat for ten years. Perhaps your cousins weren't as friendly as you would have liked." He shrugged, indif-ferent to their abuse of me over the years I had spent in his house. Now that I'd married a man he considered an enemy, the friendly, innocent façade of a doting uncle had fallen away. Was I truly seeing him for the first time? "But you had a home. You had food and clothes and support."

"You were my family. You should have cared for me. You shouldn't have robbed me blind!"

"Robbed you?" He shook his head. "My only sin was to take very little interest in that account. It's not my fault you've allowed it to be frittered away."

"Frittered away?" I took a step closer to him. "Do you have any idea what you're saying? I didn't have access to the accounts until I married or turned twenty-four a few months ago. Where did the money go before I inherited?"

"I'd ask your lawyer." My uncle's cheek ticked as he clenched his jaw tightly, and he was flushed red with anger. "He knows much more than he's ever told you."

Shaking my head, I took a step away. "No. I will not doubt Caleb. Or my husband. They've been honest and treated me well."

He roared as he lunged toward me, gripping my arm and standing over me as I cowered at the sight of his rage. "I treated you well. I refused to send you into the foster system. Your loyalty should have been to me! How dare you believe them over me?"

A tear trickled down my cheek, and I shook my head. "You lost it, day by day, every time you ignored your daughters' mistreatment of me. You lost it every time you acted like a brainless fool, too naïve to know what was occurring in your own home. You lost it when you didn't tell the police about the missing money." I swallowed and firmed my shoulders. "You never really loved or wanted me, did you?"

He sniffed as he backed away, running a hand over his fine suit, the illusion of the composed businessman in place again. "You're right. Why would I want the daughter of a woman who ran off with a trucker to whore her way through the nation? Why would I want the burden of raising you? I'm only thankful you're someone else's burden now." He strolled away as though he'd just exchanged pleasantries with a close acquaintance, leaving me quaking and stunned by all he'd admitted.

~

NOLAN

That evening, I returned home to find Theo outside wandering in a field near a paddock. After I shut off my truck, I sat for a few minutes, joy filling me as I watched her stroll through the waist-high green grass as sparrows and swallows swooped overhead, their delighted chirps a counterpoint to the meadowlark's sweet song.

Tonight, Theo wore jeans, a faded light blue T-shirt, and an old flannel two sizes too big for her as her hands skimmed the top of the grass. She'd taken no notice of my arrival and now stood with her head thrown back and face tilted up to the sun, soaking in the day's last rays. "*Teo,*" I breathed, overcome with love for her as I watched her. How was a woman so fine my wife?

I hopped out of my truck and approached her, frowning when I saw her stiffen at my approach. "Bella," I murmured, running a hand down her back as I kissed her forehead. "Do you want time alone?"

"No." Spinning, she threw herself into my arms, and I caught her with a grunt as she knocked the air out of me.

I frowned at her urgency but held on tight. "Everything's fine, bella. You're safe."

She shivered at my words, clasping onto me. "I miss you when you're away."

God, when she said things like that, I felt like my heart would explode. "You do?" I backed away, my hands playing with the hair loosened at her brow. "I thought it was just me acting like a lunatic." I jumped when she tapped me on my belly.

"I never said I was a lunatic," she teased, chuckling. Her bewitching eyes now shone with humor rather than the desperation I'd sensed when I approached her. "Although I am mad about you." Twining her arms around my neck, she stood on her toes and kissed me.

Groaning, I opened for her, my tongue dueling with hers. "I promised you'd be willing to cavort with me in a field." I fell to my knees, and she followed, our presence hidden by the waist-high grass. "Love me, Teo." I tugged at her shirt, pausing when she cried out. "Teo?" That hadn't been a cry of passion. How had I hurt her?

"It's nothing." She kissed my chest as she shimmied out of her shirt.

"No." I cupped her face, stilling her frenetic movements before I rested my forehead against hers. "Damn, you know how much I want you. I want you every moment of every day. But not if I hurt you. I'm so sorry I hurt you, my Teo."

She covered my mouth and stared at me, her eyes shining with tears. "*You* didn't, Nolan. My uncle did." Sighing, she lowered her flannel from her right forearm, and I saw fingerprints.

"The hell he did this to you!" I traced over her bruised skin gently as I stared at her with fire in my gaze. "Bella?"

She nodded, tears cascading down her gorgeous cheeks. "He never wanted me." Her words emerged as stammers as she cried over her tears. "He said I should be happy I didn't end up in foster care."

"Oh, my darling." I hauled her onto my lap and rocked her side to side as though she were a little girl. Resting my head on top of hers, I felt like there was no other place I wanted to be on this April night. Alone with Theo in our pasture was pure heaven, although I'd prefer it if she wasn't crying.

"He said my mother left with a trucker and was a prostitute," she whispered against my throat.

"Shh, bella, it doesn't matter what he said. It's probably a lie. And if it isn't, I don't care." I kissed her head. "He should know better than to upset you by bringing up the past like this." Easing away so I could look into her gaze, I rubbed the backs of my fingers against her silky cheeks. "I'll kick his ass if you'd like."

She giggled and kissed my chest. "Not needed."

"You already kicked it?"

When she giggled even more, I smiled and kissed her head.

"No. I'm realizing that being in your arms is all I need. You're my family, Nolan."

My grip on her tightened as I buried my face into her hair. Fuck, she knew how to unman me. For so long, I thought I was unworthy of having a family. Unworthy of love. Unworthy of being happy. Now with her, I knew I'd have what had always eluded me. "And you're mine."

The passion of a few moments ago had faded, and I twisted us so we rested on the ground together. Rubbing a finger over her cheek, I watched her as she now lay on my chest, her head propped up as she gifted me with an adoring smile. She turned her face into my touch as I caressed her skin with my fingertips. "Your family is mine too."

"God help you," I muttered. When I shifted, she clung to me and refused to allow me to rise.

"You've avoided telling me much about them. About your childhood. Will you tell me now?"

As I stared into her green eyes, I knew it was time for her to know more about me. She knew my most shameful secrets and hadn't turned away from me. She deserved to know everything about me. "My mother was Italian. Maria Evelina, although everyone always called her Evelina. She came here to learn English and fell in love with Montana and with a man and stayed. She never returned home to Rome."

"Rome," she breathed against my chest. "How romantic it must be there."

"I want to go there some day with you, bella."

"Do you still have family there?" She leaned back, her eyes filled with hopeful curiosity.

"My grandparents are there. And more aunts and uncles and cousins than I'd know what to do with."

She sighed, resting against me again as her fingers played over me. "That sounds heavenly. A big Italian family eager to smother you in love." My grip tightened on her as she sighed wistfully. "I'd love to meet them."

"Someday, *tesoro*." I kissed her head as I dreamed of our future spinning out together. "Someday."

~

A week later, I walked into Caleb's office, smiling impersonally at the secretary. All Montanans by the age of five had perfected the impersonal smile that acknowledged the presence of another but discouraged any real conversation. When she nodded and continued with her work, I let out a sigh of relief that I wouldn't be expected to make small talk with her today. I wanted to see what was bothering my cousin and get home to my wife. I hoped the honeymoon stage would last until we were in our nineties.

"Cay," I said as I entered his office, shutting the door behind me. I frowned as he looked like hell. His hair stood on end, his tie was at an angle, and it looked as though he'd been in the same suit for days. I froze at the rage I saw in his gaze. "Cay?"

"Sit," he barked. He raised a hand, swiping it over his face before settling back in his chair and crossing a leg over one knee. Lifting his coffee cup, he scowled into it upon realizing it was empty. "I've looked through the things you sent me. What Theo thought was interesting and what confounded Alessia."

He paused, his face reddening and jaw ticking.

"Caleb, it can't be that bad." My whispered protest sounded weak to my own ears.

"Oh, it's worse than you can imagine. I won't show you the reports," he waved at his computer, "but I'll explain it all to you." He sighed, and the fight seemed to leave him with it. Now, he looked dejected and sad. "You have a traitor living in your home."

"Not Theodora," I protested.

"No," Caleb snapped in exasperation. "*Your* home. Your father's home." He pointed to his computer again. "I asked one of my buddies from law school who specializes in white-collar crime to see if he could help." Rubbing at his head, he raised his brow. "Said it was the easiest job he'd looked into in years. Didn't do a good enough job of covering their tracks."

"Who? What are you saying?" I asked.

"Someone in your home has been stealing from Theo and then padding your books. Although all that's been stolen from Theo hasn't shown up in your bank account, so there's another account somewhere. That's why the books make no sense."

"From my house?" I sputtered. "Not Alessia." I breathed her name like a prayer. I couldn't survive another betrayal from a family member.

"It's either her or your father. You always said your dad could only use the Internet for porn. Seems unlikely he'd be adept enough to pull this off." Caleb stared at me with sympathy mixed with pity.

"No!" I roared. "She wouldn't have done that. She likes Theo. She..." I rose, pacing the small office as my breath sawed in and out of me. I remembered her reaction when I married Theo. Her words. *"If we had a vendetta we would have ruined them."* I shook my head to dispel any doubt. "She's my right hand. I can't run the ranch without her."

"I know," he whispered. "But you have Theo now."

I stood with my back to Caleb, my shoulders shaking as I fought not to fall apart in sorrow or rage. Taking a deep breath, I rasped, "She has her own dreams. She shouldn't be forced to help me with mine." Another breath rattled in and out and then I cleared my throat. "How long until we know who it is?"

"If I were at your ranch, I'd be able to tell which computer it is." He stared at me. "But you'll have trouble figuring it out."

"Because I can't read," I said in a dull voice. Must I continue to suffer forever? "Come to dinner tonight. Alessia will enjoy seeing you and you can snoop around."

Caleb nodded. "I will." He rose and approached me. "Act normal, Nol, or this won't work, and we'll have lost our chance to know who's been stealing from your wife."

I stared at him from pain-dulled eyes. "Either way, it's a member of my family. We've been hurting her for years, and I didn't have the brains to know it." I spun on my heels, storming away before Caleb could say anything more.

I yanked my truck door open, climbing inside and sitting there for long minutes. I knew I needed to calm down before driving, or I'd get a ticket or get in an accident. The rage boiling through me wouldn't calm, and I didn't know how to ease it. Through it all, I saw Theo, brave and strong as she attempted to restart her life at her ranch. *Our ranch*, my mind stubbornly demanded.

Letting out a deep breath, I rested my head on the steering wheel for a moment as I envisioned her. I imagined all she would have had, had my father or sister not robbed her blind. She wouldn't have needed to marry me. She would have had so much more. Now, she was saddled with an idiot husband who didn't even have the sense to discover what his family was doing before now. Somehow, I had to find a way to make it all up to her. Or let her go if she no longer wanted me.

CHAPTER 14

THEODORA

I sat at the kitchen table, a space I was enjoying using as my desk, although I knew I needed to find another place soon to set up as my office. Today, I continued to dream about turning the ranch into a horse farm, but I knew I didn't have the funds for it yet. I refused to believe it would only ever remain a dream, though.

Sitting at the table, I glanced at the clock and smiled. Although an impractical desk, it allowed me to be in the kitchen so I could see Nolan the first moment he walked in the door. I flushed as I knew I was acting like a lovesick schoolgirl, but I decided that's how I should be during the first months of our marriage. If not now, when?

Smoothing my hands over my hair, I attempted to act nonchalant as I heard his truck pull up. Although I tried, I couldn't prevent my heart from racing with anticipation at seeing him again and from kissing him again. I never would have thought I'd find this much joy in our marriage. "Hello, darling," I said with a wide smile when he entered.

Although he attempted a smile, no happiness entered his gaze and he seemed somber. Rather than the passionate embrace I yearned for, he gave me a peck on my cheek and moved toward the rest of the house. "I need a shower," he called back at me.

When the bedroom door shut, I sat in shocked silence. "Alone," I muttered to myself. "He clearly wants to be alone."

Swallowing down my frustration and concern, I rose to check on supper. I had a stew in the slow cooker, and I hoped we would snuggle on the couch after we had dinner. Snuggle and make love. I sighed, realizing I was a hopeless fool for my husband. I was never happier than when we were together.

When he returned to the kitchen, scrubbed clean with damp hair I itched to run my hands through, I smiled. "Dinner will be ready soon." I fought disappointment when his attempt at a smile faded.

"Damn, I should have called you. I forgot." With a sigh, he tugged at his hair and then shrugged. "We're having dinner at my family's ranch. A bit of a family get-together."

"Tonight?" I asked. "Why didn't you warn me? I would have done something with my hair and...and..." I couldn't think of anything to add after the *and*, but I knew there was more I should do to prepare for my first family dinner. Panic bubbled to the surface, and I didn't know how to push it back down.

"You look beautiful as you are now, bella," he whispered, his eyes glowing as he looked at me.

I flushed and smiled. "You're biased. I have to change." I squealed as he snagged an arm around my waist, tugging me back to him so he could nibble on my neck.

"Hell yes, I'm biased." He worked his way down to the juncture of my neck and shoulder. "You're gorgeous and brilliant and mine. Why shouldn't I be proud the whole world knows it?"

Suddenly breathless, I stared at him in wonder. Kissing him

deeply, I pressed against him, desperate for more. For his hands to caress me all over.

With a reluctant sounding groan, he broke the kiss. "Theo, you know I always want you. But not now." He mumbled more, but what he said I couldn't understand, although it seemed to sadden him.

When he kissed my forehead, his lips lingering longer than usual, I felt a flare of panic in my belly. What was wrong with him tonight?

"Come, get ready for supper. Everyone will be there soon."

I smiled up at him in a flirtatious way, although I'd never mastered the art of being a siren. When I saw the appreciative gleam in his gaze, I knew I'd succeeded. "I won't be long."

My smile faltered as the whispered words I knew I wasn't supposed to have heard after he broke the kiss floated through my mind. I shivered as I feared he was trying to find a way to let me go.

"Not now. Not ever."

~

NOLAN

I hugged Alessia as we entered, thankful she had been eager for a family dinner. Although I had hated disappointing Theodora, as I knew she loved our quiet evenings at home for just the two of us, I knew we needed to act tonight. As I released my sister, I prayed I wouldn't discover her betrayal.

I nodded to Caleb as he entered, relieved to see he had dragged a few of his sisters along, making it seem much more like a true family dinner. Tara and Quinn squealed at the sight of Theo, pulling her into hugs and exclaiming how excited they were to see her again as they prattled on about girls' night and the next time they planned on getting together, this time at Quinn's house. I relaxed as I saw Theo's relieved smile at their friendliness. My father sat at the head of the table, distant and bitter as he glared at me and my wife, refusing to join the conversation.

Thankfully, Quinn was a fantastic storyteller and loved to tease her brother. She had us in stitches by the time Alessia pulled out the pot roast. Caleb rose, ostensibly annoyed by his sister's antics, but I suspected he had another purpose.

I forced myself to remain calm and relaxed as I played with strands of Theo's hair. Thankfully, I didn't have to feign my enjoyment in watching her interact with Tara, Quinn, and Alessia. Her face glowed with excitement and mischief as she leaned forward to hear everything Quinn or Tara said, her eyes lighting with joy as she laughed. I could happily spend days staring at her when she was like this.

After Alessia had ensured everyone had been served, and Caleb had returned appearing satisfied, I relaxed. Before tonight, the computer had never been hidden, and I hoped Caleb's calm expression meant he had found it.

I joined the conversation just as Quinn was about to launch into another embarrassing tale about Caleb and me. "You tell stories so we never reveal what a hellion you were," I teased, laughing when she flushed.

"What was she like?" Theo asked.

"No, Nolan!" Quinn shook her head as her eyes gleamed with humor. "That's not fair!"

"Oh, so it's fair you spend an hour telling Theo all our misadventures," Caleb said as he grunted while pulling a wine cork free, "but we can't do the same to you?"

"Why shouldn't I mention the time you tricked us into believing poison oak was aloe?"

"You did that?" Theo breathed with horrified delight as Quinn glared daggers at us.

"I was eight. I didn't know better." Quinn sat with her arms over her chest, her face flushed and eyes sparkling with mischief although she attempted to act irate.

I burst out laughing. "Or the time you didn't cinch your saddle right and ended up in the pig muck?"

Tara spoke up, although there wasn't much humor in her voice. "Or the time you wanted to be just like us and insisted on riding the rope swing over the pond?"

Caleb shivered. "That wasn't funny. You couldn't swim well yet and you let go. You weren't supposed to let go."

Quinn shrugged. "I lived."

I sobered. "Yeah, because we all jumped in and saved you." My hand had clamped down on Theo's thigh at the memory. "Scared ten years off my life."

"You always were a pansy," my father sneered as he finally joined the conversation.

I flinched at his words but shook my head. "No, I've cared. There's a difference." I heard the collective gasp from my family as I'd never spoken to my father in such a manner in front of them before. I'd been deferential and respectful. As I stared at him, a deep certainty filled my soul, and I knew he was the one who'd robbed Theo blind.

"You don't know the meaning of the word," he hissed.

Caleb cleared his throat and shook his head at me. "Well, on that note, we'll head out." He rose, leaving to grab his briefcase and their jackets. They left through the informal kitchen door, with him whispering he'd be in touch tomorrow or the next day.

Soon, I was bustling Theo out the door and into my truck, absently listening to her chatter away about the stories Quinn told. I hated that I was going to ruin her lighthearted mood, but I couldn't conceal this from her. She had a right to know.

When we sat on the couch and I didn't scoop her into my arms, she stared at me warily. I hated the uncertainty in her expression. The look of a lost little girl. I wished I never had to cause her a moment's worth of doubt or pain.

"There was a reason for tonight's dinner." I met her gaze, swallowing as I saw her marshal her courage. "Caleb had to come to the house."

"It wasn't to welcome me to the family?" she whispered, unable to hide the hurt from her voice. At my quick shake of my head, she leaned into the cushions, tugging a throw pillow to her chest. "What aren't you telling me, Nolan?"

Although I could easily reach out and caress her foot, I had never felt like there was such a great chasm between us before. Swallowing, I spoke in a low voice as I clasped my hands on my thighs. I promised myself I would not touch her, even though staring at her as she attempted to control her emotions nearly killed me. All I wanted to do was yank her into my arms and reassure her that everything would be all right. Reassure myself that we would be fine.

"Caleb took the information you found and gave it to a friend of his from that fancy law school he attended. He specializes in white-collar crime." I cleared my throat and then rose, pacing in front of the large picture window. I needed some activity and also to have more space between us. "He told me today of his suspicions, although I had trouble believing him."

"What?"

I regarded her with unutterable sorrow. "A member of my family's been stealing from you. Some of that money has been filtered into the ranch account. *My* ranch account. Some of it's in another account somewhere. I don't know where all of it went." I froze, clenching my hands into fists as she burst off the couch, her cheeks flushed and eyes wild.

"Who?" Her breath caught in agitated gasps. "Alessia? Your father? A hand?" When I shook my head, she hit me on my shoulder. "Who?" she screamed.

"I don't know. Not yet. Caleb copied the laptop tonight

when he disappeared for a while. He should know more soon." I cleared my throat as she collapsed to the floor.

"You had me blame my family. You had me believe they stole from me and never cared for me. I've shunned them and belittled them." A keening wail emerged. "They were all I had left! I have no one now!"

"Theo," I murmured as I fell to my knees. I swallowed a sob as she curled over herself, refusing to seek comfort from me. When she shrank away from me when I ran a hand over her back, it was as though she'd stabbed me. "*Teo*," I pleaded.

Arching away, she toppled backward onto her butt, her feet digging into the floor as she put space between us. "Don't touch me!" Tears continued to run down her cheeks while her eyes were wild with grief and disillusionment. "Don't ever touch me again!"

I sat on my heels, panting and heartsore as I watched her push herself up with a moan before racing away from me. Flinching as the door to the bedroom slammed shut, I groaned and fell forward, rolling onto my back to stare at the ceiling. How had everything seemed so perfect this morning? How had I already lost her?

As I listened to her muted sobs, a resolute determination filled me. I might be separated from her for now, but I would not lose her forever. She was *mine*, dammit. Mine to cherish, honor, and love. There was nothing I wouldn't do to ensure she trusted me again. Loved me again.

With a sigh, I fought panic as I had no idea how to inspire such feelings in her again.

~

THEODORA

I woke the next morning curled on my side in my childhood bedroom. My eyes were puffy and felt as though they were swollen shut when I pried them open. Staring at my reflection in the mirror on my closet door, I wrapped a protective arm around my middle, irrationally wishing Nolan was holding me. Soothing me.

Instead, I was alone. Listening to the sounds of the house, I knew I was the only one in my home. There was no creak on the floor from his pacing. No audiobook playing on low. No scent of coffee wafting in the air, enticing me to leave my bed.

Against my will, tears started to leak out again. I thought I'd cried every tear I had in me last night, but I was being proved wrong again. It seemed Nolan would always prove me wrong.

Closing my eyes, all I saw was Nolan. Laughing at something I said, his eyes flashing with delight. Tugging me close, his gaze smoldering as I knew he was about to kiss me. Watching me with concern as I navigated his family.

I had thought I could count on him. Instead, I had been deluded and deceived. "Idiot," I whispered. "Naïve, trusting fool."

Thinking about my family, I shuddered with shame. I'd been so certain they had robbed me and stolen my dreams from me. My cousins had been cruel, and my uncle had allowed their cruelty through his benign neglect. Although I had every reason to despise him for how he had allowed me to be treated during the time I lived with him, he hadn't deserved my disdain the last time I'd seen him. *He* hadn't robbed me.

I shivered as I recalled his mean words to me and admitted I'd never been wanted by him, either. I felt so alone again, just like I had when I lost my dad.

Wrapping my arms more tightly around myself, I huddled under my blankets, wishing I never had to leave this bed. I wanted to hide forever.

CHAPTER 15

NOLAN

Life sucked. I'd been away from Theo for two days and it felt like two centuries. How the hell was I going to fucking survive the rest of my life? I groaned as I settled on the back steps of my family ranch house, staring out at the fields and hills in the distance as I took a long swig of a cold beer.

The evening was chilly, but I didn't care. It came nowhere near close to matching the glacial chunk that was my heart. I'd been a bastard to work with the past few days, and I knew it would only grow worse the longer the separation continued. Poor Alessia. She really might abandon me now.

Sighing, I lowered my head to rest onto my arms. I was waiting for Caleb, but he was backed up at work. I only hoped it wouldn't take him too long to do what I needed him to do.

When the back door opened, I fought an irrational hope that Theo had lost patience with me and was barging into my life and demanding I man up. Instead, as I looked over my shoulder, I saw my dad. Fuck. "What do you want?"

"Always charming. No wonder your wife wants nothing to do with you already."

I huffed out a breath and faced away from him, stiffening when his bootheels sounded on the wooden deck. When he leaned against one of the poles to the railing, I glared at him. "Go away. You're not wanted."

"No, Nolan, you have it ass end backward. You're not wanted. You never have been wanted." His dark brown eyes smoldered with resentment. "Since the day I learned you were to be, you haven't been wanted."

I rose and spun to face him. "Do you want to have this out now, old man?" I stepped forward, feeling my blood boil. "Do you?"

Jameson shook his head and snickered. "No. You aren't even worth fighting." He hooked his thumbs into his faded jeans pockets. "And that's what you find so hard to accept. You're not wanted, and no one considers you worth fighting for."

"That's a lie!"

"Is it?" he asked with a sneer. "Look at your siblings. Has one ever been concerned about you? They wouldn't care if you lived or died, except they'd miss the check you send them. And your wife sure as shit ain't fightin' for you. She's thinkin' good riddance. Finally has that huge place to herself." He shrugged. "Wouldn't be surprised if she divorces you and finds someone better."

"Bastard," I hissed.

He chuckled as he nodded. "Takes one to know one, boy." He strolled away, the slapping of the screen echoing around us.

I spun, hearing his words over and over again in my head even though I tried to ignore them. *Not wanted. Not worth fighting for.* Damn him for always knowing all of my most tender spots and jamming a hot fire poker into them.

I took another swig of my beer and wished everything were different and I was in Theo's arms once more.

~

THEODORA

Three days later, instead of me hiding forever, I realized it was Nolan who was hiding from me. He hadn't been home since the night of the dinner and the revelation that someone in his family was stealing from me. When I'd gone to his ranch, I'd watched him ride away at a gallop. So, I waited. I feared I'd wait in vain for him as he appeared to have no desire to return.

To pass the time, I'd started to price out what it would cost to restore the ranch to its former glory, although I was determined it be a horse ranch. I had no idea how much money I would eventually recover, but I hoped it was sufficient to put my most basic plans into motion. Perhaps over the next few years I'd be able to bring a few of my dreams to fruition.

I had spoken to Caleb a few times on the phone. He'd been friendly in the "I'm talking to a client" manner, but not as though he were speaking to a family member. I knew I failed in my attempt to appreciate how challenging it was for him. I should have known Nolan would always have his loyalty.

This evening, I was sitting at the kitchen table, determined to act like this was a normal evening and my husband would return home. My head jerked up from scratching at rudimentary plans when a truck door slammed. "Nolan," I breathed, rising to head to the front window to look down at who had arrived. My shoulders slumped with disappointment when I saw a truck other than my husband's from the ranch.

Spinning to face the kitchen door when it opened, I stared at Alessia, unable to smile at her.

"Theodora," she said in a soft voice. "I know I'm here uninvited, but I needed to speak with you." At my silent nod, she entered, following me into the living room.

"Where is he? Is he well?" I blurted out, unable to hide my anxiety about Nolan. "He's been avoiding me."

"He's at the ranch. It's like calving season. He sleeps in the office, and he's as surly as a bear." She grimaced. "It's worse than calving season."

A long silence stretched out between us as we stared at each other. She took a deep breath and then let it out. "I didn't know, Theo. I'm so sorry, but I didn't know."

"How could you not have?" I asked. "*You* can read." I flushed at my barb and closed my eyes in shame. "I didn't mean..."

Alessia looked at me, her eyes filled with sadness and disappointment. "Of course you did. You meant it. If he'd been able to read, you'd never have been in this predicament. If he'd been able to read, you'd never have felt compelled to marry him because you would have the money your father left you. If he'd been able to read, you'd never be stuck in this marriage. It's all his fault."

"No," I whispered. "It's your father's fault. Or a ranch hand's. Or yours." I swallowed, pushing down the tears and sobs that wanted to escape. "Whoever stole the money is to blame. Not Nolan."

Striding toward me, Alessia was like a warrior princess with her honey-gold hair flowing behind her and her eyes gleaming with determination. I stood stock-still, waiting for her attack. However, she stopped just short of me, her cheeks flushed and eyes flashing. "Do you mean that?" When I gaped at her, she demanded, "Do you promise you don't blame him?"

I gazed at her in wonder and nodded, a rush of air leaving me as I fell to my knees at the realization of what I knew to the depths of my marrow to be true. I shook my head dumbly as emotions overwhelmed me, and I was unable to speak. Staring up at her, a certainty filled me. Nolan would never hurt me. He'd done everything he could to protect me. To safeguard my legacy. He was the most honorable man I'd ever met, and I was so fortunate to call him my husband.

I looked at Alessia, trying to find the words, but dumbly shook my head again. She stared at me in concern, although I wondered if it was truly for me or for her brother.

After a long moment, Alessia sighed and stepped around me. She stood for a long moment, staring out the large picture window at the valley spread out below us. "This is the best land in the area. Better than ours," she whispered. "I can see why it was coveted." She sighed. "Listen to him when he comes in. Please." She spun on her heel and left me, aching and alone.

∿

NOLAN

I eased the door open, listening for her. I closed my eyes, hoping to hear some movement, some hint that she was inside waiting for me. I knew it had been cowardly to remain away. To drive off and leave her here without a means to escape. I hadn't wanted her to escape. For if she'd had a means to leave, I feared I'd never see her again.

No matter her ties to this land, I worried the betrayal had been too great, and that she'd decided she would have a better life somewhere else. Somewhere far away from her dullard of a husband.

Taking a deep breath, I slipped off my jacket and dropped my keys on the kitchen counter. Moving into the great room, I crouched in front of the fireplace, stoking the embers and adding a log.

"You've been gone a long time," she murmured from the couch.

At her voice, I jerked. "Theo." I gazed at her like I always imagined how Colter had felt upon discovering Yellowstone—

awed and terrified at the same time. How was this beautiful, brilliant woman my wife? Why would she want to continue to be my wife after the betrayal suffered at the hands of my family? "I'm sorry." She stared at me with an impassive expression, and panic filled me. Theo always smiled or glared or frowned. She was never like a frozen statue, cold and impersonal. Who was this woman? "Theo?"

"What have you learned?" She remained on the couch with a blanket covering her like a suit of impenetrable armor. I'd never felt so far away from her.

Sitting on the hearth with the fire warming my back, I stared at her. Unable to hide the bleak despair in my gaze, I shrugged. "My father stole the money. Caleb's working on all of the legal shit, but he'll soon be arrested. Some fancy talk about wire fraud, bank fraud, and other charges that will keep him in jail for the rest of his life."

"And the money?"

"Gone." I stared at her bleakly. "We think it's in an offshore account somewhere, but we haven't found it." I closed my eyes. "They haven't found it. I've been no use in any of this."

"Why do you say that?"

My eyes fluttered open at her gentle tone, a tone I thought I'd never hear again from her. Meeting her eyes, hope bloomed in my chest that I might have a second chance. That she might be generous and forgiving and truly love *me*. Truly want *me*. I swallowed, battling down the longing as I knew it too often only led to despair. "I can't read, Theo. I can't investigate." Her soft "no" was a dagger to my soul.

An uncomfortable silence ensued as the fire crackled behind me and she stared out the window. I studied her, as the light of the fire played over her features. The high cheekbones. The lustrous hair. The pert nose. How had I ever thought her a mouse?

"I have something for you," I said as I rose, moving to the

kitchen for the papers I'd left there. I returned, handing them to her before I faced the window and stared outside. Absently, I heard her flick on a lamp, and, after a moment, a startled gasp.

"No!" I heard the *thunk* of her feet and then her hands were on my shoulders, spinning me around. "No, Nolan, I won't let you do this." Tears poured down her cheeks, and the ice princess had dissolved into the passionate woman I had married. The woman I loved.

"I have to, Theo." My voice broke. "Don't you see, I have to." I closed my eyes as she cupped my cheeks and pressed herself along my length, the papers now scattered around us. Unable to stop myself, I wrapped my arms around her, groaning as I buried my face in her hair, breathing in the scent of peonies. The scent that always reminded me of my childhood, and a time when all was right in my world. A scent that now filled me with hope and longing. "God, I've missed you. Missed this. Us."

"Nolan, please, don't," she cried, soaking my shirt.

I held her as she sobbed, grateful for every moment I was gifted with her in my arms. When she calmed to stuttering breaths and hiccuped sobs, I eased her away, my fingers and thumbs tracing over her silky soft skin. "If I were another man, I would have known what was going on. I wouldn't have been too stupid to…"

"No," she said, her eyes fierce and protective. "I will never allow you to speak of yourself like that. Never." She shook her head and pressed more tightly against me. "You're brilliant and kind and loyal. It's not your fault your father has none of those qualities."

"Jameson's not my father." At my whispered confession, her eyes widened. "My father, Lorenzo, was killed when my mother was pregnant. He was out in the fields and was killed in an accident when Mama was four months' pregnant."

"Lorenzo?" Her bewitching eyes were wide with shock.

I nodded. "Lorenzo. He'd inherited the ranch from his

father, Lorenzo the elder. My grandfather had been in an Italian internment camp in Missoula during the War, and then he stayed. Bought land and started a ranch." He stared at me. "Mama and Lorenzo met and fell in love. She was never supposed to stay more than a year. She was never supposed to be a rancher's wife, but she was happy to give up Rome for Lorenzo."

"And then he died," Theo whispered. "Oh, how tragic." She stared at me with a furrowed brow. "Who's Jameson? Is he related to any of your siblings?"

I groaned as I paced away, gripping the back of my neck. "Jameson was Lorenzo's best friend." I paused. "Jameson was the foreman at the ranch."

Her eyes bulged. "When your father died, your mama married Jameson so she wouldn't have to raise you alone?" At my nod, she shook her head. "I still don't understand."

"None of us do, but she did." I gazed at her.

She frowned, deep in thought. "That's why Jameson hates you and dotes on Alessia. She was his first child with Evelina." She bit her lip and then spoke in a low voice. "That's why it's the LBarM, not the JBarM." She studied me. "That's why the ranch is yours, and not also your siblings'."

"See, you're the brilliant one—although it was my grandfather Lorenzo who founded the ranch with my grandma, Maple. She died when I was a baby." I ran a thumb over her cheek, my heart skipping a beat when she turned her face into my touch. "Jameson wanted my mother. Loved her to distraction, but she never loved him like that." I swallowed. "She was loyal and kind, but a part of her died with Lorenzo. I realized that when I saw pictures of her with my real father. She never looked at Jameson like that."

"And he resented her and you because of it." She stared at me, her eyes filled with compassion.

I sighed, my hands now cupping her face. "When Mama

died, Jameson lost any restraint in his bitterness and rage. It was then he realized the ranch, which he thought was his, was mine. My mama ensured the ranch, Lorenzo's ranch, was left to me." My eyes swam with tears. "Her son who couldn't read." I turned my face into her palm, taking comfort from her soft touch.

She smiled softly at me, her expression filled with tenderness. "She honored your father, and your legacy, by ensuring the ranch was yours."

"Yes. My father—Jameson—has been mad at the world ever since. He detests Caleb and Caleb's father for ever agreeing to write her a will that excluded him. He swore he would beggar us fighting it, but she had cunningly had him sign a prenuptial agreement, long before they were in fashion."

"You didn't know any of this."

I shook my head as I stared into her shocked gaze. "I swear I had no idea about his vendetta against you. I thought all of his hatred was focused on me. The only reason he didn't try to kill me to regain what he'd lost is because he knew I'd written a hasty will, leaving everything to my siblings. He knew he'd receive nothing." As I looked into her eyes, I saw no doubt. "How can you believe me?"

"I trust you." She stood on her toes and kissed me. "I trust in you. In us." She flushed, an embarrassed glint in her gaze. "One of your cousins hinted that you weren't Jameson's son at our girls' night in March. I didn't ask because I wanted you to tell me."

Swallowing, I let out a stuttering breath. "And?"

"I was so relieved to know you weren't related to him. I never want to see him again."

I nodded. "I'd bar him from the ranch tonight, but I can't act in a way that might cause him to flee. Caleb's orders."

She grimaced as she glanced down at the papers littering the floor around our feet. Placing her hands on her hips, she glowered at them and then at me. "I'll never agree to this." Pushing away from me, she picked them up and moved to the fire.

"*Teo*, no."

Ignoring me, she removed the protective covering in front of the fireplace that prevented sparks from flying out and stuffed in the pile of papers, watching with glee as they caught fire and burned brightly. When the papers were no more than ash, she spun to me, her hands on her shapely hips. "If you believe, for one minute, that you signing over your ranch to me before we divorced would make me happy, you're delusional!"

I stared at her, glowing with righteous fury, and my breath caught. I'd never seen anyone more beautiful in my life. "What are you saying?"

"I'm saying I married you for better or for worse. I refuse to divorce you. I refuse to steal your birthright. I refuse to allow you to ruin my happiness."

"*Teo*?"

"I love you, Nolan." She stood tall with her head back and eyes daring me to disagree with her. "I won't allow that man to destroy what we have." She shook her head in absolute defiance. "I won't."

"You'll fight for me. For us. You think I'm worth it."

Her beautiful witch's eyes filled, and she nodded. "I'll fight the devil himself for you. I've never met a more worthy man, and I love you so much."

With a groan, I rushed to her, yanking her into my arms. I squeezed her so tightly she squeaked because she couldn't breathe. "God, how I love you." I scattered kisses over her face as my shaking hands rose to rove over her head, tangling in her long hair. "How can you still believe in me?"

"How can I not?" She traced a finger over my lips, her nose rubbing against mine as she clung to my shoulders. "I know you, Nolan. You're good and honorable and everything I ever wanted."

I slammed my mouth down onto hers, wanting to devour her with my passion. My tongue dueled with hers, and I wanted to feast on her. To have this moment last forever. The anticipation of what was to come burned through me, and I was mad for her. Somehow, someway, I hadn't lost her.

Spinning her away from the fireplace, I urged her backward toward the sofa. My hands roved over her, stripping her of her button-down shirt, easing her bra off, and lightly stroking over her breasts. When she shivered, I broke the kiss, smiling as I nibbled down her neck. "Your skin is like silk." I worked on the button of her jeans, groaning with relief when I pushed them off and filled my hands with her bountiful flesh.

Backing away for a second, I jerked my shirt over my head, tossing it behind me. Groaning again as her hands played over my chest, I arched into her touch. "God, that feels good."

After she tumbled onto the couch, I followed her down, kissing and sucking one nipple until she whimpered in need. I continued to play with it as I moved to her other breast, giving it equal attention.

"Don't leave me alone again, Nolan," she whispered, gasping as she arched up as I feasted on her. "Please."

I paused in my loving of her to meet her gaze. Her sage-green eyes held me captivated, and I knew she'd hold me in thrall until the second I took my last breath. Heaving out a breath, I prayed it was seventy years from now. "Bella, beg me for pleasure,"—my hand rose to trace her eyebrow—"but you never have to beg me for my attention." I leaned over to kiss her. "For me to spend time with you."

"Nolan," she gasped as she clung to me while a sob burst out. "I've felt so alone. I thought I'd be alone forever in this house. Haunted by you and my dad."

"Oh, love," I whispered, as I edged to her side, hauling her onto my chest as she cried against me. "No." Running my hands over her back and shoulders, attempting to find any way I could to soothe her, I spoke in a soft, earnest voice. "No, my darling. I didn't want to come home until I had something to offer you. Until I knew what—who—had stolen from you."

"Offer me?" she asked, raising her head to stare at me as tears trickled down her cheeks. "I don't need anything more than you."

I shook my head. "I needed to prove to you my sincerity. Don't you see?"

She kissed my chest and I shivered. "No, Nolan, my darling love. No. I never needed that. And poor Caleb wasted hours putting together fancy words to fuel our fire for a few moments." She grinned at me, although the pain remained in her eyes. "We made a promise to each other."

"We did." I swallowed, my voice low and reverent as I stared deeply into her eyes. I rolled so my hips pressed into hers, and I was completely focused on her. My elbows were propped by her shoulders, and I cradled her face. "I promise to cherish you. To ease your aches. To rejoice in your triumphs and soothe you when you're disappointed. To laugh with you." I paused as my voice caught. "To always love you, *Teo*, mi bella."

She gazed at me as though I had hung the moon, her eyes wide and her breath hitching. "Nolan," she stuttered out. "I promise to believe in you. To trust in you. In us. To adore you." She smiled as a tear tracked down her cheek. "I promise to share all my passion with you. To dance in the moonlight with no music with you. To wake every day grateful you are my husband." She raised her hand to brush over my forehead. "To never go to bed angry. To love you forever."

I rested my forehead against hers. These were our vows. Not the perfunctory ones we'd said in Caleb's office when we barely knew each other and had yet to be tested. These were meant for *us*. "Let me love you," I whispered, my mouth meandering to one side as I kissed my way down behind her ear and down her neck.

"Yes. Make me forget the past few days."

I lifted away, stripping away the rest of my clothes, dumping them beside the couch. Words were no longer enough. I needed to touch and kiss her. I needed her like I needed air.

My fingers stroked to her center, and I groaned at finding her wet. "I can't wait, bella."

"Don't wait," she gasped, arching up, chasing the stroke of my fingers. "Show me how much you've missed me. Let me show you."

She gave a small shriek as I thrust into her, my eyes rolling back at the feel of her tight and hot around me. All thought fled as I thrust into her, again and again, my groans melding with her cries. God, she was so tight. So wet. So perfect. When I felt her gasp and then flutter around me, I roared, spilling into her as my hips continued to rock, chasing every one of her tremors.

I'd found my heaven on earth and there was nothing I wouldn't do to safeguard it.

CHAPTER 16

THEODORA

The following day, after a lazy morning with my husband, I continued to lounge in bed as he made me a very late breakfast. I heard him answer his phone and hoped whoever called wouldn't ruin our interlude. When I looked up from my pillow, I knew my hope would be dashed. "Bad news?"

"My dad's been arrested," he said, his jaw clenching for a moment. "I should go to the ranch. Or town. Or..." He stood there, with shoulders stooped, head bowed, and a lost look in his beautiful eyes.

Tumbling out of bed, I threw myself into his arms. "You're not alone." Wrapping my arms around him, I held on tight. "I don't blame you. I'd never blame you." When he shuddered, I held on tighter.

"I have to go, Theo."

Kissing his chest, I peered up at him. "I know. Can you give me ten minutes to shower and change and I'll come with you? I want to be with you." I saw the shock and relief in his gaze a moment before he hauled me close, squeezing me so tight I thought I'd never breathe again. At his whispered, "thank you," I remained in his arms for an extra moment.

After backing away and kissing him, I ran to the bathroom to shower and get ready. I didn't care about having perfect hair or makeup today. I wanted to support Nolan, and I knew he wanted to already be on the road. Within fifteen minutes, we were out the door, my hand in his as he helped me into the truck. I cupped his face, kissing him softly before he could back away and shut the truck door. "Whatever happens today, I love you." I smiled softly as his eyes flashed with relief and pleasure before he backed away.

When we were on our way into town, he reached over to grip my hand. "We're owed a day in bed," he murmured.

"We are, although I'm uncertain we'll have one before next winter. I know how much work there is on a ranch."

He cast an appreciative glance in my direction and then smirked. "Perhaps a day out in the fields would be just as enjoyable."

Flushing, I nodded, relishing this short respite before the tension I knew was to come. "As long as we're certain none of the hands will search for you."

He chuckled and shook his head. "On pain of death," he teased, raising my hand to kiss my knuckles. "Thank you." He let out a deep breath. "For wanting to be with me. For sharing this burden." He glanced at me as he slowed down the truck to drive over the cattle guard.

"I know you could do this alone, Nolan, but it's important to me to support you however I can. As long as you want me to."

He paused at the end of the drive before merging onto the highway into town. "I do. Every moment of every day, I do." He kissed my hand again before focusing on the road.

I sat, content to hold his hand as I looked at the passing scenery. I loved early May in Montana. The birds had returned and filled the fields and forests with their song, and the hills were a beautiful green. In the distance, the mountains remained snowcapped, providing a striking contrast to the green hills and fields.

I rolled down my window, laughing as my hair blew around, and I grabbed at it as I didn't want it to be a tangled mess when we arrived in town. However, the rich scent of loamy fields and the promise of another fruitful year was in the air, and I breathed in deeply. Oh, how I loved this place.

When I opened my eyes, I noticed Nolan casting furtive glances in my direction. "What?" I asked as I flushed.

"I love seeing you relaxed and enjoying yourself. You don't allow yourself to be constrained. You throw your arms wide and embrace life."

This is how he saw me? My flush deepened as I gaped at him while he continued to glance from me to the road. "Only with you." I cleared my throat from my raspy emotion. "Only with you am I free."

He nodded, slowing as we entered town. I saw him take a deep breath as we continued to slow as the speed limit dropped. Soon, we'd passed the beautiful downtown buildings and Caleb's office, and I suddenly realized we were headed to the jail. I took a deep breath, praying I could be strong as we neared a confrontation with the man who had hurt us both so terribly.

~

NOLAN

Focusing on Theo kept me from concentrating on the agony in my soul as I neared the time I had to face the man who had raised me. Betrayed me. Hurt Theo. I took a deep breath as I tried to force a smile while I squeezed her hand. When I saw her staring at me with unveiled concern, I knew she didn't expect me to hide the anguish I felt. The knowledge I could return home and hold her in my arms as I mourned was a balm I never realized I needed.

Entering the police station, I nodded to Jerry, the sheriff, and his deputy, Bobby, ignoring the fact their conversation came to an abrupt halt the moment we arrived. I'd gone to school with Jerry, and one of my siblings had been in Bobby's class. I couldn't remember which.

"This is highly irregular," Jerry said loud enough for me to hear, although I didn't understand the full extent of the conversation. "But this is still under my jurisdiction. I call the shots here."

Caleb entered, slapping his hand on my shoulder as he attempted a smile at Theo, although I saw the strain around his bloodshot eyes. His black suit was rumpled with his red silk tie tugged to one side, and I wished he could take a month away from work. "For now, Jer. The Feds'll be back soon with all the paperwork in place and then he won't be under your jurisdiction. They only agreed to move so quickly because they were worried about a flight risk." He sighed and rubbed at his eyes. "Damn, I'm tired."

I stared at the three men, my grip on Theo's hand tightening as though she was my anchor in this rapidly changing world. "Can I see him?"

Caleb shook his head. "No. He refuses to see you."

I paled and then flushed as a rage overwhelmed me. Even now, he tried to exert his power. Damn him.

Caleb appeared chagrined as he cleared his throat. "He'd like to speak with Theo."

I stilled, my shoulders snapping back as I hissed out a breath. "Absolutely not. Not without me there." I attempted to relax my rigid posture when Theo brushed her hand over my chest, but I feared all she felt was my heart hammering. I wanted to throttle the only man I'd known as my father. Manipulative bastard.

"Nolan." She spoke in a soft voice, as though we two were the only people in the room.

I looked down at her precious face, focusing on the loyalty and love in her gaze, and shook my head. "No." I shook my head for emphasis. "I will not allow him to hurt you with his meanness and cruelty and fill your head with doubts. Don't ask that of me, Theo."

"Nolan…"

"No, bella, no. I swore to protect and honor you. I can't do that if you go in there. I can't be by your side. I can't shield you from him."

She moved so she stood directly in front of me, her entire focus on me. I felt like I was drowning in her sage-green eyes. "I'm protected and cherished because I know you are mine." She waited for me to nod, a small smile flitting across her lips as her eyes glowed with a fervency that was only for me. "I'm safe from his hatred because he has no power over me. His words can't hurt me, Nolan."

I groaned and pulled her close, wrapping my arms around her. Breathing in the scent of flowers and Montana in spring, I capitulated. I realized I'd always capitulate to her. "Do you want to speak with him? I don't care what he wants. What do you want?"

She kissed my chest, and I fought an instinctual shudder. "Yes. I want to. Just this once. And then I want to go home and forget about him." She brushed a hand through my hair. "To live our life without his destructive presence."

"Then so be it."

~

THEODORA

My hand shook as I stood outside the door to the room that would lead me to the man who had robbed me blind. To the man who had inadvertently forced me to marry Nolan. I took a deep breath as I felt no rage or remorse at that. He'd led me to the love of my life, and although I'd never thank him for his tactics, I'd always be thankful Nolan and I'd had a reason to wed.

Squaring my shoulders, I tilted my chin back, boosting my flagging confidence, and turned the handle on the door, pushing it open. I paused at seeing this tall, always rather regal-looking man sitting in an orange jumpsuit handcuffed to the table. I should have known Nolan would do everything in his power to protect me even though he wasn't in the room with me. "Hello."

His dark brown eyes raked over me, and I fought a shiver. It felt as though he had attempted to strip me bare. Running a hand over my thigh, I hoped he thought it was due to nervousness. I also reassured myself I was still clothed.

"You think you've won."

I stiffened at his derisive tone. "There is no winning in something like this."

"Oh, there's definitely a loser." He smiled ferally at me. "And it isn't me."

I remained near the doorway, ignoring his motion that I sit on the chair across the table from him. Although he was shackled, a latent sense of self-preservation prevented me from approaching any closer to him. "From where I'm standing, you are."

"You think you've won?" he snorted. "Because you've married that half-wit?" His smile broadened when he saw me stiffen. "I won't disgrace myself any longer by calling him my son. He's not my son. He was never my son." He snorted again. "No son of mine would be stupid enough to not be able to read."

"He's not stupid!" I burst out, my breath sawing in and out of me. "He's smart and kind and honorable." I paused as I saw him staring at me strangely. "If you'd shown him the compassion and care you should have, you could have helped him. Taught him to read. Obtained tutors. But you didn't. You mocked him and used him as your verbal punching bag."

"How little you know."

"I know enough," I snapped. "I know you are such a small-minded, mean little man, that you needed to pick on a boy and bully him." I gasped as I fought a sob before forcing myself to continue. "You needed to attempt to destroy his spirit so you didn't feel so insignificant." I shook my head as I glared at him. "She didn't love you the way you loved her. That didn't give you the right to try to destroy her son. Lorenzo's son."

"You know nothing!" he roared.

"I know enough," I repeated again as my soft voice ricocheted around the room. "I know about love and duty and protecting those I care about. I know about forgiveness."

"Do you? How well did you practice that toward your own family?" He looked at me with a mocking glint in his eyes. "I'll be interested to see if you really are a woman of your words."

I frowned as he taunted me before I closed my eyes and sighed. I ignored what he said and murmured, "How can you have lost your chance to be a father to a man like Nolan?"

"I was never given the chance," he growled. "From the moment he was born, I was reminded he wasn't mine. He was the spitting image of that bastard, and I watched him grow up to be just like him too. Always making friends with everyone. Always so charming. Smug little shit. Who the hell was he?"

Frowning, I shook my head in bewilderment at the criticism of his friend and the envy toward Nolan. "I thought Lorenzo was your best friend."

"Until he stole Evelina!" His breathing increased with his agitation. "Evelina was supposed to be mine. Mine!"

The chain that tethered him rattled as he shook it, and I

inched backward, relaxing a little when I felt the wall behind me. I liked knowing I had as much space between the two of us as possible. "Surely who she chose was Evelina's decision."

"Said like a woman." The derisive scorn in his voice didn't affect me, and he frowned when he saw me staring at him impassively.

"If you had truly loved Evelina, you would have loved every child she had, simply because they were a part of her. You failed her, Jameson, by not loving Nolan. You hurt her every time you abused him, refused to support him, or turned your back on championing him." I waved around the room. "You might be here because you stole money from me." I shrugged. "I don't care about that. Nolan and I will be fine. Your true penance will always be knowing how much you failed the woman you loved because you were self-centered. Perhaps that is why she could never fully love you as she loved Lorenzo."

I saw him pale and then a red tide come up his neck and cheeks. He launched himself at me but could not get past the table which was thankfully bolted to the floor. The door beside me opened and I stepped out, leaving him alone.

"Nolan?" I whispered, suddenly shaking. I was moments from falling apart.

"Here, bella." Strong arms wrapped around me, and I collapsed against him. I knew he spoke soothing words, but all I could hear was his voice. Soft, warm, and filled with devotion. His hands played through my hair and caressed my back, and I wanted to stay like this forever. Comforted in his arms.

"Theo!"

I jerked back when I heard my uncle's voice. "Uncle?" I gripped Nolan's arm, desperate for him to remain beside me. I shouldn't have worried, as he turned so I stood with him in front of me and protecting me from my uncle. "What are you doing here?"

"How can you expect me to stay away when I learn how

you've been abused by these wicked Burkes?" He strode toward me. "You will come home now. We can put this terrible episode behind us, and you can forget this ever happened."

"Uncle, no," I said, then gasped as he reached around Nolan and yanked on my arm, tearing me away from Nolan. "Uncle!"

Nolan stepped forward, placing a hand on my uncle's shoulder, his jaw clenched tight and his blue eyes glowing with enmity. "Let go of my wife."

Uncle Bradley scoffed. "Your wife! I bet you haven't even slept with her yet. You only wanted her for the water and the land."

"I'll only tell you one more time. Let her go." Nolan stood tall, glaring at my uncle as his muscles rippled under his shirt as he restrained himself from attacking the man.

Uncle Bradley seemed to finally understand the danger. He paused and released my arm. "There's no need to act as though I'm the one who's going to hurt my niece when you and your family have already done a good job of that!"

"Nolan has not hurt me." I took a step backward toward Nolan, relaxing when I reached back and pressed my hand against his thigh. Having his support and strength near me grounded me. I took a deep breath and studied my uncle. He looked harried, wearing wrinkled jeans and a misbuttoned flannel. "What do you want?"

"I'm worried about you." Glaring at my husband and barely focusing on me at all, he spoke in a soft, commanding voice that I imagine worked well with his business associates. "Your cousins and I want you home."

I huffed out a breath and shook my head. "Never. I am home. With Nolan in my house at the ranch."

"You can't possibly want to remain with him now that you know what he and his family have done."

I took a deep breath and squeezed my hand on Nolan's thigh, hoping it would help calm him. I sensed his desire to thrash my uncle, but I had no desire for my husband to end up in jail today. Nor did I imagine he would want to be a cellmate with his father. "Nolan was unaware of his father's actions. I will not blame him for what he did not know."

"Gullible fool."

I felt Nolan stiffen behind me, and I sent a warning glance at my uncle. "Leave. You're not needed here. I have Nolan and my new family."

"You'd forsake us?" He stared at me with pain in his gaze, and I marveled at his ability to act concerned for me. Just a few weeks ago, he reveled that he no longer had to care for me. I didn't have the energy to remind him of that interaction, but he stiffened as though recalling it. His eyes flit to Nolan with concern.

"No." I spoke in a soft voice as an unutterable weariness filled me. I simply wanted him to leave. If I rarely saw him again, I knew I would be content. "There's nothing to forsake. I've been alone and miserable since my father died. You gave me a place to sleep, food, and clothes, but nothing that fed my soul. I want so much more than that. And I've found it."

I heard someone clear his throat and glanced at Caleb who stood to one side with the sheriff, deputy, and other men I didn't know. "Caleb?" I whispered, leaning even more heavily against Nolan. "What's going on?"

One of the unknown men stepped forward and grabbed Uncle Bradley's wrists, easily handcuffing him. Another began to read him his Miranda rights as they led him away. I watched the entire thing in stunned wonder. "I have to sit or I'm going to collapse," I whispered. A fine quivering had begun, and I didn't know if it would ever stop.

Nolan led me to a bench in the hallway, and I plopped onto it, uncaring of my gracelessness. All I focused on was that I was finally seated as the quivers turned into full-bodied shakes and shivers. Nolan sat beside me, his arms around me as he held me.

"Caleb? What the hell was that?" Nolan asked as he ran soothing strokes over my arms.

Caleb crouched down in front of us and spoke in a soft tone. "It appears there was more to this scheme than I realized." He looked at me with his blue eyes filled with regret. "Your uncle and Uncle Jameson were working together. They planned to split the money from the account and then split the huge fee your uncle would make when you were forced to sell the ranch for millions of dollars."

"What?" I gasped.

"Yeah, it was all there on the computer. Jameson wasn't very good with passwords for his email account. I suspect your uncle set up the financial stuff because that's been harder to trace and he had the password to your account. They used the computer at the ranch because they thought no one would think to look there."

Caleb sighed and plopped down on his butt, exhaustion seeping from him. "When you married without anyone knowing, you ruined their chance to clean out the accounts. And you merged with one of the strongest ranches in the state. The likelihood you'd sell became nonexistent." Caleb smiled. "You foiled them in more ways than one."

I continued to shake. "Nolan," I whispered. "I'm sorry. I blamed you. Your family. Mine was just as much to blame." I stared up at him with a shame-filled gaze.

"None of that, *Teo*," Nolan breathed as he wrapped his arms around me and kissed my head. "What they tried to do to you..." He let out a ragged breath. "I'd rip them limb from limb if I could."

"No." I kissed his chest. "Don't do anything that might keep us apart." I sat there for long moments in his arms, relishing feeling so protected and cherished.

I heard Nolan speak as his voice rumbled against my cheek.

"Why not arrest her uncle before he confronted Theo here?"

Nolan ran his fingers over me, soothing me as I froze at the question.

I turned and looked at Caleb, studying him as this was the first time I'd ever seen him squirm. "Caleb?" I whispered as I pushed up and away from Nolan. "What is it?"

"The Feds weren't convinced you had nothing to do with it. They needed to see you interact with him."

"The hell you say!" Nolan roared, only remaining sitting because I held a hand to his chest.

"What would I gain by emptying accounts that were to come to me and being forced to sell my own ranch?" I shook my head. "It makes no sense."

Shrugging, Caleb nodded. "I know, but they're not the most trusting, and I don't care to know all the things they've seen. But they're convinced now, and they'll leave you alone." He grinned. "Until it's time to go after your uncle's assets for restitution. I'm looking forward to throwing those cousin bitches of yours out on the street."

"You look too gleeful, Cay," Nolan murmured.

"And you don't?" he asked with a grin as he pushed himself up. "I'll see you when you surface." He winked at us and sauntered away, calling out something that made Jerry chortle.

I collapsed against Nolan, thankful his arms wrapped around me again. The day was surreal, and I couldn't believe all that had happened.

"I wish we were home, and I could hold you on my chest while we lay on the couch watching the fire." He continued to speak with me, his hands moving over me as his breath tickled my neck. Focusing on his beautiful baritone and the reverence in his voice, I breathed deeply. His unique scent—a mixture of bay rum cologne, sweat, and horses—always calmed me and excited me. Today, it was the balm to my anxiety, and I breathed him in as though it were the antidote to all my troubles.

"Love me," I whispered.

"You know I do." He kissed behind one ear. "I won't love you properly until we're home. And then I'll worship you."

I shuddered, this time from the promise in his voice. Lifting my head up from his chest, the agony and disappointment from the morning faded as I stared into the promise of his gaze. A sudden awareness filled me that there was nothing I wouldn't do to have him in my life. "Take me home."

≈

NOLAN

Hours later, after questions had been answered, Jameson and her uncle had been taken away, and we'd evaded an angry tirade from her cousins, I ushered Theo into our house, urging her into our bedroom. "Strip," I whispered, chuckling when she gaped at me in surprise. "No, not for that," I teased as I walked into the master bath. I rummaged around in the cabinets, popping lids open until I found a scent I loved. I couldn't find one that smelled of peonies, but this would do. After flipping on the taps to the bath, I returned to her to find her swaying in place by our bed. "Is this good in a bath?"

"Bath?" she asked, her dazed eyes focusing on me and reading the label. "Yes, it's for the bath." Her vision cleared. "You want me to take a bath?"

Leaning forward, I brushed my lips over her forehead and nodded. "Yes, bella, you need to relax. Soak away this day. Let me care for you." I frowned when her eyes filled. "What am I doing wrong?"

"Nothing." Her voice sounded like a frog croak, and I nuzzled her head when she collapsed against me. "I never dared to dream for you."

My breath stuttered. "I always dreamed for you." Kissing her head, I eased her away. "Your bath will be ready soon." Swiping at a lone tear, I waited for her to nod before I slipped back into the bathroom. After adding the bath gel which turned out to make a huge number of bubbles, I looked around me.

Caleb's words from today when he stood beside me, witnessing the goings-on in the questioning room, echoed in my mind. *"You have one hell of a woman."* His words, filled with admiration and envy, repeated over and over again in my mind, and I knew he was correct. I did have one hell of a woman, and I was so damn thankful for her.

"Candles," I muttered as I looked around the functional room with little softness to it. I wanted this room to be a sanctuary for my wife. A place where she could come and relax after a hard day's work on the ranch. "Soft towels."

"What are you talking about?" she whispered as she wrapped her arms around me, pressing her front to my back.

I shivered as I realized she was naked. Closing my eyes, I focused on her question. "I want candles and soft towels and that shit that smells good so you can relax in here." At her giggle, I eased her hold on me so I could stare down into her beguiling eyes. "What?"

Standing on her toes, she kissed me softly. The type of kiss that isn't about passion and the need to rush to the bed or fall to the floor in a tangle of limbs. This was a kiss filled with promise. With certainty. With the recognition that what we had was precious and priceless. When she broke the kiss, I felt shattered in the best possible way.

She cupped my jaw, her hands scraping over my stubble. "I don't need any of those things." At the question in my eyes, she murmured, "I only need you. I'll only ever need you, Nolan."

I swallowed, ignoring the cooling bath behind me and the sweet scent of lavender and verbena wafting through the room. Nothing existed for me but her. "You took my breath away today, bella."

"I don't know what you mean." She looked up at me with her

green eyes filled with confusion. "You're the one who prevented me from falling to pieces."

"No." I paused, clearing my throat as I was suddenly close to tears. "You defended me. To him." There was so much more I wanted to say, but my throat closed up and I couldn't say another word.

Her eyes blazed and she arched up, as though needing to be even closer to me. "Of course I did. He needed to understand what a fool he is. Was. He needed to understand any misery, any disappointment that he's suffering is solely his doing." Her eyes glowed with the belief of her convictions. "He was blessed with you and didn't see the gift."

"You say that as though that's the worst blasphemy."

"It is. He should have rejoiced in you. He should have given thanks every day that he could honor his friend by caring for his son. He should have loved his wife so much that he'd love all of her children." Her eyes glistened with tears. "I hate what he did to you, and when he sat there, as though he were the wronged party, I couldn't stay silent. I couldn't."

Groaning, I pulled her tightly into my arms, holding her close. "I already loved you before today, Theo." I paused, swallowing. "But today...today I realized just how deep my love is. It's infinite."

She clung to me. "I felt the same way after seeing my uncle. After learning what he did." She kissed my chest, her hands running over me. I felt her passion, but also her wonder that I was in her arms. "I knew, as you held me close after he left, that nothing mattered more to me than you. Not my ranch. Not my dream for having horses here. Nothing."

I eased back so I could gaze into her eyes. "I want you to have everything. I don't want you to ever feel limited."

"I won't be as long as you are here with me." She smiled, the radiance and certitude in it stealing my breath. "As long as you know there's nothing I want more than you."

"I do," I rasped as I lowered my head, kissing her with all the passion and devotion I felt. My hands swept down from her silky shoulders to cup her breasts and I groaned. "Your bath is getting cold."

"I'll have another one. Hopefully with you." She arched into my touch and laughed. "Make love with me, Nolan. Here, now. I need you."

She didn't have to ask me twice, and both our hands tore at my clothes. Soon, we were tumbling to the floor, and I angled her so she landed on the cushioned bathmat. When I heard her gasp of distress at the hard tile floor, I rolled, pulling her on top of me.

"Ride me." My eyes rolled back with pleasure as I bucked up, chasing the warm, wet heat of her. God, what had I done in this life to deserve her? "Jesus, ride me now, bella!"

I knew I was leaving marks on her hips and butt, but I couldn't care. I needed her too much. When she teased me, sliding on and off the tip of my cock, I thought I'd explode or die. Opening my eyes, I looked into her teasing gaze filled with love. "My *Teo*." I raised a hand to cup her cheek, awed that she loved me.

Her head lolled back as she sank down on me, a groan of delight escaping her as a soft flush covered her beautiful skin. My hand rose, cupping a breast, squeezing it as she began to move. "Yes, bella," I groaned as she found her rhythm. My other hand dropped to grab her ass, holding her tightly to me as I lifted my hips, pistoning up into her.

Her gasps and groans of delight as I thrust deep told me she was close. Freeing one hand, I flicked her clit, groaning as she tightened on my dick. Fuck, this was heaven on earth. "Bella," I begged. "Come for me."

She arched back, her arms anchored on my shoulders as she screamed my name, her inner muscles clamping me tight.

When I felt her let go, I sat up, wrapping my arms around

her back as her legs gripped my hips. With powerful thrusts, I worked even harder and faster into her. I felt a spooling in my back, a tightening in my balls, and I gasped as I felt her fluttering around me again. I came with a roar at the unexpected, shared orgasm, my hips continuing to lift and lower. I never wanted to leave her. I'd happily die right here.

With a groan, I collapsed backward, toppling her with me. When she shrieked, I laughed, delighted that she wriggled so we remained connected. "Let me hold you for another moment. I'm being greedy."

She sighed, her lips flitting over my face as soft as the touch of a fairy's wings. God, she made me fanciful. She made me believe in anything. Even magic.

Finally, I lifted her off me and rose, pulling out a washcloth and a towel. After cleaning her up, I placed the large towel over her as she had begun to shiver. Kneeling by the tub, I let out the water and then restarted the taps. "Let's have a bath together."

"Yes," she murmured. "There's nothing I want more."

~

THEODORA

I watched the muscles of his back tighten and relax as he got our bath ready. I relished just watching him, enjoying this time with him where no words were needed. Today had wrung me out, and somehow he knew I needed pampering. "Thank you."

He turned to stare at me at my whispered words, his brow furrowed. "For what, bella? For caring for you? For making sure you are okay?" He shook his head as a smile lifted his gorgeous lips and delight lit his eyes. "I'll always do that."

"Thank you," I whispered again. "I needed you so much today, and knowing you were there gave me strength."

He knelt by me, frowning at my words. "You don't need me to be strong, Theo. You're the bravest woman I've ever met."

I sat up, uncaring that the towel fell away. "I know I am strong, but for so much of my life I've had to be strong on my own." I traced a finger over his brow. "Don't you know how much it means that I'm not alone anymore?" I paused as he ducked forward to kiss me. Groaning as I lost myself to the kiss, I wrapped my arms around his neck. After we broke apart, I whispered, "I trust you and know you'll be there to support me." My breath caught at his incandescent smile.

"It's the same for me. We've both felt alone since our parents died." He shrugged. "Although I've had my siblings." He kissed the top of my head. "Come. It's time for a bath and then sleep."

I rose, groaning as I'd stiffened up on the floor. After easing into the large tub, I scooted forward so he could get in behind me. I sighed with pleasure as I leaned against his front, his hands stroking over me and eliciting goosebumps. God, I hoped I was always affected by his touch.

He sighed, resting his head beside mine and nibbling on my throat. "Let's have a bath every night. This is paradise."

Chuckling at his murmured comment, I ran my hands over his strong forearms now wrapped around my waist. "Not every night. Then it wouldn't be special."

I felt him relax underneath me, and I realized how difficult today must have been for him too. I froze as I thought about who might have listened to my conversation with his father. "Who was behind the glass window? Who listened in?"

"Caleb, Jerry, and I were there."

I heard the subtle hint of resignation in his voice. "Jerry. He didn't know, did he?" I wriggled and sloshed around until I faced him in the bath, my legs on either side of his hips. When I looked deeply into his gaze, I saw the echo of shock and shame he must have felt earlier today. "I'm so sorry." I raised a hand, covering my face as my head fell forward. "I never meant to hurt you."

He gripped my head, pulling me closer so I lay on his chest, his arms banded around my back. A heavy sigh heaved out of him, and I felt him quiver underneath me. "I was ashamed," he admitted in a barely audible breath. "But Jerry can keep a secret, and he's not mean." He shuddered, his hold on me unrelenting. "When I heard you defend me, when I heard what you said, it changed everything, Theo."

My fingers were digging crescent moons into his sides where I was holding on to him tightly. "How? I hurt you!"

"No, my darling love, no," he kissed my neck and cheek. "No. You made me see how he'd failed me. I should never have had to pay for being Lorenzo's son."

"You were always enough, as you were. As you are."

"Yes. As you are." His hold eased, although he kept his arms wrapped around me. "I realized you could shout it out to the entire town, as long as you believed in me like you did today while confronting Jameson."

I sighed with pleasure as I relaxed in his embrace. "There's no need for that. And he's gone now."

"Leaving us to finally have a honeymoon."

Nolan and I had woken numerous times in the night to make love, and I slept like the dead until noon the following day. I woke to the smell of pancakes, bacon, and coffee. With a groan I rolled over, irrationally disappointed to find Nolan out of bed even though my stomach grumbled with appreciation for breakfast.

He poked his head into our bedroom and smiled. Today, he looked like a little boy on Christmas morning as he stared at me. As though I was the gift he'd always dreamed of receiving, and he couldn't believe his good fortune I was actually there. "Bella." Even the way he said that endearment made me shiver. "Don't get up. We'll have breakfast in bed." He winked at me and disappeared.

I disobeyed him just to run to the bathroom but groaned with relief to crawl back into bed. When had I become so lazy? I hugged a pillow because I couldn't hug him and relaxed again as I thought about last night. We'd stayed in the bath until we were prunes and the water was cool. Then he'd dried me off, and we'd snuggled and loved all night long.

"You seem pleased with yourself," he teased as he entered our room with a tray laden with food.

I stared up at him, sporting a wicked gleam in my eyes and a satisfied smile. "I am."

He set the tray down on the bureau and leaned over me, kissing me softly. "You should be." His husky voice gave me shivers. "God, I want you again already, but I know you must be hungry."

"I'm hungry for you." I tugged him forward, feeling no resistance from him. "Although I appreciate you making breakfast."

"Fuck breakfast," he groaned as he fell into me.

Soon, I was swallowed up in a kiss and a full-body embrace. His hands were everywhere, eliciting gasps and shivers as I spread my legs wide and arched up into him. His mouth on my breast nipped and sucked one nipple and then the next, gently biting until I had bowed off the bed in ecstasy. "Nolan!"

His hands pressed my thighs even farther apart before he dove down to kiss my pussy. His tongue licked and stroked over my clit, driving me mad as he pushed me toward an orgasm. "I want you with me," I pleaded.

Shrieking, I clung to his shoulders as he heaved up, impaling me in one long stroke. He filled me completely, and it was ecstasy. "Nolan!" I screamed again, unable to say anything more than his name. Soon, I knew I would be reduced to moans as he began to pound into me.

"So fucking good," he said between clenched teeth, his head thrown back.

He hit a spot inside me, and I arched up, thrown over the edge in an instant. I screamed as I convulsed all around him. His hips pumped a few more times until he groaned and twitched, and I felt his release deep inside of me.

"Bella," he rasped as he collapsed forward into my arms. I continued to pulse around him, and I loved these moments when I could hold him in my arms. When passion had been as overwhelming for him as it had been for me, and we were lost to each other.

I felt his heart hammering against my chest, and I turned my head to kiss his ear. "I love you."

"God, how I love you, my bella." He didn't move. "Give me a minute and we'll have breakfast. And then a long nap."

I giggled and ran my hands over his back, feeling lighter and more at peace than I ever had. Marrying my family's enemy was the best thing I'd ever done.

CHAPTER 17

NOLAN

A week later I continued to live in the pleasured, half-dazed world of a newly married man. I longed for every moment with Theo, but I also had to run a ranch. Theo never resented the time I spent away from her, although she had begun to drop by my ranch more and more, now that my father was gone.

"Do you miss him?" I asked Alessia eight days after Jameson had been arrested.

She flushed as she looked at me. "A little," she admitted. "He was good to me. Until Mama died. Then everything changed." She looked away.

"Alessia? What is it?"

She rubbed at her head. "We all have secrets, Nol. Even me." She shook her head. "Today is not the day for mine to see the light."

"Has someone threatened you?" I strode toward her, ready to do battle.

"No." She sighed and relented a little. "I received word that Chase is coming home."

"Chase?" I asked, rubbing a hand over my jaw. Chase had been one of my best friends when I was a kid. Along with Caleb, he'd made up the third in our trio of best friends. We'd splintered apart with Caleb going to law school and Chase disappearing around the time Mama had died. He hadn't even been at her funeral. I rubbed at the ache in my chest, thankful Caleb had come home after law school. I don't know what I would have done without him. "Chase? Why would he come back now?"

She shrugged and refused to say more.

I stared at my boots, lost to the memories of my best friend. Filled with life, he had a ready laugh and was full of joy. I never understood why he abandoned the valley—abandoned me in my grief—ten years ago. "Why would he come back now?" I asked again, unable to push aside the hurt at his absence for ten years.

Alessia forced a smile and ignored my question. I didn't have time to focus on her evasiveness when she blurted out, "There's more news." She wrung her hands and then shrugged in resignation. "Our siblings are coming home. This weekend."

"This weekend? All of them?" My eyes bulged at the thought, and my heart raced with joy. "But they hate me."

Frowning at me, Alessia shook her head. "No they don't. They love you."

I scoffed and paced away, moving to the window in our office to stare out at a part of the paddock. "They have a funny way of showing it. They each left as soon as they could after Mama died."

"You don't understand, Nolan." My sister stared at me in dawning comprehension. "You believe they were angry because you got the ranch."

I lifted a shoulder as though that were obvious.

"That's not it at all. They saw what Dad was doing. How he treated you." She swallowed. "How he would treat them if they stayed. He'd already started picking on them. Telling Sofia and Carmella they were no better than two-bit whores wanting to ply their trade for dreaming of being bakers. And that Giulia was a slut for going into fashion. Or that Ward was pathetic for his scribbles and desire to be an architect."

I gaped at her. "How did I not hear any of this?"

"You had your own battles. They fled the first chance they got because they knew you would never abandon them. You'd always support them in ways Jameson never would or could." Her gaze overflowed with sympathy as she stared at me. Not for the first time, I gave thanks that her eyes, so much like Jameson's, had always been filled with warmth and love when she looked at me, rather than the cold disdain in his. "They've always felt guilty for leaving the two of us behind. And so grateful you've supported them through everything."

"Of course I have." My voice was scratchy as I thought about my beloved siblings. We hadn't all been together since the funeral. One or two had come home for sporadic visits in the past ten years, but it wasn't the same. "I love them."

Alessia approached me and gripped my arm. "Forgive them for staying away."

I nodded, a smile bursting forth. "As long as they forgive me for believing they resented me." I let out a whoop of joy and swung Alessia around before setting her down. "How long do you think they'll stay?"

She shrugged, grinning as my joy was infectious. "I think a few might want to return to live."

"I can't wait to tell Theo." My excitement faded when I saw Alessia grimace at my wife's name. "Ally?"

Her eyes filled with shame as she stared at me. "I'm so sorry about Theo and the money. I didn't know."

I frowned, gently gripping her shoulders. "I know you didn't. I don't blame you. Theo doesn't either." I paused as I saw doubt on her face and then grinned at her. "Theo hasn't invited you to dinner, and I've turned down all of your invitations, because it feels like we're having a belated mini honeymoon." I shrugged. "Even though I'm still working."

"It's not because she resents me?" She rubbed at her head, something she only did when she was really worried or upset. "I was afraid that she'd believe I was partly to blame and wouldn't want to see me."

"No, that's not Theo's way," I whispered as I pulled Alessia in for a hug. "She'd tell you if she was upset." I backed away and smoothed away a piece of honey-colored hair. "She'll help you with the preparations for the welcome home celebration. She's always wanted a big family."

Laughing, Alessia hugged me. "I have too. A happy family."

I let out a breath of relief as I realized that we now had the opportunity for the family we envisioned.

I returned home with an extra spring in my step, anxious to see Theo and to tell her all about my siblings' return. When I couldn't find her in the house, I traipsed over to the barn, breathing in deeply of the rich scents of spring. Birds trilled and I paused, closing my eyes as I listened for a meadowlark. After a minute or two, I heard its lilting song, and I relaxed further. This was home, and I couldn't wait to see what Theo and I could create together.

I entered the barn and stilled, listening for her. When I heard a muttered "ow!" from a stall at the opposite end of the barn, I walked in that direction. "Theo?"

Her hand lifted out of the stall. "In here!"

I reached the stall and peered inside, bursting out laughing as I saw her covered in dust and hay and looking thoroughly disgruntled as she attempted to wield a crowbar. "What are you doing?"

"There's a trunk in here and I wanted to see what's in it." She held the crowbar up. "But I can't pry the lid off. It has a lock, and I can't find the key." She sat with a huff, smiling up at me. "Hi, love. It's so good to see you." Her smile broadened as I approached and leaned forward, kissing her softly. "How was your day?"

I stared at her in wonder as I realized this was how my life would be. Working with her or coming home to her. Sharing the events of my day. My worries. Knowing she would support me through everything. "Wonderful." I pointed to the trunk. "Do you need to know what's in it?"

She shrugged and tossed the crowbar down. "No. A mystery to solve another day. I'd much rather have a shower with my sexy husband."

Laughing, I hauled her close when she rose. "Never change your perfume. I love it."

"It's nothing special," she said as she snuggled into me.

"It's ambrosia," I teased, remembering the word she'd used the first night we met. "My mother had a peony garden, and you smell like that garden. Like everything good and new and hopeful." I kissed her head before easing her away. "How was your day, bella?"

"Good. I did some work here after I went into town for groceries." I felt her grimace and backed up to gaze at her.

"What happened?"

"I ran into my cousins. They were even more unpleasant than usual and very angry with me."

"They should be pissed at their dad, not you. He's the asshole."

She giggled and nodded. "Yeah, he is." She flushed. "But it was embarrassing to have some of the townsfolk listen to them scream and carry on. I wish they'd leave Burnside Creek and never come back."

I shook my head. "From what Cay tells me, they have no

plans on leaving. They'll be here to torment us for longer than we'd like. Although they'll be much poorer after Cay finishes bankrupting them so you receive part of what is owed you."

With a sigh, she pressed against me. "In the end, it doesn't matter, Nol. They can't hurt us."

"No," I whispered as I kissed her head. "I have the most exciting news."

She gasped, backing away to stare into my eyes. "Why didn't you tell me right away?" She tugged on me to sit beside her on the trunk. "What has put that sparkle in your eyes?"

"You put that sparkle in my eyes." I brushed the back of my hand down her cheek as she stared at me in awed wonder. Unable to help myself, I beamed at her. "My brothers and sisters are coming home. All of them. This weekend."

She goggled at me, her hand gripping mine. "Really? All of them?"

I nodded, my eyes filling as I admitted, "I thought they hated me." Her grip tightened on my hand at that admission, but she remained quiet as she waited to hear what I would say. "Because I got the ranch and they got nothing. I've done everything I can to support them. They get quarterly checks, as much as is possible." I cleared my throat.

"Why are they coming home now? What's changed?" She paused, nodding in comprehension as her quick mind deduced the reason. "Jameson's gone."

"How could I not know how much they loathed him?"

She cupped my face, smiling broadly. "They love you as much as you love them." She sobered. "Can you forgive them?"

"Always. They left me to him, but I can't blame them. I'd never want anyone else to suffer his hatred the way I did." I sat in shocked silence a moment. "I never realized how much he only really cared about Alessia."

Squealing with delight, she threw herself in my arms and squeezed me tight. "I can't wait to meet your siblings. To have a big, messy family party with Caleb and his siblings too. And the ranch hands and any of your friends you want to invite." She gazed at me in hopeful wonder. "I want this ranch—our ranch—to be a place of joy and where our family and friends want to gather."

I looked at her and nodded. "I do too, bella. I do too."

On Saturday, I woke early beside Theo. I'd loved her hard the night before, and she slept soundly beside me. Immediately, my mind started spinning with all that could occur today. Although I wanted her with me when I saw my siblings again, a tiny part of me wanted to see them alone for the first time in years. To reassure myself that Alessia was right —that they didn't resent me. I didn't want to look like a fool in front of Theo.

After slipping from bed, I moved to the living room. I stood, staring out the windows as dawn lit the distant mountains in a beautiful wash of pinks and yellows. Sipping a cup of coffee, I thought about my siblings. About their close connection. A connection I had always felt excluded from.

As her arms slipped around my waist, I closed my eyes, relaxing at the feel of her pressed against my back. "Everything will be all right."

"I shouldn't doubt Alessia." I shivered when she kissed my back.

"What do you want, Nolan?" When I remained quiet, she spoke in an even softer voice. "What do you need?"

"To see them alone the first time." I waited for an outburst or some sign of distress from her. When none came, I relaxed, opening my eyes so I could see her reflection. She waited, patiently, for me to say more. "I don't want to hurt you."

A confused frown marred her features for a moment before

she smiled and kissed my shoulder again. "Why do you think you're hurting me? I can't imagine what today will be like. If you want a little time alone with them, I understand." She paused. "Although I hope I'll meet them."

I spun, cupping one cheek with my free hand. "Of course you will. I want you there." I kissed her for a moment. "I just need a little time alone with them at first."

The sound of doors slamming shut jerked my attention from her and I stilled. There, in the drive, emerged my siblings from various vehicles. Laughing and chatting and well. "They've come here."

She kissed me again before easing away from me. "Then I will go back to bed for a while before getting ready for the day. I'll be in our bedroom." She ran a hand over my jaw, smiling at me as she spun and walked away.

Taking a deep breath, I ran a hand through my black hair. A few of us shared blue eyes. It had come as a shock to learn I wasn't truly Jameson's son as I looked like my siblings. I should have known, though. None of them struggled with schooling, whereas I always had. I tugged on a flannel and moved to the side door, throwing it open. They stood in front of it, uncertain if they should knock.

"Alessia will kill us," Sofia proclaimed as she threw herself into my arms, her black hair loose around her shoulders and her cognac-colored eyes shining with unshed tears. I caught her, overcome at seeing her again. She'd been home twice since Mama died after running away at age sixteen. The last time had been seven years ago, and she'd been barely more than a teenager then.

"You're all grown up," I whispered, awe and wonder in my voice. I glanced at the gaggle of siblings huddled around the door and motioned for them to enter. Soon, I was hugging and slapping everyone on the back. Tears were swiped away, laughter burst forth, and it was like we were the family I had always dreamed about. How was this possible?

I must have murmured that question aloud as the exuberant reunion calmed.

Ward, my oldest brother and the third sibling among us, sobered first. He'd always been somber, but he seemed even more solemn than usual. I hadn't seen him in years, and I knew little of his life since he'd left home. He'd cut his black hair short, and it was overstyled with hair products, which seemed odd as he'd never liked fashion as a boy. He'd always been responsible and too serious when we were children. "I speak for myself, but I think also for many of us." He waited as they nodded, and Logan held his coffee cup up as though Ward were making a toast. Logan, the youngest of us, had always been the most exuberant sibling.

Ward ignored Logan and focused on me. "We stayed away because of him."

Carmella's blue eyes filled with tears as she approached me. "I'm so ashamed I didn't support you. I ran, hoping to escape him and his anger. I only thought of myself."

Reid nodded. "We never thought of the toll it took on you to stay and to keep the ranch running. To protect it and preserve it while sending us quarterly checks." He flushed and ran a hand through his shaggy light brown hair. "You must resent us."

I shook my head as I stared at them. "Never. I wish I could have left. But the ranch was mine, and I was damned if I'd let him have any control of it." I shook my head again, staring dazedly from one sibling to the other, noting that Giulia cried softly while I spoke. "I thought you hated me."

At that a roar of dismay rose, and they surrounded me like a rugby scrum, enfolding me in their embrace. After another round of hugs and slaps on the back, I eased away. "Let me go get my wife, Theo. She wanted to give us time alone, but I want you to meet her."

Striding to the room I shared with Theo, I listened to them marvel at the view down the valley. I entered our room, finding Theo sitting on the bed, showered, dressed, and ready to join us. *"Teo,"* I breathed, momentarily overcome.

She rose, opening her arms to me. I pulled her close, needing a few minutes to control my emotions. "I want you to meet my siblings. They're all here, drinking coffee."

After kissing my chest, she murmured, "I hope we have enough food for breakfast for everyone."

I chuckled. "Such a practical ranch wife," I teased, inordinately pleased at her taking everything in stride. "I'll call Alessia and we can pool what we have."

When we emerged, I realized I must have been with Theo much longer than I realized as Alessia was here, cooking with Sofia and Carmella while Reid and Giulia told them stories about life in San Francisco. I paused, watching them in our kitchen, overwhelmed all over again.

After breakfast had been served, we crowded around the table I had once thought of as large. They'd met Theo without any comment about her father, and I knew I had Alessia to thank for that. "How long can you stay?" I asked during a lull in conversation. At the glances between them, I froze. "Shouldn't I have asked that?" I played with a piece of bacon, uncertain what I had missed. Dammit, why was I always saying the wrong thing? Would I always be the outsider among my siblings?

Theo gripped my hand and gave it a gentle squeeze, relaxing me as I saw my siblings glance at each other, as though determining who would speak.

Ward spoke up. "We all want to move home. Not to the ranch, but to town at least. We're tired of living away."

I gaped at them as they stared at me with a mixture of hope and dread in their expressions. "All of you want to come home?" I sputtered.

"Oh, how wonderful," Theo breathed. "We can have family

dinners and impromptu breakfasts like this all the time." She beamed at them as she squeezed my hand again. "That is the best late wedding gift we could ever have received."

I nodded, overcome with joy that my siblings would return home after all their time away.

∼

That evening, we had a bonfire in an empty paddock at my ranch, and a few of the hands pulled out their fiddles. An impromptu party became a dance and social gathering. It was fitting after the hard calving season, and I swayed with Theo in my arms. Word had spread to my neighbors and friends, and a slow trickle of trucks arrived, the parked cars filling the drive. Kegs of beer, bottles of wine, and spirits were on the table, and I suspected our homes would be overflowing with those unable to drive home tonight. I found I didn't care. As long as I had Theo in my arms, everything was fine.

Theo kissed my neck as the sweet tones of a waltz carried on the wind. "This has been the best day."

"One of many we've had," I whispered.

She smiled up at me. "The best part is knowing we have so many more to come." She frowned as she glanced over my shoulder. "Who is that man speaking with Ally? She doesn't seem pleased."

I glanced and froze. "Chase," I breathed. "He was my best friend, along with Caleb, when I was younger. I told you a bit about him." When she nodded, I continued to stare at him as though he were a ghost returned to us. "I never thought he'd come home, although Ally said he had. I thought she was wrong."

I watched as Chase said something to Alessia that made her tilt her head up in defiance, her shoulders back and eyes blazing. "He always could irritate Ally."

"She's not irritated," Theo said as we now swayed in place and watched the other couple. "It looks to me like she's devastated at his return. That's her attempt at bravado." She stroked a hand over my chest. "I think they have a past you know nothing about."

I shivered at her insight as I remembered Alessia referring to secrets she wanted to remain buried. Holding Theo close, I wondered what it could be as I continued to watch the nearby couple. When Chase left my sister's side, I watched Ally force a smile as he slipped into the crowd.

"We'll know soon enough," Theo whispered, urging me to start moving around the dance floor again. "He seems the type of man to provoke her." She grinned up at me. "Should be fun to watch."

I focused on her as the party around us faded away. "Fun?" I shook my head as I smiled my devilish smile that always made her shiver. "No, bella. Fun will be watching our ranches prosper with our family around us." I kissed her neck, whispering in her ear. "Fun will be watching you grow big and round with our child." I nibbled on her ear as her breath caught at the thought. "Fun will be every moment I spend with you."

She sighed, resting her head against my chest. "Heaven."

I nodded, kissing her head. I knew we'd have challenges, but with her by my side, there wasn't anything we couldn't face. "Heaven."

EPILOGUE

NOLAN

Today was an important day for us, and I wanted it to be perfect. Theo rested on her side, breathing softly and sound asleep. I'd worn her out last night, and I had a feeling I'd wear her out again soon. Kissing her shoulder, I wrapped the blanket and comforter around her and slipped into sweats.

After making breakfast, I carried the tray into our bedroom, beaming at her as she looked at me with love and desire in her gaze. "Happy anniversary, Teo."

She sat bolt upright in bed, the blankets falling down around her waist as she gaped at me. "Anniversary? That's three days from now!"

I chuckled and set the tray on our bureau. Shucking my clothes, I climbed into bed and eased her into my arms. "To me, we have two anniversaries. The day we met and the day we married. Today is the first one." She looked devastated and I frowned. "What is it, bella?"

"I don't have anything for you today." A tear slipped down her cheek.

Huffing out a breath, I cupped her head and stared at her in awe. "Are you kidding me?" I reared up and kissed her senseless, toppling her backward so I leaned on an elbow and caressed her and kissed her until we were both breathless. "You give me everything. Every day. Your love. Your laughter. Your joy. I don't need some material item from you, bella, when I have *you*." I dropped my hand and caressed her belly. "And soon, we'll have a child."

She nodded, another tear leaking out. Rubbing a hand over my face, she whispered, "Why do you seem nervous?"

"I have something for you." When I eased away, she sat up and tugged the blankets to her chest, covering her perfect tits.

"Will you finally tell me what you've been hiding from me?"

I stilled, gaping at her. "You knew?"

"I know you've been keeping something from me for months."

"Bella," I breathed as I saw the doubt and fear in her gaze. "It's nothing bad. I promise. I wanted to surprise you." When I saw her take a deep breath and nod, I hoped this would be a good surprise. She'd never let me down, and I refused to doubt her.

Rising, I moved to the breakfast tray and lifted it, carrying it to rest on her lap. "I wore you out last night. You need your energy."

She smirked at me. "Considering I know we'll have round two soon."

"Two? I think it's round five." I chuckled as I kissed her lips and settled so I could watch her.

She stared at me a long moment before focusing on the tray, snagging a piece of bacon to munch and then taking a sip of orange juice. She stilled reaching for a fork when she saw the envelope. "Nolan?" Her sage-green eyes widened, and she met my nervous gaze.

When I nodded, she let out a deep breath and picked up the

envelope. Biting her lip, she flicked it open and tugged out the card. Reading it, her teeth bit in more deeply to her lip, and when she flipped it open, she gasped.

Tears coursed down her cheeks, and I panicked. "I'm sorry. I thought you'd like this." I picked up the tray and set it aside. I had to feel her in my arms. Undo the damage I'd done. "I'm sorry, *Teo*."

"Sorry?" she croaked, crawling into my arms. "Sorry—for writing me a love note?" She pressed her head to my chest and clung to me. "Oh, my love," she whispered, "how?"

I shivered at the wonder in her voice. "Caleb helped find a tutor. I've been meeting her in town at his office."

She pushed back and regarded me thoughtfully. "That's why Sofia mentioned seeing you with another woman."

"Dammit!" I muttered. "I love having my family home, but I never thought they'd meddle." I'd murder my sister Sofia for upsetting Theo. Brushing my thumbs over her silky skin and smoothing away her tears, I leaned forward to kiss her cheeks. "I wanted to surprise you."

I felt her let out a deep breath as she fell forward and clung to me again. "I'm sorry I doubted."

My hand stroked over her back, earning a subtle shiver. "Was it hard?"

"Yes," I murmured. "The hardest part was to stop hearing his voice calling me an idiot. Instead, I focused on you. On your belief in me." When she pressed on my chest, I sat back and met her incredible eyes. Turning my face into her soft caress, I kissed her palm. "I heard your voice, over and over again, telling me I could do this. That even if I failed, you'd still love me."

She nodded, her witch's eyes luminous as she wrapped her legs around me. "Yes. Always. I love you, Nolan. Now and forever."

"I give thanks, every day, for you. You are my everything,

Teo. I adore you. I love you, my precious wife." I recited the words I'd painstakingly written her in the card.

"Nolan," she breathed, kissing me through her tears. "I adore you and love you and treasure you. So much."

"Never stop sharing this life with me."

She beamed at me. "Never."

～

Do You Want More Nolan And Theo? Sign Up For My Newsletter For A Bonus Epilogue you don't want to miss!

SNEAK PEEK AT SECRET
MONTANA LOVE

Yay! *Secret Montana Love (Burkes of Burnside Creek, Book Two)* will be here before you know it in July. I can't wait to share Sofia and Chase's second chance at love romance with you. Here's a sneak peek from Chapter One.

CHASE

Finally, I'd see the woman of my dreams again tonight. After ten years of her haunting me, of having long winded one-sided conversations with her memory, of wondering if she even remembered me, I'd see her again. Speak with her. Smell her perfume. Hear her laugh. And, if I was a really lucky bastard, kiss her.

Alessia Burke. Tall, slender, spirited and gorgeous. I closed my eyes as I remembered her sitting across from me in her dorm room as we crammed for a test, taunting me as she knew all the answers, but was patient enough to tutor me so I'd pass my tests, too. Of her jumping up and down, screaming at the top of her lungs as I scored the winning soccer goal, her gaze filled with love and pride. Of her sitting astride me, her thick honey colored hair flowing down her back as her Godiva rich chocolate eyes hinted at the secrets, mischief and pleasure to come. God, she'd been my match in every way. How had I been stupid enough to lose her?

When I'd left ten years ago, I'd thought a year would be my penance. Then two. Somehow purgatory had spun out to ten years. Ten years without her in my arms. Without her wise counsel. Without her smart ass comments and stupid puns to keep me on my toes. Why had I ever allowed her to push me away?

I parked my truck in the long driveway of the LBarM ranch next to another pickup truck and took a deep breath. The air felt crisper, clearer, fresher here. It smelled like home in spring-time and I resented every spring I'd been forced to be away. Life in Nashville had been fine, but their country wasn't my country. Their rolling hills never eased the need in my soul to see snow topped mountain peaks blanketed in pine forests. I'd long ago tired of hot, humid weather and I longed to feel cool, crisp air, even on a July morning.

As I climbed out of my truck, I heard the distant sounds of the party, the laughter and music carrying on the breeze along with the faint scent of woodsmoke. The Burkes would have a large bonfire as it wasn't yet the dry season and it would encourage many to linger and enjoy the festivities.

I paused by the side of my truck, tossing my keys from hand to hand as I considered joining this party. Was I an ass to crash my best friend's party? He had to hate me as much as his sister did. I'd left town, without a word, right when his mother died and I'd never written. I'd never called. Hell, I'd never even attended his mother's funeral. As far as he knew, I'd died.

But, when I'd heard in town that the wandering Burke siblings had decided to move home and that Nolan was throwing a party to celebrate the news, I couldn't fight the temptation to drive to the ranch and join the festivities. I hoped

I could blend in and mingle. See my old friend again without starting a brawl.

"Dipshit," I muttered at that idiotic idea as I tugged at a strand of my red hair. Although not as fire-engine red as when I was younger, it was still red enough and far from the more acceptable auburn that women found attractive. I'd stand out like a beacon on a foggy day, unless I kept my Stetson on, which only made me feel like an imposter. I was no rancher or cowboy.

With a sigh, I put it on and pulled the brim down, hopeful few would recognize me as I wasn't the gangly boy who'd left. Now, I was muscular and broad chested. Strolling with a confidence that was all for show, I ambled toward the party, my eager gaze searching for Alessia or Nolan.

Just as I was about to join the line for beer, there she was.

More beautiful than ever. Her head was thrown back in laughter at something a tall, handsome blond man said and I wanted to punch him senseless for making my woman laugh. Fuck. How was she even more beautiful than I'd remembered?

Just seeing her was like being sucker punched. How was I supposed to talk with her when I had to continue to lie to her? Would she ever want to know the truth?

I stepped into the shadows, away from the light from a torch and studied the man with her. He looked too polished, too refined. Like a player. How couldn't she see he'd only use her and leave her? When he shifted, I froze, feeling like a fool. "Caleb," I breathed, staring at my other best friend from childhood.

Memories rushed back. Impromptu wrestling matches in the fields as we helped Nolan with his chores. Secret signals as we attempted to stay awake in Miss Nolte's English class. Learning together how to decipher the nearly indecipherable female code of attraction. Did a hair toss and a roll of her eyes mean she was interested or not? Nolan, Caleb and I had been inseparable. No matter what happened to any one of us, we supported the other. We knew all of each other's worst secrets, greatest triumphs and biggest dreams.

Well, until I betrayed us all and left with no word.

Caleb Doyle was not only one of my former best friends, he was Alessia's cousin, too. Embarrassment flit through me as I realized she'd been laughing and enjoying her cousin's company rather than that of some idiot dandy passing through town.

I froze as she looked in my direction, unable to move as her gaze clashed with mine. I was as ensnared now as when I was seven and she'd smiled at me with her guileless gaze, offering to share her mittens with me because I'd forgotten my gloves. I'd started tumbling into love with her then, and I'd never tumbled out of it.

Now, her gaze was guarded, haunted, tormented. No gasp of welcome surprise or smile of joy. Instead, she stood as frozen as I, horrified to see me. My heart splintered a little more as her arms crossed over her chest and she hunched her shoulders as though she had to protect herself against attack. Protect herself from me. *Me*, dammit.

"No, sugar," I whispered. I'd allowed her to believe I'd betrayed her. Abandoned her. But I hadn't. I'd come to make things right. I'd come to make her mine again. And nothing, and no one, would stand in my way.

Preorder Secret Montana Love Now!

NEVER MISS A FIONA CULLEN UPDATE!

Thank you so much for reading *Forbidden Montana Love*! I can't wait to share more of the series with you.

Are you missing Nolan and Theo already? I've written a bonus epilogue, just for my newsletter subscribers. Join now to read about their adventure meeting Nolan's grandparents! You'll also have access to the bonus short story prequel- yay!

Become a Fanatic! Join my Facebook group for Fiona's Fanatics, and be the first to know about updates, cover reveals, fun give-aways, and so much more!

Follow me on Facebook or Instagram!

ALSO BY FIONA CULLEN

Sexy, heartfelt romance set under the big Montana sky

The Burkes Of Burnside Creek

Unexpected Montana Love- prequel- only for newsletter subscribers!

Forbidden Montana Love- March 2022

Secret Montana Love- July 2022

Blazing Montana Love- November 2022

ACKNOWLEDGMENTS

It's impossible to thank everyone who's helped me on this journey, but I'll try!

Thank you to all my amazing readers! I couldn't do this without you!

Thank you to all the bloggers and everyone on Instagram and Facebook who helped spread the word about Forbidden Montana Love. I can't thank you enough!

Thank you Sarah for being my first reader and for being so enthusiastic and excited about this new series. I don't know if I would have continued with this without your enthusiasm. Thank you!

Thank you to my family for understanding when I disappear into my imagination as I write. Your support and encouragement is priceless.

Thank you, Linda and Foreword PR, for your excitement about this new series and for taking a chance on me.

Thank you to the Editing Anns for their hard work in helping me polish my MS. You're the best!

DB, you've always been such a great support and cheerleader, thank you!

Thank you, Margo V, for your friendship and for listening to me ramble on about my ideas and dreams.

ALL ABOUT FIONA

Fiona Cullen likes her tea strong, loves a long-winded story, and is always rooting for the underdog. An author of sexy, small-town contemporary romance, her heroes are men you'd want to bring home to meet your parents for family dinner and her heroines are women you'd want as your best friend. Fiona calls Montana home, and is happiest when she's fly fishing a cool, clear Montana river, hiking a trail, or immersed in the beauty around her.

Made in United States
Orlando, FL
03 April 2024

45399759R00150